Sean Sinclair is handsome, brilliant, and completely self-centered, so it is no surprise that his main ambition is to succeed as Master of one of England's oldest and most prestigious universities—St. Thaddeus's College. And while working his way up the academic ladder, he is more than happy to fill his days with as many sexual conquests the life of a successful gay university fellow can throw his way.

But when an embittered former lover goes missing under grisly circumstances, and suspicion falls on him, Sean is dragged into a world of ancient horror hidden behind the dreaming spires of St. Thaddeus's, and into a centuries-old war between light and darkness.

Hounded by police and stalked by monsters, Sean must fight to find the truth of "The Shadow College". What are its plans for humans? And for him?

In the shadows, it's hard to tell friend from foe, lover from killer, and as the darkness deepens, Sean is forced to make choices that will cost him far more than just his life.

DARK MASTER

Jack Stevens

A NineStar Press Publication

www.ninestarpress.com

Dark Master

Printed in the USA

ISBN: 978-1-64890-297-0

NineStar Edition, May, 2021

Also available in eBook, ISBN: 978-1-64890-298-7

CONTENT WARNING:
This book contains sexually explicit material which is only suitable for mature readers, murder, torture, and death of a secondary character.

For Huw, who thought this was my Pride and Prejudice.

Chapter One

When does something begin?

Yes, I know, stupid question. That's what I would have thought. Until this night. Now, I'm standing here in the gothic gloom of St. Thaddeus's College central quad, staring into the bloody-golden eyes of the creature that has offered, or threatened, to make me immortal, and part of my stupidly still-human mind is trying, even now, to work out just when the train of events began that led me here to this, the most important and possibly final decision of my life.

It could have been the day I first entered the college, of course, the day my path first crossed that of Richard Farjeon. That would be the easy answer. Or the day I first met Lee? Or that first afternoon in Rufus's study? Always men. Always me and men. Someone, and I really should know who, said that character is destiny, so maybe I was fated to come to this end right from the day I was born. Or should that be from the day Richard was born, centuries earlier?

Go figure.

On the whole, I tend to opt for that bitterly cold November night less than a month ago, when the rain was pelting down in stinging pellets just short of ice, the wind was shaking every window in its frame, and I was in my rooms at college fucking the brains out of one of its most promising graduate students.

Lee was a brilliant kid. The work he'd done with me the previous year on medieval lyric poetry had been some of the best I'd seen, short of my own of course. But that night it wasn't his skill at textual analysis that had my full and undivided attention: it was how much hard reaming his small arse could take before he shot his hot load over the starched white sheets of my college bed.

St. Thad's rooms are old and draughty at the best of times, their small coal fires generally a source of more smoke than heat, but after an hour and a half's energetic thrusting and pumping, screwing like horny undergrads, Lee and I weren't even noticing the cold. By then I'd got him right where I wanted him, on his back, his thighs pressed into my chest as I banged my rock-hard cock again and again into his tight hole. His mouth was open, and he was panting as if he'd just run a marathon, his gasps and grunts mixed with inarticulate words that might have been pleas for me to do it more gently or demands that I do it harder. I did it harder.

Even then Lee had what they used to call a "scholar's pallor"; pale skin, probably from Celtic ancestors, accentuating the black of his hair, sweat-plastered now on his head and chest, trailing down over his belly in that sexy crooked thin line.

He'd seemed nervous when he'd turned up at my rooms that night, most unlike his normal cocky self, but we'd kissed, I'd rested my hand on his arse, he'd rested his on my arm, I'd stroked, he'd closed his eyes and sighed, and the next thing we were pulling each other's shirts off and heading for my bed, so I'd naturally thought no more of it. And then the "normal" Lee had been back with a vengeance, the studious graduate of one of England's most prestigious and ancient universities gagging for the rough fuck I was more than happy to give him. Even then, though, with my thick dick deep in him, pounding at his aching prostate like there was no tomorrow, he managed to look as if he was challenging me: the glitter in his eye, the curl of his lip. Generations of well-to-do county blood ran in those veins, and Lee tended never to forget it, even when a nine-inch iron-hard shaft was being rammed up him and he was begging for it to be more brutal. A shake of my head and my sweat spattered down on him, showing him just what I thought of his moneyed connections. "Take it boy! Take it!" I grunted, relishing the coarseness of it, the sheer bloody lack of lyric poetry.

He shouted out then, something unintelligible, unable to help himself, and I grinned and redoubled the pace of my pistoning. That was the way I liked it. Nice and loud. Gasping like a fish out of water, Lee threw his arms back behind him to grab hold of the metal bars of the bedstead that was squeaking and creaking so alarmingly at the violence of our sex. I wished then I'd thought to leave something handy lying around to lash his wrists with, but I was way too close to coming by that point to want to pull out and faff around looking for ropes or cuffs in the habitual mess of my small rooms. Besides, Lee knew what he was doing, holding on to the metal rods as he arched and yelled, the not-so-subtle suggestion of bondage without any actual restraints. Oh yes, he knew what I liked. "Oh God, yeah! Oh yeah!" He pushed his arse hard into my thrusts, timing as spot on as ever, driving me even further into him as he came out with all the corny shit that really makes me hot. Cheeky young bastard! He was trying to make me come before him. No way!

I paused, saw his eyes widen in surprise at the abrupt lack of motion, the sudden stilling of the protesting bedsprings so that our ragged heavy breathing became the only sound to be heard over the howls and beating of the wind outside. Then, without warning, I thrust into him more savagely, far harder, far deeper than even before and held myself right up there, my implacable cock smack up against the hot nub of his sweet spot. The arrogance in his eyes vanished completely. He was totally mine and I laughed down into his face, before pulling right back and nearly out, waiting, then driving back in, faster and even further. Three more shaftings like that and on the last his resistance broke. He screamed and his cock, hard up against his flat belly like a veined tent peg, shot streams of thick cum up the length of his body and into his own howling face. "Gotcha, fucker!" I shouted, loving the way his habitual sneer had collapsed into a pained grimace of gasping helpless ecstasy, covered in the shower of his own hot spunk, milked from his balls by my ruthless ministrations. Only then, as his thick cream was sliding down his cheeks and chin, only then did I let myself give way to the sweet urgency of my own balls, and I jettisoned the copious jism my aching cobs had been screaming to release for over an hour.

"You just don't care, do you?" Lee said to me afterwards. We'd slept for a short while by then—well, I knew I had—and were wrapped up in each other's arms, as much for warmth as for any other feeling, under the triple duvet that was essential at that time of year in St. Thad's Halls of Residence.

"Care about what?" I said, nicely relaxed and not really too fussed about whatever sort of mushy drivel Lee felt the need to come out with. If anything, I suppose I was mildly surprised. Lee was a graduate student after all. In my experience grad students tended to have got over the need for romantic small talk that undergraduates, especially in the arts, so often seemed to have. And that was just fine as far as I was concerned. As it turned out, however, romance was the last thing on Lee's mind. Things would have been considerably easier if that hadn't been the case.

"About most things. But right now, I mean about the noise. You really don't care who hears you."

I smiled. "I like the noise. I like to hear the 'groans that thunder love with sighs of fire.' Hadn't you noticed?"

Lee's eyes narrowed in thought as he stared up at the ceiling. "*Much Ado About Nothing*?"

I tutted. "*Twelfth Night*. Act one, scene five. That's what you get for staying away from me for so long. Your faculties begin to decay." I didn't bother to keep the disapproval out of my voice, both for the misattribution and his apparent insistence on talking. I hoped he wouldn't continue with either. "And that wasn't a pun by the way."

"I've been...busy."

If he expected me to ask at what, or with whom, he was disappointed. I'd assumed he'd been enjoying himself with someone or other in the two weeks or so since we'd last seen each other, and that was fine, although it had crossed my mind that he might actually have been working on his thesis. Whatever. Speaking for myself I had very definitely been "busy": firstly, with a very promising anthropology specialist from one of the neighbouring colleges, then with a surprisingly versatile theology student from our own college. Most recently, though, there had been the most extraordinary exchange student from the Sorbonne. Ah yes indeed. Jean-Philippe. Now there was a project that might even outlast a term. I had a momentary stab of regret that it wasn't Jean-Philippe in bed with me right then. I quashed the thought. It was a little ungenerous, even for me. And there was always tomorrow.

"And I know about the French guy."

I blinked, slightly unsettled for a moment that Lee seemed almost to have been reading my mind. "I'm not surprised," I said. "Someone as...talented as he is must have quite a reputation." I sighed. Lee was a good shag, one of the best I'd ever had to be honest (though not in Jean-Philippe's league), but that was all he was: a fun time in bed now and again. I'd hoped he'd understood that, but it looked as if I was going to have to add a dose of cold reality to an already freezing night.

"Aren't you worried you'll be caught?"

I raised myself on one elbow to look down at him, puzzled and faintly irritated by the line he seemed now to be pursuing. "We're not doing anything illegal." His damp hair lay around his head on the pillow like a dark halo. I couldn't resist winding a lock of it around one finger, just tightly enough to make him frown and then wince. "Unless you have something more in mind?" I tugged, quite gently really.

He swatted my twining finger away, and for the moment I let him. "Bedding one of your students?"

I sank back onto my pillow and laughed. "I don't think I've heard it called 'bedding' in anything other than Victorian bodice rippers. And besides, you are not, technically, one of *my* students. I helped you with your MA. That was more than a year ago. You are now Professor McCafferey's student, and he is much too old to want to sport it with your flesh as I have, and much too deaf to hear it if I do, which is a great blessing seeing as it is he who has the rooms across the corridor."

"I spend more time with Professor Hamilton actually."

I shrugged, as much as one can shrug lying in a bed under heavy duvets, not really paying attention to his little burst of vainglory, hoping that was the end of our little chat. Without looking at me, Lee moved his hand deliberately under the covers and began slowly stroking up and down the inside of my thigh. Well, that seemed to have put an end to the pointless chatter, and I was torn between wanting to enjoy the afterglow of our sex just a bit longer and the undeniable stirrings this new contact was creating. A delicious new image filled my mind: that proud, clean-cut young face of Lee's under my arse; that witty tongue and mouth put to much better use deep up my crack, rimming me hard, making me erect again as I pressed down onto him, pulling his hands up my body, to my chest, my nipples...

"I really envy you your rooms in college, you know."

Sod it! We were back with the chat. I frowned briefly, unwilling to tear my mind away from such stimulating images. "Even with the neighbours?" I said, not really paying that much attention to what either he or I was saying.

"Even with them." Lee paused, then, "I should like to have rooms like these."

I pulled back slightly, and his caressing of my thigh stopped. I was aware that Lee was looking at me very closely and the mood of our conversation had changed, or perhaps I had misinterpreted it from the start.

"They have a certain ambience and comfort," I agreed. "Maybe one day you'll get something like them." I moved my leg closer to his body, but he didn't take the hint and resume his stroking.

"'One day' sounds a long way off. I don't like to wait."

"I noticed."

"You know what I mean. Academic life doesn't offer too many privileges. I'd like to make the most of those it does while I'm still young enough to enjoy them."

I began to see the way things were heading, or at least the way Lee wanted them to head. I laughed again, but more for the effect than because I found anything particularly amusing. "You have a while yet before the decay of senility begins to set in," I said, with mock reassurance. "You should complete your PhD in, what, two maybe three years? And from what I've heard it should be pretty stunning."

"From what you've heard! You don't even know what it's about, do you?"

I gazed up at the age-spotted plaster above the bed while I searched my mind. Rather to my surprise I found I didn't. "Some Jacobean poet?" I suggested vaguely.

"Some Jacobean poet!" he repeated bitterly, with really rather poor rhetorical technique.

"There are rather a lot of them, you know," I countered, "most forgotten for very good reasons and not worth the effort of exhumation." I could see him rising to that particular bait and quickly moved in to cut off the line of thought. The very last thing I wanted when naked in a bed with a man was to hear all about his fascination with the minutiae of another man's life, especially when that man has been dead for nearly five hundred years. "In any case, it doesn't really matter what you're writing about. It could be on Elizabethan recipes for hamburgers. What counts is the quality of the scholarship and yours, shaped as it was by me, will be superb I'm sure. And with that under your belt, you shouldn't have too much trouble finding a junior place at almost any university you care to mention. They'll all have accommodation of some kind to offer. Quite probably something more modern, with central heating that actually works."

Lee's laugh was scornful. "A ground floor flat in a high-rise block, you mean, attached to some nice little redbrick university? Or maybe a shared house in a council estate next to some crummy little polytechnic pretending to be a university? I don't think so."

"Something like this university then?" I said, with feigned innocence.

"No. Not a university *like* this one. I want to be a part of *this* university. And not just for its accommodation."

"Really?" And now I couldn't be bothered to keep the sardonic tone from my voice. I knew it would sting him, but sometimes sleeping with a Fellow can give a student, even a graduate student, an overinflated idea of his own abilities. "You realise of course that's pretty unlikely, don't you? For the moment I mean," I added, to soften the blow slightly. I didn't want to piss him off completely. I was still harbouring vague hopes of a good rimming before I sent him on his way into the cold night like Porphyro in *The Eve of St. Agnes*. *"Ah, bitter chill it was..."* "This college isn't renowned for the youth of its lecturing staff, you know. Most of them had to work for years in their fields, publishing mountains of research before they were allowed to give even a visiting lecture."

"But you..."

"I...am special," I said, and now it was my turn to slide my hand under the duvets into the dark warm hollows of his body, between his legs, to the promise of his crotch. "Or is that something else I have to remind you of?" I felt the impressive meat between his legs against my fingers, the pleasing jump of it at my touch, the encouraging stiffening.

Lee smiled coldly, with that hint of challenge again in his eyes. "Maybe I could be special, too, with a little help."

"And what sort of help would that be?" I asked, pushing my hand in deeper, caressing the curve of his hairy balls, gently squeezing and releasing the weight of them, extending the tip of one finger down to the deliciously sensitive, spongy spot behind them. I was sincerely hoping I could turn his thoughts away from the path they so obviously wanted to take into the direction my own fast-rehardening dick was pointing.

Lee took a deep breath. "College rumour is there could be a new Chair financed before the start of the next academic year. You could...put in a word for me."

Gently I massaged that yielding spot, wanting to kiss him, as much to silence his babbling so that we could get back to some serious fucking as for any other reason, but

I held back. Regretfully, I forced myself to acknowledge that a line had been crossed, the moment had passed, and so I pulled my finger back from its probing, trying not to think about how the motion just made Lee's cock stiffen even more. "You overestimate my influence," I said. "It would take more than a word from me."

"Maybe. But an outstanding result in my PhD vivas would maybe do the rest. And you could help me with those too."

"Ah." I leaned back, away from his slim body. It's funny. My own naked ambition had always been sexy to me. In anyone else I've always found it a real turnoff. "You don't need that kind of help, Lee," I said. "You'll get your PhD. And it'll probably be brilliant. Pay your dues. Work your way up the academic ladder, lecture at the various universities, and one day...?"

"...after ten years I could get to the place the great Sean Sinclair got to in a year?"

I shrugged again. "What can I say? Like I said, I'm special." It was now, I decided, time for my chicken to leave our little love nest. The damp patch was turning cold anyway. But then Lee's suddenly soft voice made me pause. "He that climbs highest has the greatest fall."

"*Revenger's Tragedy*. Act five, scene three," I said, automatically. Some habits are hard to break, even at the most inappropriate moments. "I'm impressed. Not a play many people can quote from. Or did you learn that particular phrase especially for tonight?" There was no answer, so I suspected I'd hit a truth. "It's not especially apt, you know," I added, just to discomfit further. "My climb may have been swift, but it hasn't been particularly high. Yet." I turned to look down at him, forcing him to look me in the eye, "And if I remember correctly, which of course I do, the character who says that, Lussurioso, a decadent and debauched Duke, is just about to be murdered."

He tried to maintain the eye contact, but he couldn't, and when he did look away, he licked his lips, the arrogance he simply couldn't help now touched with nervousness. I have to admit, I found that tiny sign of my small victory mildly erotic. I wondered if I could parley it into something physical, maybe forcing him to swallow my cock and more of my cum as well as his words. Only to teach him a lesson, you understand.

"A swift climb can lead to an equally swift fall."

"Now you're merely paraphrasing. You'll be misquoting next. And just what exactly is supposed to precipitate such a fall?" I asked, though I knew what he had in mind. One of the first things you learn as a tutor: don't ask your students questions you don't already have the answers to.

"Improprieties." He coughed to clear his throat and make his words clearer. "Lack of professional conduct. Indelicacies."

"You mean fucking the students?" It amused me that I could say the plain truth with more ease than Lee could utter the euphemisms.

"Sounds ugly. doesn't it?" he said with an attempt to recover the upper hand.

"Actually," I said, "I think it sounds bloody hilarious." And now I did get up, pulling the duvets around myself as I did, making sure that I had hold of all three, leaving Lee to scrabble for some cover in the chill air as I drew them with me away from the bed. Sangfroid is all very well so long as it isn't literal. "Like I said earlier, Lee, you're not my student. You're not even an undergrad any more. You're a graduate, old enough to drink, smoke, go to war, and be shagged by a devastatingly good-looking and brilliant lecturer in medieval English. You could shout it from the chapel rooftop that I've had you in a dozen ways in as many different college rooms and the most likely reaction from our crusty Senior Common Room would be a chorus of jealousy. We might study the Dark Ages here, Lee, but even in St. Thaddeus's we don't live in them. So now"—I reached for his jeans that were hanging across the back of my solitary armchair and threw them across the room to him—"it really is time for you to go. I hate to throw you out into the snow"—I glanced through my cloudy windowpane out onto the Quad below—"so if you hurry you might get home before it begins."

"You think you're so clever," Lee spat as he dragged his jeans on.

"I *know* I am clever, Lee," I sighed. "We established that. remember?"

"What was it? Assistant Professorship here by the time you were twenty-six."

"Twenty-five!" Call me a queen if you like but I wasn't having some peevish prick adding years onto my age.

"Right. And you still haven't got a clue what really goes on here, have you?" He rammed his feet into his shoes, and before I could ask him what, if anything, he meant by that, demanded, "So what next?" Now that one definitely didn't deserve an answer. It was really quite obvious. I'd gained full professorship long before I was thirty, almost certainly the youngest man to hold such a position in this college's very long history. "What next?" I pulled Lee's coat from its peg and held it out to him. He snatched it from me but didn't put it on, just stood there staring at me. "What next?" he repeated. I didn't feel the need to spell it out for him. But then he didn't wait for me to do so. "Master of the College, yes?" I didn't deign to reply. "You're just going to sit here and wait for it to fall into your hands, aren't you? Master of the fucking College before you're forty."

"Long before I'm forty," I couldn't help adding. "Though your good friend Professor Hamilton might have something to say about that."

Lee either missed my sarcasm or was too bound up in his own visions of my future to rise to it. "You don't deserve it."

"Let's not get bitter, eh?"

"You don't fucking deserve it. And maybe...maybe you won't get it. Shall I tell you what *is* going to happen to you, Sean?" I didn't answer. I could tell he wasn't expecting me to. "I'll tell you. You'll get old, just like everyone else. Your theories will become less brilliant, less original. Out of date. And your chasing around after students, graduate or otherwise, will become faintly embarrassing, then downright disgusting."

I smiled. I knew that would really piss him off. "I don't chase after them, Lee. They chase after me." *Like you did*, I considered adding, but I didn't think he needed reminding, and I had no time anyway as he blazed on, fuelled by this curious anger.

"Fewer and fewer young men will make their way up those stairs to this room, until the only ones you'll get into your bed, and it'll still be that one there"—he jabbed a vindictive finger behind us—"will be the kids who've really pissed their time away in the bars and clubs and who need your 'help' in their last term to keep them from getting Thirds or failing altogether."

"Sic transit gloria mundi," I said quietly.

"And you'll never, *ever* become Master! But it doesn't have to be that way." And his tone changed. Suddenly the fire of his anger seemed to burn out leaving...something else. I wasn't sure what. To be blunt, at that moment I'm not sure I cared any more. I was standing at the door by then, ready to open it and usher him out, but Lee stood there before me, coat held in one hand, looking at me with an expression I couldn't read. "It doesn't have to be that way, Sean," he repeated, and that addition of my name did surprise me a little. Even sitting on my cock, grinding his arse down into my crotch, he rarely used my first name and now he was throwing it around like confetti. "Don't you know what really goes on in this college? How can you of all people not know?"

Again, that strange accusation. "Look, what the hell do you mean?"

Lee's face twisted then, as if with an effort to expel something from inside, or to keep it hidden. "I didn't want... That's why I came to you first. But I have to...I thought you could..." He held out his hand to me then, as if in supplication. "Sean, please."

I looked at him, at the pleading, the naked need in his eyes. I'd never seen him like this before.

I opened the door. "Goodbye, Lee."

Am I sorry about that now, after all that has happened? Yes. I suppose so. I'd have to be some sort of monster to say no, wouldn't I? If I could go back, if I could turn back time, if I could rewrite history, etc, etc, etc. But there's no use denying what I did then. I opened the door and I stood back to make it clear that I wanted Lee to leave. It was late. I was tired. He was incoherent. And yes, I admit it, he had stung me with his potted version of my future career at St Thad's. Implausible bullshit though it was. "Goodbye, Lee," I repeated. "Let's neither of us ever mention this again."

For a second I thought he was going to ignore me, going to try to speak again, and I had visions of a "scene" on the stairs, perhaps with Professor McCafferey poking his bleary grey head round his door (glass of invariably splendid port inevitably in hand) to enquire with his unfailing politeness what was going on at that late hour. To my enormous relief, however, that didn't happen. With a visible effort Lee pulled himself together again and stalked past me, into the freezing corridor outside without even bothering to put his coat on. "I'm sorry," he said in a low whisper that seemed empty of any real contrition. "Just remember, later on, that I came to you first. That I tried to do things...properly." And then he was finally gone.

With a huge sigh I turned back to my failing fire, piled on the last chunks of coal from my scuttle, and stirred them up into a quick blaze. "That was doing things properly?" I muttered, poking the fire. "If that was doing things properly, Lee, you should stick to what you're good at: shagging and poetry analysis. There are worse things to be proficient in." I sat, staring into the glowing caverns and ghostly faces I'd always been able to see in the burning coals of a fire while outside the wind and the rain continued to beat against the weathered stones of St. Thaddeus's College.

The next morning, of course, Lee was reported missing, presumed dead, and I would shortly come to understand I had been set on a path that would eventually lead me here to St. Thad's Quad and to the brink of an existence of appalling beauty and darkness, beyond anything I had ever imagined, at the end of a journey I had begun, in all innocence, so very long before.

Chapter Two

There's a kind of telepathy that operates in universities. Or perhaps just in old universities. Or maybe just in St Thad's.

Soon after joining the college I'd found I could walk from my rooms of a morning, through the arches that lead to the Quad, partway round that patch of green to the clock tower and then through the gatehouse and into the lecture rooms, and somehow, without speaking to anyone, I could have picked up on the mood of the day, have been prepared for the first thing I would be told when, finally, I spoke to someone. A psychologist friend tried to explain it to me once, talking at length of subliminal impressions processed by the mind without conscious thought: the expressions on faces of passing students and dons; the sounds and lack of sounds from the various rooms passed, smells, pheromones, memes, and a whole host of other things I didn't really understand. Or maybe, he'd added, it's something in the old stone of the buildings talking to us. Then I knew he'd been taking the piss.

However it happened, I knew even before old Harry the Porter hobbled towards me with that gallows expression on his face that something had happened, and somehow I already had a pretty good idea of who was involved. I'd seen the looks one or two of the students had given me as I walked by them. I was sure I'd heard Lee's name whispered behind my back, and even though I wasn't consciously willing it, the events of last night were beginning to replay in my mind.

"Mr. Sinclair, sir."

"What is it?" Apprehension made me unusually sharp with Harry. He was a good old stick and I genuinely liked him. Plus, it was always wise to keep on the right side of the Porter of your college. You never knew when you might need to sneak back in late after the gates were closed, alone or with a "friend."

"Some people to see you, sir, in the gatehouse. To do with Mr. Barker, sir."

"With Lee?" For just a second I thought maybe he'd gone through with his semi-articulated schemes of blackmail, but I dismissed the thought as quickly as it had arisen. What I'd said the previous night about the futility of his implied threat still held true in the light of this day, and besides, somehow, I knew that wasn't what this was about.

"He's dead, sir."

I'd like to say the half-whispered words hit me like a thunderbolt, but I could never bring myself to say something so clichéd. Besides, they didn't. I'm not sure how I felt. I don't know if I believed what I'd just heard or not. It was just...words. So, I looked at Harry to see if what I saw could help me make sense of what he'd said. I saw the look he gave me, a sort of sideways glance as he tried, discreetly, to read my reactions. Harry was old and a bit bumbling, and absolutely no one's fool. You didn't get to be Porter of one of the country's most prestigious seats of learning by being an idiot. He'd seen Lee come to my rooms enough times to know the score. I kept my face down, unwilling to let him see my reactions, at least until I knew more clearly myself what they actually were. "How?" It seemed the safest thing to say.

"I don't rightly know, sir," he said, his tone making it clear to me that he did, or at least had a pretty good idea.

He showed me into the gatehouse and a room like most of the others in the college: small, irregular, dimly lit through clouded old glass and with whitewashed stone walls adorned only by shelves full of books and several dingy portraits, some of which could quite possibly turn out to be long-lost masterpieces if only the time and enthusiasm could be found to take them down and clean them. That much was typical; what was unusual about this room today was the presence of two police officers, a man and a woman.

"Good morning," I said. I addressed the man, not because I am inherently sexist but because he was by far the sexier of the two, so much so that it didn't seem wrong to notice the fact even in the circumstances. Midtwenties, I guessed, though his close-cropped hair was already receding at the temples in a way that was curiously not unattractive; a good, powerful build, strong jawline with a bluish beard shadow already showing after that morning's shave. He'd claim to be a top, I thought, but if I got him in bed his face'd be in the pillow and his arse up in the air begging for it. Even I am sometimes surprised by the speed of my erotic imaginings.

"Good morning, sir." It was the woman who answered, and I don't know if the frostiness in her voice was due to my having overlooked her or to her having picked up on my purely instinctive reaction to her colleague. "I'm Detective Inspector Marrin and this is Sergeant Taylor." Was it my imagination or was there just a bit of emphasis on that "sergeant"? She continued without giving me a chance to say anything. "You are, I believe, Mr. Sean Sinclair?" I nodded as we both pretended she hadn't already been damn sure of that. "We understand you are a friend of Mr. Lee Barker."

No mistaking the very definite and sarcastic emphasis there. "Friend" indeed. "Yes," I said, "we have been 'friendly'". I returned the sarcasm, like a tennis player insouciantly returning a volley with a backhand.

"May I ask how friendly, sir?"

The verbal ball play had been amusing but now I was just insulted by the pussyfooting. There was no point in trying to pretend I was anything other than I was. I had nothing to hide and it made more sense to make it quite clear from the outset what my relationship with Lee had been. Did I care what that made this policewoman think about me? No. "More than simply friends, detective inspector," I said crisply, "but considerably less than lovers. We had a sexual relationship. MBF."

The detective inspector raised an eyebrow. "MBF?"

"Mutually beneficial fucking." I'll give her credit, she didn't flinch. I glanced across at her hunky oppo. Was that a hint of a blush, a flush of the thick neck over the tight line of his crisp white shirt collar? A bit of blood rushing to the extremities? Always a good sign.

"Do you have sex with many of your students, Mr. Sinclair?"

"In point of fact, detective inspector, I have sex with none of them. That would be unethical. Mr Barker, Lee, was not one of my students."

"A fine distinction, sir. He had been, I believe."

"Fine, but real, and very important. And much like myself I see you don't ask questions without having researched the answers carefully beforehand. May I ask what this is all about?"

DI Marrin fixed me with her undeniably formidable gaze. "At six o'clock this morning we received a call regarding Mr. Barker that gave cause for concern. Subsequent investigation of his lodging revealed Mr. Barker was missing. There were signs of a struggle and—" she paused, and I had to give her credit again for her ability to create drama and tension, even if her official police diction was laughable. "—quantities of blood."

I'll admit it, the word "blood" knocked some of the uppitiness out of me. That wasn't an image I'd been expecting. "Lee's?"

"The reports aren't back from the lab yet but yes, we believe the blood to be Mr. Barker's."

"I see." I didn't of course, but DI Marrin's next question came as no surprise to me.

"We understand you were with Mr. Barker for most of last night, sir, before he returned home?"

"I think you know very well I was, detective inspector."

"Then would you mind telling us what happened? What you did? As precisely as you can, please."

Needless to say, a flip answer rose to my lips. Did she really want to know about the nipple play, frottage, sucking, and fucking, and was the exact order they took place in important to her? Wisely, I bit my tongue. This had suddenly become far too serious a matter for such flippancy, and I was beginning to suspect that my obvious innocence might be very far from obvious to these two representatives of the law, especially if I was foolish enough to tell them the exact nature of the argument Lee and I had ended our night on. So, I told the DI and her silent sidekick almost everything, except the finer details of my lovemaking and that we had parted on such a distinctly sour note. She listened to it all and said nothing. Sergeant Taylor took down every word in a small notebook pulled from his suit pocket and didn't look up at me once. I wondered if that was because he didn't want to catch my eye, for whatever reason, or because he had to concentrate on his spelling.

"So, there you have it." I took a deep breath and licked my lips. "Can I conclude that this means I am a suspect?"

"Suspect for what, sir?"

I gave a short grim laugh. Clever, though a bit obvious. "You have blood and a missing person, detective inspector," I said. "It doesn't take a finely trained police mind to see that we could be talking about murder here."

"You're right of course, sir," she said. "But, as you say, we don't have a body yet. And though there was a quantity of blood discovered at the scene—" and again I caught her looking directly at me as if to gauge my reactions to the grisly picture she was painting "—there was not sufficient to prove of itself that Mr. Barker is dead. The exact nature of the crime, if indeed there is one, is still open to conjecture. So no, sir," she added, "you are not, at the moment, a suspect."

"Oh," I said, surprised, though pleased of course, even though I had caught the implicit underlining of *at the moment*. I couldn't help asking, "Why not?"

"Mr. Harry"—she nodded to the door on the other side of which St. Thad's Porter almost certainly had his ear pressed—"has already vouched for your presence in your rooms throughout the night."

I briefly debated whether to treat Harry to a pint at his local for that or kick him in the shins on my way out for not having told me beforehand he'd given me an alibi.

"We won't keep you any longer, sir," Detective Inspector Marrin said stiffly, heading for the door. "I'm sure you have much to be getting on with. Thank you for your time." The words were formulaic, doing little to disguise the glacial undercurrent. She didn't offer her hand and neither did I. I had, however, hoped for a bit of flesh-to-flesh contact with the handsome Sergeant Taylor on his way out, but he contrived to be putting his notebook away as he passed and he merely mumbled something as he exited, head down, still avoiding eye contact. *You know you want it*, I thought, as the door closed behind him.

Almost immediately the door reopened, and for a second I wondered if St. Thad's telepathy had cranked up a notch and the fit sergeant had picked up on my thoughts. My aroused libido was quickly put back in its place by the sight of Harry's wrinkled walnut of a face. "All well, sir?" he inquired, as if he didn't already know. "Anything I can get you?"

"All's well, Harry," I said. "If I could just have a minute or two by myself?"

"Of course, sir." With his usual deference Harry stepped back and began to close the door behind him.

"Oh, and Harry?"

The door opened again fractionally. "Yes, sir?"

"Thanks."

He nodded. Neither of us needed to say anything more.

Left by myself I sank down onto one of the creaky settles in the room and began to try to sort out events. *All's well,* I'd said. For me, yes. But maybe not for Lee. The boy had proved to be an idiot at the end but that didn't mean I'd wished him ill, certainly not the kind of ill involving violence and blood loss. Was he dead? Somehow, I didn't think so, but did I have any rational reason for thinking that, or was it just a knee-jerk refusal to accept something so awful? A refusal to accept something for which I might be expected to feel some kind of pity...or even guilt? Should I? What did it make me if I didn't?

There was a knocking at the door. Relieved to be dragged from this unprofitable and unusual soul-searching I called out, "Who is it?"

A heavily accented voice said uncertainly, "Sean?"

"Jean-Philippe? Come in!"

The door opened and Jean-Philippe, my philosophy student from the Sorbonne, Paris walked in, and the room seemed to shrink even more about his massive proportions. "Old 'Arry said you were in here," he said, almost as if he was apologising. It never failed to amaze me how someone so big, so brilliant could be so self-effacing. And it never failed to turn me on either.

I sprang from my seat, throwing my arms as far around his huge frame as I could and hugging him tightly before planting a passionate kiss on his surprised lips. Our greetings were generally enthusiastic when no one else was in sight, but I guessed that Harry must have prepared him for finding me in a sombre mood. Well, I had been, and Jean-Philippe was just the thing to lift me out of it. I knew exactly what I needed to set my confused thoughts back into some kind of order. "C'mon," I said, pulling him to the door and leading us both out of the gatehouse. "I want you to fuck me senseless."

Chapter Three

Nothing like an engorged French penis stretching your sphincter till next Wednesday and beyond to take your mind off things I always say.

When they'd told me of a prospective exchange student who wasn't sure whether to make his career in academia or on the rugby pitch, and who had the potential to be world class in either, I was intrigued. When I saw the papers Jean-Philippe had submitted in his request to join St Thad's for an exchange year I was impressed by his mind. When I saw him on the rugby pitch almost single-handedly trouncing our college's First Eleven, I was very impressed by his body. But it wasn't until I'd seen the enormous bulge straining through his terribly fashionable Paris couture house trousers during the post-game drink in the college bar that I'd hoped we might become more than just passing acquaintances. And when I'd invited him back to my rooms to see my impressive Quarto, he'd accepted with an enthusiasm that made it quite clear neither of us was talking about a book.

I'm not one to get too caught up in the whole "tops and bottoms" debate. The simple truth is I like fucking and I like getting my own way so I'm pretty much always a top. With Jean-Philippe I can't really say that the question had ever had a chance to be aired. Any philosophical training in precise niceties seemed to fly straight out of the window the first time the door to my rooms had closed behind us. His clothes had flown off, mine had followed, and I'd been pinned under the bulk of a seventeen stone French bear with a caveman's club for a cock and an internal sat nav programmed straight for my arse. On our first "date" Jean-Philippe had been up and in me with such vigour I'd wondered whether I'd ever walk again. Which was just what I wanted after my little interview with DI Marrin. None of the complicated double talk and half-truths of the night before with Lee, and none of the suspicions and uncertainties the morning had left me with. A good healthy dose of raw sex to clear the head was what was needed and was exactly what Jean-Philippe proceeded to deliver.

His jacket was off before the door to my rooms was closed; the shirt thrown aside and shoes kicked away before he'd gone more than a couple of steps; the socks slung all ways while I was still struggling to get my own coat off. Not much of a clothes horse myself, I have to admit that one of the advantages of expensive tailoring does seem to be that it comes off quickly when you need it to, and I always found it really sexy that Jean-Philippe didn't give a toss about his fancy wardrobe. Getting naked with me was always more important to him than ruining the cut of his expensive glad rags by chucking them to the four corners of a room. He was down to his silk boxers and advancing on me while I was still hopping on one foot trying to pull off my first sock. It made me feel horribly... English! "Hang on a minute, I..."

My protests were smothered by his mouth on mine, his tongue hard in, demanding, his powerful arms that swatted university rugby players away like flies on the pitch enveloping me, pulling me tightly into him. Even his comparatively baggy silk boxers couldn't hide the jutting pride of his Gallic manhood, and now I felt its hard length jabbing into me as Jean-Philippe moaned in my ear, "Oh Sean, Sean," in that crazy accent of his. I swear he exaggerated it to pull the guys, and that was fine by me.

Already panting hard, I pulled back to tear off the rest of my clothes while Jean-Philippe slid his boxers down over his tree trunk-like thighs, letting them fall with a whisper to the floor around his feet and then bringing his hands up, rubbing them slowly over his hairy chest, pecs the size of dinner plates, down over the thick ridges of his six pack belly, down further to the frankly incredible size of his dick, jutting out like a flag pole from the forest of his crotch, grasping it in one hand, looking at me hungrily as he stroked himself, pulling down on the shaft, rubbing his thumb over its already slick swollen mushroom head.

Down to my briefs at last I paused to take in the sight of him. As ever it made my heart hammer in my chest, even as the sight of his mammoth erection made me hesitate. This was going to hurt. It always did, at first, but then...

...then Jean-Philippe was on me again, his muscled arms drawing me helplessly into the hairy warmth of his body, and any further hesitation was purely academic. Being with an aroused man like Jean-Philippe was like surrendering to a force of nature: you were in for the ride and had to hope you'd come out of the experience at the other end reasonably intact.

Out of bed and off the pitch Jean-Philippe was quiet and gentle, diffident even. On the pitch and between the sheets he played hard and he played to win. The hands he used to write essays about the world's greatest thinkers, calloused from hours of rugby training, gripped my flesh hard, pulling, twisting, rubbing, slapping. He liked me to slap him back; at first, I'd done it playfully, but as his mauling had grown more heated so my slaps had become more real, more urgent, until now the crack of my palms on his hairy arse, his wide back, his broad shoulders was as much a part of the soundscape of our fucking as our grunts and cries.

Jean-Philippe laughed as he mauled me, bit me, sucked me, dragged the sharp bristles of his immaculate goatee over my nipples, down my chest, and over my stomach as I struggled and gasped, bang on the borderline of pain and pleasure. Within minutes he was shoving his thick fingers up my arse, laughing again at my helpless, inarticulate gasp, working me roughly before flipping me bodily over with ridiculous ease, giving me just enough time to scrabble for the lube left close at hand in the bedside cabinet while he stretched one of the special XXL condoms he used over his incredible boner, before dropping back down onto me with the full weight of his mountain of a body, amidst a shriek of protesting bedsprings, and driving into my arse with what felt like the full force he'd use to drive into a ruck of straining burly rugby players. I held on, bit hard into the pillow smothering my face, held on, till the white-hot stab of his meat in my ring gave way to the blessed wash of sexual electricity from my prostate as Jean-Philippe's broad cockhead banged it into a heated frenzy. As best I could against the weight of the hirsute bulk pinning me to the bed, I shoved my arse back and up, and clamped down hard on the continental cock fucking me like a crazed gorilla, all in a potent cloud of male musk and expensive French cologne.

I came quickly, I always did with Jean-Philippe, literally stretched to my limits by him. Mercifully so did he. The first time, I'd been worried that I might have disappointed him (and believe me, I am not used to worrying about how my performances are received) but I'd quickly realised that what our sex might have lacked in duration it more than made up for in intensity. There weren't many men who could have coped with Jean-Philippe at all, let alone for hours on end, but another on the list of my candidly rather remarkable achievements was that I was one of them, and mixed in with the cosy fuzziness of postcoital satisfaction was also always a real pride at knowing that.

Now we lay side by side in my bed, the same one I had fucked Lee in the night before. I hadn't even had time to change the sheets, something that gave me a guilty and rather adolescent glow of pleasure. I'd be carving notches in the bedposts next. We were warm, but I couldn't say we'd exactly worked up a sweat. Matters had been far too quick for that. But our frantic fucking had indeed helped me. My mind felt clearer and I was definitely more relaxed than I had been before. (Parts of me were considerably more relaxed, but that was essential with a man as big as Jean-Philippe!)

"So, what were the police asking you questions for?"

I smiled, already feeling a little drowsy, and noting that Jean-Philippe's accent was considerably less marked during postsex pillow talk than it was before. "It's a long story," I said, which was a lie really, given that it was actually a very short story, and I was only a minor character in it.

Jean-Philippe sighed and lay back, his arms thrown over his head. I nuzzled happily at the dark fur of his armpit, trying to tell what part of the delicious smell was him and what came from a tiny and probably fantastically expensive bottle. "The problem with you," he said, "is you spend too long on the medieval lyric. You have no time for the long story. *Le roman*."

"The novel," I translated, knowing even as I did that Jean-Philippe's English was considerably better than my French. "But thank you for reminding me."

"Of what?"

I leaned over and kissed him on the mouth. Drained as I was by my thinking rugby player's lovemaking, even now I felt myself stirring at the thought of another session between the sheets with him. Well, he was used to games of two halves. I put the thought firmly to one side. "I have a lecture to give on Layamon and then a seminar with half a dozen hot young guys, all positively dripping at the thought of what I have to tell them about Thomas Malory and the legend of the Grail." I elbowed hard against Jean-Philippe's reclining bulk which hardly moved at all, and reluctantly clambered out of the bed.

"You English and *les devoirs*," he said. "You should find more time for *l'amour*."

"Come again tonight, *mon brave*," I said, heading for the chill porcelain splendour of my antiquated bathroom, "and I'm sure I'll find a few minutes to squeeze you in again."

Chapter Four

A good hard fuck from Jean-Philippe had certainly helped me put things back into perspective, but I could hardly say that it had put the matter of Lee out of my mind altogether. My lecture on Layamon was a formality, one I'd delivered half a dozen times already. It had been great the first time I gave it so I'd seen little reason to revise it since then and I could practically deliver it with my eyes shut. But as I worked my way through Arthurian legend and the influence of Chrétien de Troyes, I couldn't help my mind drifting off to Lee from time to time. At one point I even thought I saw his face among the rows of students when I looked up, but when I tried to focus, I realised it must have been a trick of the light or of my imagination. And I hoped the suspicious glances I was getting from the young people gathered that afternoon in one of St. Thad's dingiest and mustiest lecture halls were also just in my imagination. It was far too early for them to have heard of what had happened to Lee and of my interview with the police. Wasn't it? I sighed and pressed on, moving on to Marie de France. No, probably not. The speed of gossip and rumour in old English colleges defied all laws of physics.

The seminar that followed with the half dozen students who were assigned to my direct pastoral care was lacklustre and unproductive, not least because some cruel twist of destiny had given me six of the ugliest lads it had ever been my misfortune to tutor. I had never yet stepped over the mark with a boy for whom I was responsible, but I did take it as a sort of right and recompense that such restraint be rewarded with at least a good view, and this shower didn't even provide that. And by then I had very little doubt about what they knew. They weren't saying anything, but I could tell from the avoidance of my eye when they thought I was looking, and the stares when they thought I wasn't, that my students were very well aware of what was up. *If you know more than me*, I thought bitterly, as I droned on about medieval aesthetics, not even really listening to myself, *why don't you tell me*? Where the hell was Lee?

The obligatory two hours up, they all left the seminar room very quickly, none of them hanging around for the usual last-minute hints on essay technique or none too subtle questions as to what might be coming up in that term's end of paper examination. Even Dean, the plump blond lad from Bristol whom I suspected was going to come on to me when he'd got over his first-year nerves and who was going to be very disappointed if he tried it, left without any of the excuses he usually managed to find to hang around. I sighed and began to pack my briefcase with the papers they'd given me to grade. I wondered if Jean-Philippe had actually stayed in my rooms, maybe sleeping off his energetic lovemaking. Mind you, was my arse up to another French reaming quite so soon after the last? I wasn't sure it was, and nothing less than getting the full ten inches all the way in really satisfied Jean-Philippe.

Besides, what I really wanted just then was the warmth and support of a strong man's arms around me, not his cock deep inside me.

I paused, Dean's substantial and almost certainly half-plagiarised essay halfway to my briefcase. Shit! There was a thought. A hug! Rather than a shag? I was pining for a *hug!* I shook my head, shoved the essay roughly into my case with the others, and snapped it closed. Unpleasant memories of what Lee had said about growing old echoed faintly in my mind. Not yet. Not by a long chalk. If Jean-Philippe was there I suddenly fancied making such a rumpus with him that even deaf old McCafferey next door would be able to hear it. If he wasn't, then maybe I'd see what the trade was like in one of the rougher pubs on the outskirts of town. Even a college of dreamy towers and spires like ours has its seamier nooks, thank God.

A sudden rattle at the window made me jump. I span to see what it was but there was immediately a knock at the door, and I thought that must have been where the first noise had come from. The door opened and Sarah, the English Department's rather mousy secretary, poked her nose round. I had long suspected that Sarah didn't approve of my hunting the buck rather than the doe, and I also suspected this was due more to frustration than moral rectitude. Whatever the cause, she hardly ever let more than her nose enter my room, and today was no exception. "The Master would like to see you, Mr. Sinclair," she squeaked. "Now," and then her nose was gone and I could hear her scuttling back to her desk at the end of one of the less well-lit corridors. *Ah yes*, I thought grimly. *I really should have seen that one coming.*

*

I like to think I'm fairly catholic in my sexual tastes. Young, old(ish), black, white, left wing, right wing. I think the rainbow is a fairly garish symbol for gay manhood but I approve of the theory behind it. The only thing I draw the line at is women but then that's only natural. On the whole, though, I'll admit the guys who end up in my bed tend to be on the younger side of forty, but maybe that will change when I get to that age myself. If I ever do. And if I get there the way most people do.

Rufus Hamilton, Master of St Thaddeus's College, was definitely older than forty. He was almost certainly older than fifty, though by exactly how much no one seemed to know. The basic biographical details available on most academics of his stature seemed unusually fuzzy on that detail. Still, however many years there were on his clock, there were certainly more than was the case with most of the guys I'd slept with, although I should make it clear right now that I never had slept with Rufus. Though I would have done in a heartbeat if he'd asked. He'd have had me, too, I knew. And I knew he knew. And neither of us ever said anything about it. Maybe that was why he was the only man in the whole world I could really say I trusted. Maybe even loved a little. Like a father. But definitely (and sadly) not like a daddy.

I know I will never forget my first meeting with him, over ten years previously, when I'd been a callow sixth former, already promoted beyond my actual year group on account of my precocious talents. I'd gone up to the college by train for my admission interviews, the longest journey I'd undertaken alone, to try out for one of the very rare unconditional offers of a place made to students of supposed outstanding ability before they had even taken their end of school examinations. Alone, nervous, conspicuously younger than any of the other students trying for the coveted places, I'd been submitted to a barrage of interviews in a succession of cold drab rooms by a series of grey boring individuals who'd fired question after question at me that left my head spinning and my heart sunk. The questions they asked were all so obvious, so unchallenging. I'd begun the interviews feeling nervous. In what had seemed like no time at all the nervousness had transformed to boredom and then disenchantment. I couldn't believe this was the famous seat of learning students were supposed to be ready to sell their grandmothers to get into.

And then I'd been called into my final interview with the Master of the College, Rufus Hamilton, and within seconds he'd reignited both my love for my subject and my ambition to claim a place at venerable St. Thaddeus's. He also stiffened my young cock in my neatly pressed best interview trousers to a degree that made standing up in front of him almost impossibly embarrassing for the awkward adolescent I then was.

Even now, a decade later, whenever I knock on that dark oak door of his study and walk in, the smell that greets me transports me back effortlessly to our first meeting: that spicy mix of rich pipe tobacco, smoke from the small coal fire that burned winter or summer, and the leather from the deeply upholstered armchairs that shone like polished wood but yielded to a person's weight like eiderdown. I'd entered that room the first time well and truly pissed off by the facile process I had been subjected to, more or less determined this was going to be my last interview and that whatever came of it I would be on the train in an hour's time and on my way back home to seriously reconsider my plans for the future. Angry young novelist, I seem to remember, was top of my list of "Things to Become," though I do think I'd considered porn star either as an alternative or, at least, a preliminary. Even then I could sense a natural aptitude for it.

I remember stopping in the doorway, struck by the difference between this room and the spartan chambers I'd been allowed into so far. I didn't even notice Rufus at first, so I'd jumped when his deep voice had said softly, "Enter freely, and unafraid."

I couldn't help myself. "And leave behind a little of the happiness you bring with you?"

There was an equally deep chuckle. "At last. A student who knows his *Dracula*. Good. Very good. Come in and tell me what you think about Stoker."

I closed the door behind me, walked across the thick carpet, and sank into the chair Rufus offered me. So many things about his interview were in such stark contrast with the others I had had. At last, I was being asked to talk about what I "thought" not simply what I "knew." And the person inviting me to share my opinions was sitting in a chair opposite me, both of us either side of his cheerful fire with no vast expanse of desk between us. And then there was Rufus himself.

I'd been a precocious adolescent in more ways than just the academic. I was long past sexual innocence even then, though my confidence still far outstripped my actual experience as is typical of most very young men I suppose. Rufus, though, was an experience beyond anything I had ever known up to that point. I think if I were to meet him for the first time even now his presence would have the same impact upon me. He has changed remarkably little in the last ten years. His hair is white now but it was then, thick and strong. I like to imagine it turned at a very early age, if indeed it hadn't always been white. And Rufus's age is hard to tell from his face, so much of it being concealed by the splendid luxuriousness of his beard and moustache, also white. His frame is large, and a careless observer might at first think this was the corpulence of the typical college professor, fond of his food and drink and not so keen on exercise. Wrong.

Even sitting there that first day, I could feel the strength Rufus radiated. It was like being close to a furnace or some kind of dynamo. You might not be able to see the energy, but you could feel it, sense it in some way. He excited me then, intellectually and physically. Even as we talked about Stoker and then Blake and Austen and Chaucer, I was looking at his wrists, noticing the black hairs there, such a startling contrast to the white of his beard and hair, and wondering whether his chest hairs were white or black, whether the hair swept down over the swell of his belly to the black (white?) nest at his legs? What it would be like to suck at his cock here in the old-world charm of his Master's room, breathe in the smell of leather and tobacco and male musk, and reach up to stroke his heavy belly? What it would take to make a man like Rufus cry out in pleasure? What it would take to make him come?

I blinked and shook my head to clear it of the images. Ten years on and they still hadn't lost their power over me. I wondered which was sadder: the thought that I might one day actually get to live my daydreams with Rufus and find reality so much less exciting than fantasy, or the thought that actually I never would. I knocked, stepped in, closed the door, and just took a second to breathe in the smells.

"Good morning to you, Sean. I hear you seem to be in a spot of bother."

Harry had been busy, I thought. "Good day to you Rufus." I walked to the chair, the very same chair I had sat in for the first time so long ago, nodded, and sat down. "I am caught up in an...unpleasantness," I said cautiously. "It is regrettable but not really my fault." I shifted uncomfortably. That was nothing less than truth, but I still felt like a naughty schoolboy in front of the headmaster. If only my headmaster had been more like Rufus. I think I might positively have begged for the cane at school if that had been the case.

Rufus nodded. "Lee Barker is a very promising student. I'm sure he's learned much under you."

I looked up sharply at that one, but Rufus's attention seemed suddenly to have switched to a sheaf of papers on a small table by his side, and I couldn't tell if this world-renowned expert on late eighteenth/early nineteenth century gothic literature had actually stooped to the depths of a double entendre.

We had spoken about much together over the years, Rufus and I, when I'd been undergraduate, postgraduate, and now I was a Fellow. But we had never spoken about my love life, certainly never about his. For some reason, though, I'd always worked on the assumption that he knew everything about it. If St Thad's did have telepathy, Rufus was its Master. "I gather he has gone missing," he said. DI Marrin's words came back to me: *"quantities of blood."* I pushed them to the back of my mind and merely nodded. "Let us hope for the best," he said with a heavy sigh. "It is really all that we can do."

And that was all he said on the matter, which, I thought, was all that needed to be said. In his own way Rufus was reassuring me and making it quite clear to me that he, unlike DI Marrin and possibly all my students, didn't think I was in some way reprehensively involved. I loved Rufus, I really did, and wondered again why I would never ever tell him so.

The matter, as far as Rufus was concerned, dealt with, he leaned forward and passed me the papers he had been shuffling through. "In the meantime, we have more mundane matters to concern ourselves with. Glass of sherry?"

I hate sherry, and it was much too early in the day. Like I always did, I accepted. We silently raised our small crystal glasses to each other and drank. It tasted superb, the way it did only in that room with him. I put the glass down, still savouring its rich warmth, and looked for myself though the papers I'd been given. *Why now*, I couldn't help thinking. *He obviously knows I have other things on my mind. Or is that the reason, to take my mind off that...other business?* "The new chair?" The new academic position Lee had spoken to me about, that he had tried to get himself appointed to. Rufus's motives might have been kind, but his choice of subject to divert my attention was ironically unhappy.

Rufus nodded. "It is perhaps unfortunate that you have become embroiled in such a...difficult situation"—I attempted to protest at the word "embroiled" but Rufus waved it to one side as unimportant—"but this is a matter than needs to be dealt with now. The company that wishes to sponsor our new chair is anxious to speak with us as soon as is possible."

All credit to Rufus. Most of the other Fellows of the College, even the ones who weren't as old as him, would almost certainly have invested that single word "company" with as much venom as they could. The worlds of Education and Business, Academe and Mammon, never coexist comfortably, and in venerable establishments like our own they were thought of as being about as compatible as wild dogs and kittens. But that attitude might have been fine and dandy when St. Thad's had first been founded, or possibly even for three or four centuries afterwards. But in the twenty-first century, biting the hand that fed you, even if it belonged, metaphorically, to a grocer rather than a gentleman, could only lead to starvation, and Rufus was far too wise to allow that. So, he spoke the c-word with supreme neutrality.

I glanced at the name embossed at the head of the papers he had given me. "'Aegis'. Is that meant to be reassuring, honest, or just pretentious?"

"They're based in America so probably the first, never the second, and definitely, if unintentionally, the third."

"Careful, Rufus, you'll be referring to the Colonies next."

"I still mourn their loss," he said with mock solemnity.

I returned to the papers. "You know, I still can't say that I've ever really heard about these people."

"You should try speaking more to our colleagues in the Economics department."

"I find it hard to do so and stay awake."

"Quite. Although I have heard that young Edwards is quite a...conversationalist." Again, I looked for some expression, some hint that I was being teased. I, too, had heard about Edwards, though what my sources had told me about his oral skills had had nothing to do with conversation. He was on my to-do list. "Be that as it may, Aegis, it seems, is more of an umbrella name…"

"As the word suggests."

"Indeed, given to the parent company. If you look through the portfolio there, I think you will definitely recognise some of the other smaller companies that are to be found under its corporate shadow."

I scanned through the pages Rufus indicated and whistled. "Talk about household names. Why on Earth are people like this interested in funding a chair at an English university?"

Rufus spread his hands. "We do have something of a reputation, Sean," he said dryly. "It cannot hurt any commercial enterprise to have its name associated with one as prestigious as our own."

"So you say, but I remain dubious. And why should I be the one who has to deal with this unholy representative of filthy capitalism?"

Rufus laughed. "Sean my boy, I know you take possibly sinful pride in the fact that you are by far the youngest Fellow of our college. This, as I believe the young say, is the 'payback.' You are by a long way the best suited of all of us to deal with this emissary from the modern world." His words became gentler, less obviously amused. "And I also thought it might take your mind off your present woes." He leaned back and his tone changed yet again into what in someone less august might have been described as bantering. "Besides, I have a feeling you are particularly well-suited to deal with

Aegis's representative."

I flicked suspiciously to the last page of the document. "Christopher Bailey."

"Chris," said Rufus with mild reproof, gazing towards the ceiling and waving his pipe stem vaguely. "I am assured you must call him Chris."

"Why? Is he unable to cope with a name of three syllables?"

Rufus tutted. "Overweening pride, Sean," he said. "Remember, that was Lucifer's sin."

"Lucifer never had to wine and dine American businessmen."

Rufus looked thoughtful. "Actually, given the number there are bound to be in hell, I'm sure he must have."

We finished the sherry over a few suggestions of what I should and should not say to this wretched businessman I was to have the dubious honour of escorting to the next formal college dinner in two days' time. Rufus rose with me when I stood to go and, rather surprisingly, took my hand. It wasn't a handshake, rather the closest this quiet, reserved man could come to a reassuring hug. I was absurdly touched and determined not to show it lest it embarrass us both. "Don't let this business with young Barker worry you, Sean," he said. "I'm sure everything will turn out well."

I nodded, thinking silence was the best response, and turned to go, but as I did something Lee had said came back to me. "He said something about working with you on his thesis. I hadn't known that. I thought he was working with Professor McCafferey."

"Did he say what on?"

"No."

"Hm. I fear young Mr. Barker was...*is* inclined to, shall we say, embellish situations. McCafferey is indeed the tutor in charge of his thesis."

"Right." Of course, he was. Rufus was the Master of the College. He probably hadn't taken a personal interest in a student's thesis in years. Not since mine in fact. "Typical. Lee certainly was prone to exaggerate."

"True. But he said some remarkable things about you."

Rufus sat back down in his leather armchair so I knew our interview was at an end and I had no choice but to leave his room with that last comment buzzing around in my head. Now that had to be a tease, didn't it? If only Rufus knew how close to home it had struck me. *Remarkable things.* Now what the hell did that mean? Good things? I'd forgotten or wilfully overlooked the fact that at some stage, possibly even right up to last night, Lee had actually admired me. Maybe if I'd thought a bit more about that and a bit less about how irritating I'd found him I'd have let him stay in my rooms. And then he wouldn't...

I shook my head and walked determinedly on to my next appointment. Nothing that had happened had been my fault. Besides, Lee *was* going to turn up again. He had to.

Chapter Five

I changed my mind about "Chris" the instant I saw him.

I hear some colleges around the country have formal dinners once a term. The more determinedly traditional might have one once a week. St Thad's, of course, insisted on three a week: all tutors present, all staff and students (did I mention we're an all-male college, one of the last in the country—just another of my alma mater's good points) in suits and gowns. Mr Bailey had been invited to one of these, I had no doubt, to wow his American sensibilities with a little traditional pageantry. Normally, I confess, I do rather like it. It makes the young men at least look very handsome, and I do quite enjoy sweeping around the place in my full graduate's gown, its deep-red trim signifying my degree subject. Tonight, though, as I was putting it on, I was irritated again, feeling rather like a monkey being dressed up to perform tricks for money. Until, that is, I laid eyes on Mr. Christopher Bailey. Rufus was, of course, there and he merely smiled, still somehow managing to convey an entire *I told you so* vibe.

Chris Bailey was gorgeous.

All right, so there was a certain American-corporate-wholesomeness about him, that plastic transatlantic sheen of high-powered businessmen, politicians, and movie stars, but above and beyond that he had a chin and shoulders that were all nature and not art, and a knowing twinkle in those astonishingly blue eyes that said, "You know this is a joke and I know it's a joke. Let's just get through it, okay, and later on, when we're alone..." Like I said, my erotic imagination wastes no time.

We'd met for premeal drinks in the Fellows' room adjacent to the main dining hall, and amid a gathering of about a dozen Fellows all decked out in their academic finery, he stood out in a simple dark suit and deep-red tie. He turned towards me the minute I entered and smiled, and I admit those perfect teeth created agreeable little flutters in my heart, tummy, and cock. I paused only to check the cut of my gown before walking over to him to take the hand he was offering.

"Hi, I'm Chris."

"Sean."

His handshake was warm and firm, and did it last just a fraction of a second longer than it needed to?

"Sean Sinclair, yeah?"

"I'm afraid so." Unlike Jean-Philippe, diffidence isn't normally a strong suit of mine, but with this man I found myself falling into the role of the reserved Englishman. Well, they like that sort of thing don't they, Yanks? Olde-worlde charm and all that. Pulls them like a magnet in New York clubs so I'm told. *No harm in trying a bit of it here*, I thought. I tried not to notice that Rufus was arching his eyebrows in the background at this show of unusual humility on my part.

"Expert on the medieval lyric?"

"I wouldn't say 'expert,'" and here I had to contrive to turn my back on Rufus while still facing Chris. Before I'd entered the room, I had been hoping that Rufus would stay with me so that I wouldn't be stuck on my own with a boring businessman. Now, I was quite happy thank you to be left quite alone with Chris.

"You're too modest," he said.

Aren't I just? I thought, shrugging.

"I read your recent paper on the *Pearl* poet. I thought it was brilliant."

"You've read that!" I'll admit it, his comment surprised me and jolted me for a moment out of my role play.

He smiled again (white, strong teeth—very American, very sexy) and I got the strong impression he knew very well the game I'd been playing and was amused to see me startled out of it. "I like to get to know as much as I can about people I'm going to meet and be doing business with. I'm actually very interested in Middle English writing too. In fact"—and he leaned oh so slightly in towards me, lowering his voice as if delivering some secret—"I think you'll be pleasantly surprised at just how much we have in common." He waggled a finger between us and for a second I wasn't sure what he was signifying. "Same taste in colours for a start."

Of course. His tie was the same shade of red as the trim of my gown. I laughed. "I'm afraid mine's a bit more than a fashion statement."

"So's mine," he said.

While I was digesting that one Rufus raised his glass of sherry and tapped it with a spoon. With everyone familiar with the routine, the small sound was enough to bring the genial chatter of the room to a stop. "Gentlemen, shall we proceed to dinner?" One by one the Fellows finished their drinks, replaced their glasses, and made their ways into the dining hall. I saw Rufus approach Dr Wilson, a mathematics professor whom, rumour had it, was only in his forties, though a life of devotion to dry numbers and statistics had left him looking like he was in his sixties. "Gerald," I heard Rufus say quietly, "I wonder, would you mind taking a seat with Alex and Frank tonight, just so I can make a place for our important guest?"

"Of course, Rufus," Dr Wilson said immediately in that clipped way of his, but I saw his lips thin and caught the sharp glance in my direction and knew what it meant. Fellows of course sat apart from the student body on a raised dais at one end of the hall, but even then, there were further divisions, the Fellows having three tables. The table at which Rufus sat was, naturally enough, the High Table, and to sit with him was a mark of seniority. There were four other places, two on either side of him, and only recently had I been able to lay claim to one of them after the death of an ancient professor of physics (who was rumoured to have had an undergraduate fling with Albert Einstein). My relief at the promotion to High Table had been profound as, if I couldn't have the pleasure of sitting with the good-looking undergraduates, I could at least be spared the dull conversation of most of the Fellows by having Rufus to talk with. But as the most recent person to ascend to that exalted position it should have been I not Dr Wilson who gave his place up for our guest. When we got to the table Rufus had a further little surprise for me. I had naturally expected him to seat Mr. Bailey between himself and me so that we could both talk to him. Instead, he showed Mr. Bailey to the end seat, and at first, I thought he'd made a mistake, had perhaps even inadvertently slighted our important guest. Then I thought again and understood what he had done. The only person Bailey could talk to now was me. In a crowded room Rufus had contrived to put us together as alone as we possibly could be. Chris didn't seem to be objecting.

We stood, waiting for the students to all enter and then, as tradition demanded, Rufus gave the Latin benediction. As my personal tradition demanded, I lowered my head but didn't close my eyes as the more devout did. Instead, I sneaked a look at Chris. His head was bowed, too, but then it turned, and he was looking at me. He winked. It was all I could do to smother my laughter.

The prayer done, we sat, the wine was poured, and the first course was served. Now I was supposed to carry out my task: extol the virtues of St. Thad's and secure the sizeable financial donation Aegis was dangling in front of our noses. *Sod that,* I thought. I wanted to know more about this man. "So, is this your first time in England?" As an opening gambit it was right up there with *Do you come here often?* But it was a start, and I had a feeling we wouldn't be keeping to the small talk for too long.

Chris shook his head with that half smile of his I was beginning to find so beguiling. "Not at all. I've done some research here in the past."

"For Aegis?"

"Of course."

"Where did you go?"

Chris spread his immaculately manicured hands. No rings I noticed, as perhaps he had wanted me to. "Oh, here and there," he said vaguely. "It was all work-related. I didn't get a chance to...see the sights."

"We'll have to correct that for you."

"I'd like that."

He took a moment to look around the hall and I took the moment to look at him. Everything about him conveyed the sort of manly simplicity it probably cost a fortune to create, from the clean lines of his Armani suit to the cut of his wheat-blond hair. Hard to tell how old he was. Probably older than me given his high position in Aegis, but if anything, he looked younger, in the way having an expensive facial every day can achieve. But then again, maybe he was a high-speed high-flyer, like me. He'd said we had a lot in common.

"Beautiful," he murmured.

"Yes," I breathed, realising too late we were almost certainly not talking about the same thing. "I'm sorry?"

He gestured outwards. "This hall. It's like something out of *Tom Brown's School Days*, y'know?" He laughed apologetically. "Sorry, I guess that's kind of crass. It's just so very...British."

"English," I ventured to correct, and nodded. It was, and yet at the same time, it was also completely unlike anything else currently existing in England. A piece of frozen history really.

"Who are they?" He was pointing to the portraits hung all around the hall.

"Our illustrious predecessors, the past Masters of the College," and I went on to name them all, one after the other. It had been an undergraduate tradition when I'd been a student, that the first fresher to be able to name all the past Masters in under thirty seconds without a single fault had free drinks from the Junior Common Room for the rest of that night. Needless to say, in my fresher year I had won.

"So maybe one day your portrait will end up on the walls," Chris said.

"Oh, you generally have to have been dead at least a hundred years before they get around to that. And," I added, realising I had just exposed one of my life's ambitions perhaps a little too precipitously, "you have to have been Master. Who knows if I will ever be so lucky?"

"Who knows indeed," he said, raising his glass and tipping it to me before drinking as if toasting me. "But you seem to be missing one."

I smiled. "I'm impressed. Most people don't notice." Chris was looking up at the space directly above the High Table, the one that conspicuously did not contain a portrait. "That is the Founder."

"Sorry?"

I laughed. "It's an old college tradition. Or perhaps it's more accurate to say it's an old college joke. It's supposed to have been where the portrait of St. Thad's Founder hung but for some mysterious reason, lost in the mists of time, it disappeared and was never replaced." Chris nodded seriously and I'm afraid I laughed again. "The more likely truth is that it was some ghastly daub that just fell apart from old age and no one could be bothered to replace it."

"So, there is no picture of the Founder?"

"There is no Founder, not that we know of anyway. Most likely St Thad's was founded by a group of well-to-do merchants wanting somewhere their sons could go to do better for themselves. *Le plus ça change.* Who knows, if Aegis does indeed sponsor this Chair, which I'm fairly sure we're supposed to be talking about now, maybe one day there'll be a picture of you up there," and I tipped my glass to him in an ironic echo of his own gesture. I expected him to laugh or even smile but instead he continued to gaze at the portraits thoughtfully for a few moments before turning the attention of those beautiful blue eyes back to me.

"Enough of the past for the moment," he said. "Let's talk about you."

"My favourite subject," I said, which was probably the most honest thing I had said so far that evening.

Contrary to popular opinion, the food at these college formal meals is not usually that good. Fellows and students are supplied by the same kitchens and the result is, frankly, institutional rather than cordon bleu. Tonight, however, there was a marked improvement on what was arriving on our plates, and also, I noticed after sneaking a look at the lower tables, a marked difference from what the undergrads were being served. I raised an inquiring eye at Rufus. He coughed apologetically. "I took the liberty of engaging a chef from the town to help out in the kitchens. Given the added strain of a guest." *Given the need to impress a potential source of money,* I thought, and raised my glass to him, an unusually fine Rioja, from his own cellar I suspected.

So, given the fine food and good company I was in the unusual position of regretting the speed with which the meal passed. All too soon Rufus was standing to deliver the end of meal Latin blessing, the students were filing out, and the Fellows were retiring to the side room for port and smokes. Reluctant though I was to leave the unusually well-provided dinner table, I consoled myself with the thought of more talk with Chris and, I guessed, a superb bottle of port (or two) doubtless dusted off for the special occasion. My hopes looked like being dashed twice.

The first cloud on my horizon came in the shape of Dr Wilson. Literally sidelined during the meal he took the first opportunity now to press his attentions on our wealthy visitor. "Dr Wilson," he said without preamble, virtually seizing Chris's hand. Chris was far too smooth to let any surprise or distaste show at the mathematician's uncouthness. "Hear you're thinking of coughing up a sizeable sum for St. Thad's." The man might be a genius at sums, but he has the social graces of a dockside navvy.

"Well..." Chris demurred.

"Waste of time giving it to that lot," Wilson said, pausing only to knock back a generous slug of the Masters' port and wave in the general direction of myself and a couple of colleagues from the humanities end of the college. "Man of business like yourself should be investing in the sciences. That's where the future lies."

"Sometimes," Chris said, "we stand to gain much from the past."

Wilson snorted, drew breath, and was about, I could tell, to launch into a lengthy and detailed refutation of this idea when Rufus appeared at his side. "Gerald," he said genially, one hand gently resting on his elbow, "I wonder if you would be so kind as to lend me your opinion on a small matter that has been puzzling me. Peterson over at Gladstone's says he's got the answer but I'm sure he can't be right and if anyone can set me straight it must be you. Shall we go over here? Please excuse us, gentlemen," and with gentle but irresistible pressure he guided Wilson away.

"A narrow escape," I breathed. "Forgive me if that sounds unprofessional."

Chris shook his head slightly. "Not at all. My own thoughts exactly." Once again, we were in accord, but then came the second blow to my hopes. Chris went on, "However, I'm afraid now I have to be leaving."

"Oh." My disappointment was quite genuine, and I couldn't help expressing it. "Well, I hope..." I stopped as a quite disagreeable thought struck me. "You don't mean... You are staying in Britain for a while, aren't you? You're not going back to America tomorrow?"

Chris laughed easily. "No, no. My business is going to keep me in Britain for quite a while yet. No, I mean I have to turn in for the night. I'll admit to being a bit jet-lagged. I have a long day ahead of me, and some things I'd really like to get out of the way before I go to sleep."

"Ah, right." It occurred to me that I'd been making my feelings just a little too plain there, and I determined to rein them in a little. "Are you staying in Hall? Have they given you rooms?"

"No, I didn't like to presume."

"Hardly presumption."

"The company had booked me into The Regency anyway."

"Ah. Right." Right indeed. St Thad's was full of enough history and tradition to warm any American's heart, but it definitely lacked the heating systems and insulation to warm the rest of his body at this time of year. The Regency, on the other hand, was a five-star luxury hotel, the best for a considerable distance. It could hardly have been a struggle for Chris to have decided in favour of the hotel over St. Thad's for his base. A pity though. Rooms here would have given me the pretext to walk him around the Quad, maybe drop in for a night cap, and then...? Again, I reined myself in. There really was no point in running ahead of myself.

"I wonder, though, if I could ask a favour?" Chris continued. "Would you be so kind as to walk me back to the hotel? All those alleys and small streets. I'm not sure I could find my way back in the dark."

It was at most five minutes from St. Thad's to the Regency. There were maybe two turns to make: one left, one right. I could have drawn a map on half a napkin. "Of course," I said. "It'll be a pleasure."

"Good. I'll just go and make my farewells to Rufus and then we can be on our way."

Rufus, always the gracious host, had demurred to Chris's desire to leave, so comparatively early, the dinner that was ostensibly in his honour. I caught the expression on his face as I was leaving, not quite on Chris's arm, but as near as damn it. It was odd, a mixture of resignation and concern. *Don't worry,* I wanted to say to him, *I'm a big boy who can look after himself. And I'm not about to blow the college's chances of hooking up to Aegis's cash.* All I could do was wave to him cheerily with a gesture intended to reassure, but the door closed on us before I got a chance to see how he took it.

The night air was refreshingly cold after the fug of the Senior Common Room, our breaths pluming out in front of us as we walked on, huddled in our coats, chatting idly. The stone of the ancient buildings and paths already glittered with ice. "Y'know, I hate to sound the typical American tourist," Chris said, "but this"—and he gestured around himself, taking in, well, everything really—"is so romantic."

"In the lyrical poetic sense, you mean."

"This is the Quad, right?" which didn't seem like an answer to what I had said.

"Yes. Short for Quadrangle of course."

"And what is that?" He was pointing to the centre of the square lawn, and the squat blocky shape that could just be made out in the dim light coming from the study windows on the Quad's four sides. I managed to hold in a sigh. Chatting about the College's paintings and buildings, etc was all very well, but by this time I was very keen on seeing where our conversation would go when we were on our own in a modern, well-heated, well-lit hotel room, if indeed we spent any time at all just talking. "It's the Founding Stone."

He turned to face me. I couldn't see his expression in the gloom, but the tone of his voice made it clear he was smiling. "The Founding Stone? For a college without a Founder? Is this another *tradition*?"

"I suppose it is." I made as if to walk on, but Chris remained obstinately where he was, looking at the damn stone, so I was obliged to go and stand at his side and try to make up for my shortness. "It's just a stone. Nothing special. Some say it might have been a millstone or something like that, so maybe it symbolises one of the businessmen who put his money into the college at its start. No one's supposed to touch it." I knew as soon as the words had left my mouth, I had said the wrong thing and I had delayed our hotel experience by at least a few more precious minutes.

"Why not?"

"No reason. It's just another tradition, another one of those stupid rules we live by in colleges. It's probably just meant to keep people off the lawn, a quainter version of a Keep Off The Grass sign."

"Let's touch it."

"What!"

"C'mon, let's touch it. What's the matter? You scared?"

Scared was not the right word. Irritated, yes. Horny and frustrated, definitely. And also surprised. This sort of undergraduate prankishness was not what I'd expected from a high-powered transatlantic businessman, and this frat boy enthusiasm seemed at odds with the sexily urbane man I had just dined with. But then, I reminded myself, how many sexily urbane men had I met in my time? I shrugged my shoulders. "Okay." If we must.

"Will anyone be watching?"

"Everyone in his right mind," and I couldn't help just a bit of emphasis there, "is inside eating, drinking, or making merry. If we're quick no one will notice."

"What are we waiting for then? C'mon," and he was off, trotting quickly across the short grass of the Quad lawn heading for the Founding Stone. Unable by this point to hold in that sigh, I dutifully followed.

The frost on the grass crunched softly underfoot as we made our way to the Stone. Chris reached it first and stood, looking down at it. "I'll bet all the undergraduates do this at least once in their time here."

"Actually no," I said as I joined him. "I don't think anyone's been interested enough in it to make the effort. It is just an old stone block."

Chris was still regarding it. For someone who'd made the effort to get this close, now he seemed almost reluctant to touch the thing. "Yeah. Right," he said softly. He didn't sound convinced.

I looked around the sides of the Quad at the windows. I wasn't worried that we'd be punished if caught *in flagrante delicto*. I was mortified, though, at the thought of being observed doing something so puerile. "So, are you going to touch it?" I not so gently hinted.

"What? Oh yeah, right." Drawing his hand from his coat pocket, Chris removed a glove and slowly stretched out a hand towards the stone. For a fraction of a second he held it an inch or two over its pitted surface and then deliberately placed it down firmly and held it on the cold surface.

"Mission accomplished," I said pointedly.

It was a second or two before he answered. "Yes," he said finally. "Yes, I guess it is." He withdrew his hand, looked at it for a second as if expecting to see something different, and then pulled his glove back on and stepped briskly away. "C'mon. It's freezing out here."

"Isn't it?" I muttered and followed on. Perhaps it was true what my old grandmother had always said. All Americans were mad.

Once out of the college gates, The Regency was about two minutes away. On an impulse I guided us down a side street. It might add about another minute to our journey but, unlike detours to touch old rocks, this one had a more interesting possible outcome. "They call this Lovers' Lane," I said when we were about halfway down. "The undergrads, I mean. Trite but only to be expected I suppose. I'd guess that every uni town has its Lovers' Lane somewhere near the campus."

Chris slowed and then stopped and turned to face me fully. There were no streetlights nearby, the only thing making his face even half visible the sliver of moon high above us. "And now why would it be called that?" he asked softly.

I leaned back against one of the tall buildings lining either side of the alley. "Long. Dark. Secluded."

"Little chance of interruption?"

"Exactly."

He moved closer. His breath was warm on my face. "Sounds perfect." He leaned into me, gently pushing his hands up, under my arms, pinning me against the stone as he pressed his lips to mine and kissed me long and hard. I opened my mouth to him without hesitation and his tongue slid in possessively. I could taste the fine wines we had been drinking back in Hall. Bingo!

When he finally pulled back, I'll admit to being a mite breathless, but Chris seemed as cool as ever and he simply smiled before saying, "Shall we continue on our way?" as if we'd just taken a break from a board meeting. Then his hand dropped to my crotch and he squeezed hard. I hissed, as much at the unexpectedness of it as the pressure, and reached out for what hung between his legs but I only got a tantalising touch before he pulled back and moved off again, laughing quietly. But I'd been knocking on wood, of that there was absolutely no doubt!

"Do they really call it Lover's Lane?" he asked as I caught up to him.

"No," I admitted readily, "but if I ever do rise to any position of importance in this town, I shall very definitely petition to make sure that one day it is."

He laughed again, but then suddenly he stopped and held up his hand. "Did you hear that?"

I tried to listen, though events had got my heart pounding quite nicely thank you, and though the heated pumping of my blood was doing wonders in making me oblivious of the cold, it created a distracting thumping in my ears.

"There it is again? Did you hear it?"

I had to shake my head. "'Fraid not. What?"

"Footsteps."

I couldn't help a teasing laugh. "I thought you big-city American types were used to open gang warfare on the tough mean streets. Don't tell me you're getting worried about being mugged on a quiet English backstreet?"

I've often heard it said that Americans have no sense of irony. Certainly, Chris didn't pick up on mine then. He continued to scan the area, listening hard for further noises. "I'm from Boston, not New York," he said softly, which I suppose was meant to be some kind of explanation.

"Well, wherever you're from, you really don't need to worry about being jumped here. Our crime rate is pretty low, and what crime there is tends to have more to do with local schoolkids lifting cigarettes in the corner shops than anything more serious. Don't worry. I'll protect you if anyone jumps out on us."

Chris snorted genially, and abandoned his attempts to hear any more, perhaps reassured by my promise of protection, more probably because he simply couldn't hear anything more. "C'mon," he said, "let's get out of the cold."

It had been a while since I'd gone back with a man to his hotel room, but even then, I don't think I'd ever been invited to a hotel as swanky as The Regency. I'd left my gown back at college, of course, though I was still kitted out in my best suit, but as soon as I stepped through the gilt double doors into the understated, deep-carpeted luxury of the hotel, I was acutely aware of how less than impressive my off-the-peg ensemble looked next to Chris's sartorial perfection and that of the other residents drifting elegantly around the foyer. I felt as awkward as a student in jeans and T-shirt and waited for the supercilious receptionist behind the sweeping oak signing-in desk to ask me what the hell I thought I was doing there. The staff of The Regency, however, were either far more used to the peccadilloes of their clientele or far too well-bred to mention or express them, even by so much as the raising of an eyebrow. If the white-haired buffer handing over the key to Chris had any suspicions about why Mr Bailey was bringing another man back to his room at that time of night, he didn't betray it in the slightest.

To call the suite Chris showed me into simply "a room" was a massive understatement. I'm a smug superior bastard most of the time, I'll be the first to admit it, but even I nearly whistled like a hick on walking in.

"This has got to be bigger than about four rooms put together back at Thad's."

Chris shrugged as he took off his jacket and hung it carefully by the door. "The company looks after its employees," he murmured. "Drink?" I shook my head. "Good," he said walking towards me, unknotting his tie as he approached. "Me neither. Spoils performance." And then he had his arms around me again and was kissing me as before in Lover's Lane, but even harder, pushing me back all the time. Thrilled by his eagerness I didn't notice or care where he was taking me until I stumbled against something, fell backward, and found myself sinking into the biggest, softest, most voluptuous bed I had ever encountered.

Chris let go and stood back then, looking down at me, pulling the undone tie swiftly out of his collar, removing cufflinks, unbuttoning his shirt. There was none of Jean-Philippe's carelessness here. Everything was swift but precise, and Chris didn't take his eyes off me throughout. It was a businessman's examination, thorough, exacting, taking stock of what he was about to possess. It was a fucking turn-on, and he knew it. I should have been taking my own clothes off, but I just couldn't. I was fascinated by the sight of him, hot to know what kind of body lay under those expensive designer labels. What was finally revealed was surprising. It certainly wasn't disappointing.

Even with his clothes on it had been obvious that Chris was slim and in shape, but I was wise enough in the ways of the world to know the lies skilful tailoring can create. To the joy of my hardening cock and racing heart I now saw there hadn't been a scrap of artifice in the outline Chris presented to the world. What you saw was what you got, and I was about to get it all. Chris was beautifully muscled, not the bulging beef of a Jean-Philippe, but the clear-cut lean lines of a man who always only eats the best and uses the facilities of his corporate gym to the fullest: a flat belly, defined pecs, smoothly contoured shoulders and neck, skin silky smooth, tanned the colour of light honey. No tan lines. The blood pulsed in my temples, chest, and crotch as I took it all in. I was aching with anticipation, burning to feel, smell, and taste him. It was an effort but I held back, letting the anticipation build, and Chris stood there, letting me, supremely confident, enjoying my silent devouring of his body with my eyes. "Like it?" he murmured.

"Fuck yes!" His cock was a beauty. Already smack up against his belly, jutting up strongly out of a neatly trimmed bush of light-blond hair, its cut crown thrust up way past his navel. I couldn't resist. "Outstanding!" I reached out, unable to hold myself back any longer, hungry to hold that hard veined length in my hand, to pull it to my mouth. With unexpected speed he caught my hand in his, holding it back from his erect pride. With a smile he pulled it, gently but firmly, up past his belly, up to his chest, and laid it on his left pec, over his heart. Over the other surprise I'd seen as soon as he'd removed his shirt. "A tattoo?"

But even as I spoke the word Chris was leaning down, pressing the length of his naked body against my still-clothed form, and his tongue was deep in my mouth again, making any further communication other than delighted and breathless gruntings impossible, his lengthy hard-on grinding into mine, spurting warm precum liberally over my freshly dry-cleaned trousers. I tore at my clothes, desperate for the feel of my skin against his, as much of it as possible, any questions about that unexpected tattoo driven away from my mind along with almost every other scrap of rational thought. Without leaving off kissing, Chris pulled at my buttons and zips, and my last fully coherent thought that had nothing to do with sex was to notice that he was far less fastidious with my clothes than he had been with his own. But then I didn't give a damn either. Tongue to tongue, chest to chest, belly to belly, cock to cock, we bucked hard against each other, hot to shag with a huge silk-sheeted bed and all night to do it in.

You know how it is with some guys: even when it's rough, it's a sharing thing, both of them out for what they can get but always aware of the other man, thinking about his pleasure, too, wanting him to enjoy the moment just as much.

This wasn't like that.

Within seconds it was clear it was going to be every man for himself, and that if I wanted to be more than living, breathing, moaning, groaning wanky-hanky for Chris I was going to have to work for it. Which was fine by me.

We rolled, we thrashed, we grappled, the silk sheets tangling around our increasingly sweaty bodies. It was clear we both liked being on top, and at least to begin with the honours were fairly evenly shared. "You like that, yeah?" I jeered back to the mattress as Chris rode me, his cock pummelling mine as I ran my hands up, over and round his firm smooth buttocks. He didn't reply, just looked down at me with those pale-blue eyes of his, outwardly cool even as his cock was ramming repeatedly, with increasing speed and animal urgency into mine. A twist and I was on top of him, my sweat dripping down onto his face, into those magnetic eyes. He didn't even blink, but lay there, staring back at me, his hair matted by his sweat and mine, the wheat blond darkened to a burnt gold, sticking to the sides of his face and forehead. I loved that! Loved that I had swept away that debonair "civilised" exterior, was reducing him to a sweating panting primitive male. I went to take a handful of his hair and he took advantage to twist and straddle me again. "Bastard!"

I clapped my hands to both sides of his body, pressed hard, and ran them slowly up his flanks, over his chest, down his back. His skin was incredibly smooth, unnaturally smooth I couldn't help thinking, and then I remembered that perfect triangle of gold hair curling over his tight ball sac and knew for the first time what it felt like to shag someone who could afford to go for expensive body waxes as frequently as some of us tried to go for decent haircuts. My mind was suddenly flooded with images of his arse. I couldn't get enough of the near frictionless curves of his buttocks, but what about the arse crack between? Had that received some waxer's careful attention? Would it be perfectly hairless and smooth too? Would a finger slip in as easily as our bodies were slipping on the silk sheets? Would a tongue? Two fingers? Three? My meaty cock?

Galvanised by the erotic images I heaved and was on top again, eager this time to turn him over, arse uppermost so I could make my mental wanderings reality, but swift as ever, Chris struck as I hesitated over how to achieve my goal and I was once again back to the mattress, his knees planted firmly either side of my head. For a moment he just sat there, looking down at me, and I looked up at him from between his thighs, over the wrinkled bulge of his ball sac. He rose slowly onto his knees and leaned forward until his balls were hanging in my face, soft and warm and wiry with a rich spicy musk. I lapped at them, feeling the dangling weight of them on my tongue, and from above me I heard him sigh, tasted the salt of the precum oozing down the length of his penis shaft, over his balls, felt its wet warmth in droplets on my face. I nuzzled in closer, my tongue straining for the softness at the cock base, reaching for that dark temptation I'd been fantasising about. Chris pulled back, moved his knees down to either side of my torso, leaned down, and kissed me again, and my heart thundered fit to burst as his lips met mine, his rigid cock pressed down the length of mine. I abandoned myself to him then, surrendered absolutely as he ran his hands along my arms, pushed them up higher and higher, above my head, until he stopped kissing me, pulled back slightly to look down at me with that slightly crooked smile of his, and I realised that he had pinned my wrists in his hands.

His cock sandwiched tight between his body and mine, he began to drag his way up my body, slowly, very slowly, our sweat and his precum making the passage of his stiff dick over my skin easy. Inch by inch he worked his way up my body, arching back further and further to press his weight down on me, hard, through his cock, eyes nearly closed, breath coming in small gasps as his body trembled with the sensations flooding the nerve endings of his cockhead and shaft. Over my belly, then on my chest, harder against the resistance of my ribs, and then his cock crown, warm, wet, and swollen, was nudging my chin, sliding up over it. I opened and closed my mouth, rubbing the point of my chin against the bonelike rigidity of his cock, making him hiss. He arched more and I could feel the warm, soft weight of his ball sac on my lips again, and I licked and nuzzled until this time my tongue found and pressed into the sponginess of that spot just between ball sac and hole. I could feel it beating like a small wildly spasming heart, and I knew then his orgasm was only seconds away.

I made one last attempt to twist out of his grip, to grab hold of his dick and manually pump it dry, something primal in me desperate to make him cry out helplessly in my hands. It was no good. He had a death grip on my wrists. I saw his eyes close tight completely, his mouth open in a soundless cry, and then my vision was blotted out by the gouts of cum shooting from his volcanically erupting cock and splattering down copiously, seemingly endlessly over my face, sliding into my eyes, nose and mouth.

When he finally let go of my wrists and sank down to one side of the bed I had to use both of my hands to clear my face of his balls' salvo. "Jesus! Are your cobs pressurised or something?" I gasped. I don't think I'd known anyone whose bollocks held so much of the good stuff.

I made then as if to climb on top of him. It was my turn now, and my own balls were burning for some release too. Immediately Chris half turned, raised a hand, put it flat on my chest, and pushed me quickly and firmly back onto the bed. "Hey..." I began.

"You'll like this," he said, and his hand on my chest moved down to my crotch, was joined by the other. Before I could see or say anything I felt his fingers press, swift and hard, into my body. I don't know where exactly, near my balls, near my hole, I know it sounds odd but I couldn't tell precisely where. I went to shout out, anticipating the sort of pain you get when a guy digs his fingers deep into the soft parts of your anatomy, but even as it burst from my mouth my scream twisted from one of pain to one of undiluted, unexpected pleasure. To this day I don't know what Chris did to me, some sort of feng shui/acupuncture/Vulcan nerve grip thing I suppose, but for a few seconds it felt like every nerve in my arse, balls, and cock had been wired into the mains. My orgasm ripped through me like an electric charge and I could only cry out like a teenager coming for the first time and wondering what the hell was happening. My hips arched, my whole body twisted and turned helplessly, Chris unshakably staying with it, maintaining the implacable pressure of his fingers, and I shot my load high up into the air from where it rained down the length of my body. It was intense, it was fast, and when it was over I lay there, jism-coated from his outpourings and mine, feeling like a lorry had run over me, with a stupid smile and a very, very dazed expression plastered over my face. "Where the fuck did you learn to do that? And what was it?" I panted.

"Man management," he said. "You have to know how to keep people happy in my job."

I laughed and turned to face him. I think I've already told you, I'm not a great one for pillow talk. There doesn't seem a great deal of point after you've got what you came for, and it's only human nature for the male to want to collapse into a snoring heap of happy satisfaction after he's done the deed. But I found I enjoyed Chris's dry wit, and I didn't think he'd be the type to try to feed me some romantic tripe we neither of us really felt. I was more right than I'd guessed. He was already getting up and heading for the bathroom.

I'd thought I'd drift off while he was showering. He certainly gave me enough time to, but I found to my slight surprise that silk sheets might be great for shagging in, but they're just not cosy to drowse in. The suite's windows were superbly double-glazed, but my primitive self still knew it was bitterly cold outside and missed the comfort of thick blankets. Maybe I'd become too conditioned to the simple life at St. Thad's.

When he emerged, Chris was wrapped in a thick white cotton dressing gown with the hotel monogram. "There's towels in there for you," he said, "though I'm afraid they only give one dressing gown. I don't think they expect their guests to entertain. Have that drink now? I'll have it ready for you when you've done."

Okay. I'd kind of hoped he'd get back into bed, that we could have drifted off to sleep together, at least for a while, the warmth of a male body spooning with mine almost certainly going a long way to counter the lack of comfort offered by the silk sheets. But, it was obviously not to be. "Any decent red wine?" I asked as I rose from the bed.

"Perhaps not as good as Rufus gave us tonight, but I guess The Regency will have stretched to something halfway interesting."

When I got back from my shower I found that he was right on both counts: the wine certainly not up to Rufus's standard, but considerably better than anything I could find or afford from my local corner shop. I raised my glass to him and he returned the silent toast, leaning in to kiss me on the mouth before drinking from his glass.

We stood for a moment, slightly awkwardly. I noticed that he'd turned on the lamp on the desk to one side of the room and spread around it was a pile of papers and folders and an open laptop. "Working late?"

"Not as far as my bosses back home think." He sighed, though he didn't seem too bothered really. "Different time zones, remember. I'm expecting a call from them any minute."

Ah, the *"I'd love to ask you to stay over but…"* speech. Fair enough. Bloody cold outside and, unusually, even after a pretty thorough and intimate exploration of this man, I still found myself curious about him. It'd just have to wait till the next time. If there was a next time, I reminded myself. There was no guarantee there would be. I'd given too many guys the polite (or not so polite) brush-off myself to be sanguine about every guy getting back to me the next day just because I wanted him to. It's a lifestyle thing, isn't it? But there was nothing to stop me raising the possibility of coffee the next morning, though, maybe in some quaint little coffee shop in the town that would be bound to charm the pants off him. Or maybe in my room, when his pants would be equally at risk. Then his mobile went off.

Chris looked mildly irritated. "Look, I'm sorry but I really have to get that. My bosses aren't exactly the forgiving type and If I don't report in…"

"It's okay. I'll grab my things and…" I left the words hanging. He leaned in again and kissed me once more, and I felt my cock jump under the towel I had wrapped around my waist. Even for me, that swift a recovery after Chris's exacting milking was pretty impressive. It looked like we had chemistry. I headed for the bedroom to collect my clothing.

When I emerged fully dressed Chris had withdrawn to one of the other rooms. I could hear his voice faintly but not make out the words. "Right. I'll see myself out," I said to the closed door, and proceeded to do that very thing.

Chapter Six

I took the long route back. It took me through Lovers' Lane again. (It made me smile, okay?) As I walked I replayed the events of the last hour or so. The memory of Chris's body went a great way towards warding off the effects of the cold: the smooth warmth of his skin; the heated solidity of his cock; the burnt-sugar brown of his nipples. I smiled dreamily to myself. Yeah, that would have shaken his coolness all right if I'd chewed on those babies. A few kisses to begin with, and then some gentle sucking, just to get them standing up and paying attention. Then one tender bud between my teeth, just enough pressure to tease, to pull, and then...

I heard a sound behind me. When I turned to look, no one was there, and it was only when I turned back to resume my walk home that I realised with a start I'd reached the gates of St Thad's. I'd been so caught up in what should have been, and what, if I had my way, would be, that I'd made almost the entire journey on automatic pilot.

Only when I was walking through the gates, tipping a wave to Harry who accepted my late return as stoically as ever, did my subconscious mind finally get the message through to the rest of my brain about that one detail of my erotic musings it had forgotten: the tattoo lying just over one of Chris's exquisite nipples. I stopped in my tracks. That was odd. I'd been surprised to see a sophisticated businessman like Chris had his tit inked, but I'd had my attention diverted before I could ask him about it. I'd meant to bring up the subject later, and God knows I'd had plenty of opportunity to get close enough to the tattoo to examine it in microscopic detail. Yet, somehow, I hadn't, and now, though I could recall in vivid detail the hair at the nape of Chris's neck, the cut of it at his crotch, the way his belly button was a flattened oval rather than a circle and that his mouth had tasted of mint the last time he'd kissed me, I couldn't even begin to recall the shape, size, design, or colours of that tattoo. *Okay*, I thought, as I made my way up the small flight of stairs to my rooms, *so now I have yet one more reason to see Chris again. With his shirt off.*

My room looked particularly cheerless as I re-entered it. Just the contrast with your recent brush with luxury, I told myself, and the fact the bloody fire had gone out again. And the fact I was going to bed alone. I restoked the fire, banking it up so that it would hopefully stay in overnight. I threw off my clothes for the second time that night, though with much less enthusiasm than before, and then I fell into bed and wrapped the triple duvet around myself, shivering at its chill initial contact. *It would have been nice to have a warm body in here with me,* I thought, as real sleep finally crept over me.

And then the dreams started.

It was not surprising, really, that I should dream about a man in my bed, considering the thoughts I fell asleep to, and let's be truthful here, dreams of men were not that unusual for me. I'll confess, though, that the locations are usually a little more exotic than my rooms at St. Thad's. (A particular favourite was set in the changing rooms of the British Olympic Men's Gymnastics Team, but that's something I normally keep to myself.) What was also unusual, apart from the prosaic setting, was my dream's choice of man. I'd have expected Chris to have tiptoed into my head, either reprising some of the highly enjoyable things we'd got up to, or maybe trying out a few of the ones I'd got filed away in my mind for future testing. But it wasn't Chris who entered my dream that night, and he definitely wasn't tiptoeing.

It began with a feeling, an awareness of another presence in the bed with me. *That's all right,* my sleep-fuzzy mind told me, *that's what you want, isn't it?* I rolled over, reached out, and pulled the man's body I found there close to me as if it was the most normal thing in the world to do. It was cold. Cold as ice. And that was all right, too, in the illogic/logic of the dream state. It was cold outside. I was warm. I could warm this man. So I held him close, feeling my warmth seep from my body into his cold flesh, wanting it to warm us both. But I just grew colder and colder.

And then I felt his hardness pressing into my thigh, and my own cock responding, stiffening. I felt his hand on my chest, fingers like moving icicles, tracing their way down over my belly, down to my crotch, cupping my balls till they ached, not with desire, but from the leaching of their warmth, and when they were cold and heavy the icicle fingers released them, and slowly, inescapably, wrapped themselves around my cock. I hissed through gritted teeth, aware of being asleep, incapable of waking up, unable to do anything except suffer this dream. The cold was intense, burning in the blood of my heavy erection like fire, my cock growing ever harder and harder. Like a thick ribbed icicle.

And then there were the lips. From out of the dark, a kiss, like the touch of snow, on my forehead, my neck, each of my nipples, one after the other, moving down, down. As my dream lover descended the duvets were pulled with him until I was left lying naked on the bed, not caring about the bitter chill of the room, not caring about anything except the man between my legs, his hand still firm round my cock, his mouth burning my skin with his freezing kisses.

And then his mouth was at my groin, kissing, the tongue licking, leaving a trail of saliva like gelid water on the insides of my thighs, on my ball sac, which should have been a shrivelled travesty of itself but which throbbed painfully full, along the whole length of my thickened stiff cock. It was too much! From somewhere I found the strength to cry out, to thrash in an attempt to push this iceman away, but with easy strength my arms were pushed back, held, and my crotch assaulted again by tongue and fingers, sending waves of glacial sensations along my tormented nerves that were literally, inexpressibly unbearable...and wonderful. I lay, pinned to my bed, and groaned like a man in pain or on the point of orgasm.

And then the mouth was on my broad dry cockhead, the lips around my crown and moving down, down, taking more and more of my length into a mouth like an arctic cavern, and though I thought I had felt cold before, now I felt myself being absorbed by something beyond mere cold that should have left my cock utterly beyond all sensation but which instead seemed to render it excruciatingly sensitive. I should have cum, I yearned and longed to cum but my balls were hard and heavy as if the jism bulging inside them was frozen solid.

And then came the pain. Needle sharp, stabbing, piercing the frigid stretched skin along my rigid meat, pinpoints of fierce pain blazing against the background of bitter cold. And I screamed. That is, my mouth opened, my lungs, my throat, my entire body reached for the scream the pain drove me to, but no sound emerged into the night air. The pain went on and on, utter agony, total ecstasy, and I knew there was nothing I could do about it. And I knew that if it did not stop, then it would kill me.

"No."

Through the maelstrom of pleasure/pain like a blizzard in my mind I heard the word, or thought I heard it. But the pain went on. "No," the voice said again. Slowly, very, very slowly, the pain receded, the lips slid back up the length of my dick, passing over the crown, releasing me. My cock ached terribly with the return of warmth.

The hands holding me powerless withdrew, but I could only lie there on the bed, my body something lumpish and inert that belonged to someone else. With every atom of strength I could summon I tried to move. Arms and legs failed me, only my head rose slightly. It was the hardest thing I had ever done but I put all my strength into it, straining to see. I had to know. Who or what was in the room with me?

Amongst the shadows round my bed were the silhouettes of two men standing over me, looking down at me. I tried to speak, to demand who they were, what they were doing to me, but I couldn't. My tongue was dead in my mouth. The furthest figure from the bed was tall, but the light from the segment of moon shining through the window was too poor for me to make out much of his features: his hair was silver but that could have been a trick of the moonlight which definitely had drained his face of all colour.

And then there was the other, the one standing closest to the bed, the man who had sucked the heat from my body and would have taken God knows what else if he had been allowed to continue. There was enough light for me to recognise his face. It was a face I knew very well.

Lee.

I awoke with a start. I was tied up, bound in some way! Panicked, I flailed and struck out, frantic to escape whatever was holding me. The duvets covering me flew to either side of the bed and I was left shivering in the cold of the dawn, the bondage entwining me nothing more than twisted bedsheets. Hurriedly I pulled the covers back over me. In my dream they'd been cast off. I must have recovered them at some point I couldn't remember. Or perhaps I'd never lost them at all. It had all just been a dream, hadn't it? Feeling slightly foolish but still unable to simply leave well enough alone, I gingerly slid my hands down to my crotch and gently stroked my dick. Still there. Still reassuringly whole and healthy. No pain. With a reluctance I didn't want to explain, not even to myself, I brought the hand back up, held it out, and inspected the fingers. Nothing. *Of course, there isn't,* I thought, even as I let out a pent-up breath. What had I been expecting to see?

I shivered and cast a look across the room to the fire. It was still smouldering. I'd expected it to be completely out given how very cold the room was. A sudden bang across the room made me shoot upright, set my heart racing all over again. It was the window. A breeze had caught it and slammed it against the frame. With ill grace I clambered from the bed and dragged myself over to the window to shut it, laughing, in a rather strained way, at how uptight I was. The events of the last couple of days must really have been starting to get to me. *Funny, though,* I thought, as I pushed the window catch down firmly, *I could have sworn I'd closed the window before I went to bed.*

Chapter Seven

There's really no way of getting round the fact that I was an utter bastard the next day in my tutorials and seminars. But then, to my mind, after the nightmare I'd experienced the previous night which had comprehensively wiped away any softening afterglow my session with Chris had created, the bloody undergraduates were lucky I turned up at all. To give myself credit I did try to deal with their typical inanities and ignorance with my usual professionalism, but my God they all seemed hellbent on outdoing themselves in the stupidity stakes that day. Even the two lads I might have counted on to raise my spirits, Duncan with his undeniably great mind, and Tony with his undeniably great arse, seemed determined not to show me their best features that day, and I sent both of them and the rest of their cohort packing a mere twenty minutes into their planned two-hour seminar. If they care they'll sue, I told myself.

When the first knock at the door of my teaching room came I assumed it was one or the other of them come to request that actually I did try to teach them something that day. They could play it indignant or placating. Neither method was going to get anywhere with me. "Come in!" I barked. It wasn't a student. The fact it was someone even less desirable was just one more indication of how really shit my day seemed determined to be.

"Your secretary said you'd be teaching," Detective Inspector Marrin said sourly.

I nodded a perfunctory greeting to her as she entered the room. My displeasure was only slightly mollified when she was followed by pretty policeman Sergeant Taylor. *Still looking good,* I thought. "Sarah isn't my secretary. She belongs to the faculty as a whole. And I felt my students would benefit more from a little private study time today rather than anything I could give them."

"Nice," DI Marrin grunted, in a way that rendered the word even more devoid of real meaning than it usually is. She stood there for a moment looking around my room. I forced down the irritation I felt. Ridiculous as it was, I had to remind myself that in her eyes, though she hadn't come out and said it, I was a murder suspect. I wondered if she was looking for clues among the pictures on my walls and books on my shelves. Was she trying to assess my character in the same way a gay man did when invited back to another guy's place and given the chance to poke around on bookshelves and check out the CD and DVD collection while the host went to "get the coffee"? Well, there was no Madonna and Tom of Finland on these shelves, and no lead piping or bottle of poison either.

"Can I help you?" Sergeant Taylor, I noted, had drifted over to a Hieronymus Bosch print I had up on the wall nearest the door. I wondered whether that was because he was genuinely interested or whether he was trying to blend into the background. I wondered, too, if he knew that one of the central images in that particular print of *The Garden of Earthly Delights* was a symbolic representation of the "sin" of sodomy. Most of my students never cottoned on, which was the main reason it amused me so much to have it up in the room.

"It's about the investigation into Lee Barker."

"I rather thought it would be, detective inspector." Should I tell her I'd seen him last night? It didn't take much thought to see how she would interpret that particular dream. I struggled not to say anything more. If she did have news about Lee then I really did want to hear it. But she waited, and I couldn't help showing my exasperation. It really was a palpably obvious trick: keep me waiting until I felt impelled to blurt out something incriminating just to break the silence. Well, that might have worked if I'd had a guilty conscience, but mine was magnificently, most definitely, free of guilt. With regard to Lee's death anyway. I looked again at Sergeant Taylor, still absorbed in the Bosch print. He really was trying to avoid looking at me directly, wasn't he? And when I came to think of it, so was his boss. It struck me then that DI Marrin's silence might not have been an attempt to draw me out after all. It might have been because she really didn't want to say what she had to. I leaned back in my chair and put my hands behind my head. "What about the investigation, DI Marrin?"

I caught that flash in her eyes as she caught the possible sarcasm in my emphasis on her title. Good, I'd have hated to think she'd missed it. "I have been instructed to tell you that you are no longer a suspect. Sir."

Clever, how in saying I now wasn't a suspect she had admitted that in fact I had been. I was surprised though. I knew I had nothing to do with Lee's disappearance, but she didn't. "Good. Well, I could have told you that from the start." I reined in my enthusiasm. An unpleasant thought had attached itself to the situation. "Have you... have you found Lee?"

"No, Mr. Sinclair. We have not," she said through lips almost too thin to qualify as such.

A mixed blessing I guessed. No body, but no living person to prove my innocence beyond all doubt either. I shivered. Pity dreams weren't acceptable evidence in court. Lee had been very alive in my dream last night. "Then have you caught the person who... I mean, do you have any idea...?"

"No, Mr. Sinclair. We have not."

Now it was my turn to be silent as I tried to sort out what this uptight bitch was apparently having trouble saying. "Then I don't..."

"Do you have friends in high places, sir?"

I blinked, genuinely caught off balance by both the non sequitur and the bitterness with which the question had been asked. I glanced across to the sergeant, vaguely hoping he might be able to throw some light on the matter, but he avoided my eye as determinedly as any underprepared student in a seminar. "I'm sorry, detective inspector, but you're going to have to explain to me what on earth it is you are trying to say."

"I am saying, *sir*," and the venom on that honorific didn't escape my attention, "that I have been informed by a very high source to call off my investigations against you."

"I wasn't aware that I was being investigated." A lie. Of course I was.

Detective Inspector Marrin put both her hands on my desk and leaned in closely. Her voice was low, but I'm sure that was for effect rather than an attempt to keep her words secret from Sergeant Taylor. "There is little doubt in my mind, Mr. Sinclair, that Mr. Barker is dead. There is also equally little doubt in my mind as to who it was killed him. Someone in a position of influence, however, appears to be considerably harder to convince. The word is that I am to leave you alone." She leaned forward even further. If it had been a man with eyes that burned so fiercely invading my personal space it might have been quite a turn-on. "So I have been told to come down here personally to tell you that I am doing what I have been told."

This time, her messages, spoken and unspoken, were crystal clear. I glanced again to her sergeant. He was regarding his boss with an expression I found hard to read. "Thank you," I said simply. It actually wasn't meant as a provocative remark; I'm embarrassed to say it came out because I simply couldn't think of anything else to say, but Marrin seemed to take it for deliberate stirring and shoved herself back up from the desk with an expression that could have melted metal and stalked from the room without a backward look or comment. Sergeant Taylor turned and followed with noticeably less speed.

"Wait," I said. I hadn't meant to call out but somehow it had just happened. Taylor stopped in the doorway and looked back at me. His boss's expressions were as easy to read as a large print book. His impassive regard was as indecipherable as a novice medieval monk's first transcription. He waited silently while I tried to decide what I actually wanted to say to him. "Who...?" I began uncertainly.

He cocked an eyebrow, and I couldn't help noticing that it did make him look very fetching. "Who?"

I pulled my thoughts together. "Who told her, told you, to leave me alone?"

"You really don't know?"

"Of course I don't. That's why I'm asking." I kicked myself mentally. I can be tetchy, I know that, but most of the time it doesn't matter and I don't care anyway. This wasn't one of those times.

"If it helps, I don't think you do, Mr. Sinclair. You'd better know though. She"—he jerked his thumb in the direction of his disappearing boss—"has a reputation for not following orders." For just the fleetest of moments I swear there was a smile on his face. "It's what makes her fun to work with. Take care," and he turned and left.

"Bloody plod!" I threw myself back in my chair. Taylor had left me seething and confused, and not entirely sure why.

Riled as I was, when there was another knock at my door only minutes after The Sweeney had left, it was hardly surprising I answered with a snarled, "What!" that would have given Grendel's mother pause for thought before entering. Fortunately, what entered was considerably more appealing and probably a lot stronger too.

"*C'est pas les mots d'amour!*" Jean Philippe stood in the doorway, contriving, as he always did, to make it look ridiculously small.

It was the mark of how black my mood was that the sight of his agreeably muscular frame didn't immediately dispel the clouds around me. It was, however, enough to let some sunshine through. I rose to kiss him. "Hi. I'm sorry. Bad day at the office." I stopped, knowing I would have to explain that idiom to him, and then I looked more closely at his face. "You look like shit!"

"*Merci, mon ami,*" he sighed, and let himself fall into the chair in front of my desk. Not designed for the sudden accommodation of burly French rugby players it creaked worryingly but held.

"What's up?"

He rubbed a broad hand over his face. There was a clear rasp of stubble. "*C'est rien.* I didn't sleep well last night, that's all."

You *didn't sleep well,* I thought. *If you'd only had the nightmare I had...* "Someone keeping you awake, *mon cher*?"

"Only thoughts of you."

Yeah, right.

"I came to say I will not be able to see you tonight."

"Tonight?"

"I was coming over to your rooms, yes? You said you had some manuscripts you wanted to show me. Which is usually your way of saying you want to fuck *comme des lapins* all night, yes?"

"Oh. Yes." He was right, on all counts, although I genuinely did have some old missals I thought he'd be interested in. After we'd fucked. Events had simply driven even that exciting appointment clean out of my head. "I'm really sorry to hear that." I tried to summon up a convincing show of disappointment, but after my own night of broken sleep and the visit from Malice of the

Yard, I didn't feel like a night of sexual hijinks either. "Why?" I asked belatedly.

Jean-Philippe waved his hand again in a listless way that really wasn't at all typical of him. "I really feel, what is it you say, wiped off?"

"Wiped out," I corrected, although the malapropism conjured up a nice image.

"*D'accord.* And I have an important match this weekend, as well as a paper to turn in before the middle of next week."

I nodded regretfully, and this time the regret was actually a touch more genuine. There couldn't be many hunks in the world who could postpone a night's hot sex with you because they had to conserve their strength for a varsity match and PhD level dissertation. As ever, the combination of French brains and brawn was proving delightfully stimulating, and I started to wonder whether I could change my mind, and then change his. I crouched beside his chair to give him a consolatory hug with the vague thought of turning it into something a little more heartfelt, but the comparative feebleness of the hug he gave in return checked me. I leaned back to inspect him. He was indeed looking very pale, apart from the dark smudges under his eyes. Having seen the range of skin and grooming products Jean-Philippe considered basics for hygiene, if those bags had been left unattended then he must indeed be feeling pretty rough. "You really aren't well, are you?"

He sighed again. "I thought I had said that. Somewhere between my poor language skills and your self-absorption the meaning seems to have been lost."

Harsh, but true. I stood up and, still holding on to me, Jean-Philippe got to his feet. "Poor thing. You go back home and get some rest. You need to build up your strength."

Jean-Philippe nodded, leaned down, and kissed me.

"And you might like to try a little cucumber."

"Sean. I can wait until I see you again."

"I meant for your eyes."

"Ah. *Bien sur. Au revoir, mon ami.*"

"*Á bientôt, mon amour.*"

Jean-Philippe left, and I returned to my seat behind my desk. Morosely I surveyed the pile of paperwork in front of me. Damn! The furthest thing from my mind before Jean-Philippe had come in was feeling horny, but now...

There was a third knock at the door which, fortunately for the knocker, was opened before I had time to answer. "Hi," Chris said. "I wondered if you'd like to come for lunch?"

*

"I had thought of a little Italian place I know," I said, unable to hide a little of my irritation. "Or there's even a small bistro which is quite pleasant when it's not flooded with undergraduates which it probably wouldn't be at this time of day. Or there's always my place."

Chris just laughed and waved a fork at me cheerily. He looked so damn good, and I had to admit I was so pleased he really had called me back that I let him get away with it. "Bistros and restaurant I can get back home," he said happily, "but this"—and he waved his fork again to take in our surroundings—"this really is unique."

I supposed I could see his point. It might only have been the day before since we'd last been in St. Thad's Dining Hall, but that had been Chris's first time, and the ambience of the full-blown evening meal was undeniably different from the breezy informality of lunchtime. No one was expected to wear suits and gowns for one thing, and the waitresses ("scouts" as they're known) were replaced by conventional self-service. With the warm glow of the hall's ancient electric lighting replaced by the full sunshine of a bright early winter day streaming through the windows, the clash of old setting and students in brash modern dress was refreshing. As was the sight of the handsome Chris in a light-blue suit and fetching polo neck sitting across the table from me.

"Actually, I did have something of an ulterior motive in asking you here," he said as he poked at the not-too-appetising shepherd's pie that was the dish of the day and, as I had to explain to him, naïve American that he was, had nothing to do with real shepherds.

"Really," I said, shifting pleasurably in my chair. This was looking more and more promising. I was now unexpectedly free for the night, too, wasn't I?

He smiled back, and stabbed that damned fork upwards and at a point behind me. "Yeah, I'd hoped they might be clearer in the daylight."

Puzzled, I turned round and followed the direction of his pointing. "The paintings?" Not those again!

"Yeah."

"Right!" I turned back and stuck a knife into my potato. *Okay,* I told myself, *stay calm. He may just be teasing you.* But Chris, it seemed, really was fixated on those old Masters. "You would think they'd be clear, wouldn't you?" I nodded, not wanting to suggest too much enthusiasm. It wasn't hard. "But they're not," he went on obliviously. "Not the ones round the top anyway. Even at midday. Just as dark as last night."

"It's the architecture," I said vaguely. "Sixteenth century builders really didn't worry too much about sightlines for galleries of paintings that were going to be shoved up there hundreds of years after they'd died."

"Guess so," Chris agreed, his eyes still fixed on the pictures as he talked to me. "Or even for twenty-first century photographers."

"I'm sorry?"

"I took pictures last night."

"You did? When?"

He laughed. "When no one was looking, of course. I was pretty sure it was against etiquette, and maybe some arcane copyright law too."

I had to admit he was probably right about that but what had surprised me was he'd managed to take pictures at the meal without anyone noticing. Your average mobile phone camera might have been unobtrusive but there was no way one of those could have even hoped to get decent pictures in that light and at that distance, and I already knew Chris wouldn't have been so foolish as to think one would. So, what sort of equipment had he been using?

"But like I said, they were way too dark to make out very much," he went on. "Although I did notice one thing that was very interesting."

He stopped and looked down at his plate, apparently diverting all of his attention to the remains of his meal. I counted to ten. "What?" I said, making it clear I knew I was being manipulated into answering.

He looked up again, clearly enjoying his game. "Haven't you ever noticed? The one thing they all have in common?"

What little remained of my patience was beginning to evaporate. "What?" I said again, though with more edge. "They're all dead?"

Chris raised that fork again and used it to trace a line around the upper gallery of the hall, taking in all the pictures. "With each guy, each past principal..."

"Master," I corrected.

"With each past Master there's someone else."

I waited for his words to start making sense. When they didn't I was obliged to speak again. "No, there isn't," I said simply. "They're portraits. Individual portraits. You can see that, even from down here, even the ones that are half in shadow."

Chris was shaking his head, clearly enjoying himself. "No. Nope. *Nein*. That's what I thought, too, but then I looked more closely."

"At your photos?"

"And I saw that in each portrait there's something else apart from the main subject."

"Well, of course there will be. There'll always be something in the background, usually to suggest something about the character of the person being painted. A house, a favourite horse. One of them's holding his favourite hunting bird, I think. If they were more honest they'd all have their favourite mistresses with them."

Now Chris was nodding. "Mistresses, no. But houses and animals, yes. And statues, busts, other portraits even."

I narrowed my eye. I was missing the point he was making.

"And when I looked closely at these statues, busts, and other pictures I found they were all of the same person."

He leaned back and regarded me, an expression of mild triumph on his face. In spite of myself I had to admit I was quite interested, and quite impressed. Don't knock it please, just remember: I am an academic, and in spite of my apparently endless grumblings about it, I do actually love St. Thad's. And this American seemed to have uncovered a little piece of its history that had gone completely unremarked for hundreds of years. "Are you sure?"

"Yup. For a while I thought there were a couple that didn't. You know the one of the guy holding the book in the library?"

"Thomas Ralsley. 1832 to 1857," I said automatically. I told you, I really do love St Thad's.

"Well, I thought he was one of them until I noticed he's pictured standing in front of a small window, and if you look through the window..."

"You see this other person?"

"Correct. Small and way off in the distance but definitely him."

"What kind of camera were you using? And are you always this obsessive about things?"

"That's kind of rich, isn't it, coming from a man who's dedicated his life to studying books most people wouldn't spend five minutes on?"

I passed over that one. Something about the phrase "dedicated your life" was oddly unsettling. "And the other one?"

"The other picture?"

"Yes, the other picture." Why was he drawing this one out?

Chris took his time, carefully arranging his knife and fork in absolute symmetry on his cleaned plate before answering. "It's that one," and he indicated which one he meant with a nod of his head in its direction.

It was the latest portrait. The one of Rufus.

"There's nobody else in that portrait," I said immediately.

"Like I said, that's what I thought at first. Look more closely."

Self-conscious at drawing attention to myself, nevertheless I stood up and walked over to Rufus's portrait. It was undeniably hideous, and I can say that quite openly because Rufus himself had been the first person to describe it as such. It was a source of great embarrassment to him, and consequently of mild amusement to me, and I had always assumed that was why he had insisted on its being hung as high as was possible without actually ending up on the dining hall roof. I stood now beneath it and looked up. The artist was a graduate of dear old St. Thad's, which was presumably the only reason he had got the commission. He had captured absolutely none of Rufus's mixture of fierce intelligence and bearish sexual magnetism, managing to make him look merely fat and shortsighted. He had, though, made a decent job of the study which Rufus had chosen as his background. I knew the picture well. I knew the study very well. There was, I was sure, no other image of another man, in painting, sculpture, whatever, in that portrait.

"To the right of him. That small mirror on the mantelpiece. See it?"

Chris had walked up beside me and spoke while looking round the room, so the focus of our attention wasn't so obvious. I looked where he had said. There was a mirror there. And there did indeed seem to be a figure reflected in it, a nice little Renaissance trick updated to the present day. "Funny, I'd never noticed that before."

"Yes. It is, isn't it?"

I looked back down to Chris who was looking back at me. His words had been uninflected, his expression now was carefully neutral, but there was some meaning beyond them, I could sense it. "I can't make out the details from here."

"No, of course not. I'll show you the photos back at the hotel." He stepped closer so that his mouth was very close to my ear. "Come and see me later," he said in a playfully urgent whisper.

Thank God for that, I thought. My interest in the portraits was piqued, I'll grant you that, but the prospect of a return to bed with Chris and his magic fingers was more immediately appealing.

I smiled and shivered. His breath on my neck was making the small hairs stand on end. What I would have given to have had his lips on my skin right then, just below the ear, his tongue probing, teeth grazing along...

"And tell me what you've found out." He pulled his suit jacket back on.

"Wha...? Hang on a minute. Found out what?"

"You'll be seeing Rufus, won't you? If anyone knows who else is in his picture with him it'll be him, won't it? So, pump him for all the information you can about it, then come over to The Regency and I'll..."

"...pump me in turn. That sounds...fair. There's just one flaw to your plan. It's Wednesday. Rufus isn't available Wednesdays. He's out of town. I won't be able to see him until tomorrow."

Chris finished buttoning his jacket and wrapped the smart yuppie scarf he was carrying round his neck. "Okay then, see you tomorrow night."

"You mean I can't..."

"Bye!" And he was striding out of the hall faster than I could call out after him.

"You bastard!" I breathed to myself, though obviously not enough to myself to stop the bunch of undergrads at the next table looking round and grinning at me. Maybe that was the way Mr. High and Mighty Corporate America behaved with his flunkies, but I was not one of his drones. I was a senior member of Britain's academic elite and...and... My thoughts trailed off as I watched Chris disappear from sight around a corner. Shit, but he had a great arse! I made a mental note to "drop in" on Rufus first thing the next day. I looked up and round the hall, at the pictures hanging on the walls. I was mildly curious to see if I could make out this recurring figure Chris claimed to have found but doubted I could make out any more details than I'd been able to with Rufus's portrait. Besides, I didn't want to draw any more attention to myself from the milling undergrads than I already had. I'd have to make do with Chris's photos in his hotel room. Well, we'd need something to do after we'd shagged in the silk till we were shattered.

Chapter Eight

I dreamed again that night.

In a detached, impersonal way I awoke to my dream, aware, just as I had been the last time, that I was asleep but still weirdly lucid. I was in a room I didn't recognise, a bedroom, sparse enough to make me suspect it must be a hotel room. I wasn't sure where I was standing, or even if I was standing. My vantage point seemed to change and shift as if I was some kind of camera that swept and swooped around the room, viewing it from all angles. I was completely unaware of my body. I was just eyes, able to observe but not affect. And I knew something was about to happen that I was meant to see.

A door opened and Jean-Philippe walked in. I would have smiled if I had lips, would have chuckled if I'd had a voice. That was hardly surprising. Given that two hot men had both raised and then dashed my sexual expectations in the same day (not counting the tantalisingly tasty Sergeant Taylor) it was only to be expected that at least one of them would figure in my dreams. If I couldn't get it in real life the least I could look forward to was a little action in my unconscious fantasies. Idly, I wondered whether I'd actually have a wet dream. Now that would be a blast from the past.

Somewhat less idly I wondered if my dream would also star Chris. Now that just had to raise the chances of nocturnal emission. Chris and Jean-Philippe, down and dirty! I'd enjoy watching my big French rugby player screwing the waxed arse of Mr. American Moneybags, seeing that haughty Boston smile twist helplessly into his come face as Jean-Philippe's giant cock mercilessly reamed his uptight hole. Somewhere, my heart was beating ten to the dozen. I wondered excitedly if I could force the outcome of this dream. I filled my mind with thoughts of Chris, naked, sweating, screaming, coming, willing him to walk through that door. But it seemed I was only this dream's camera, not its director. My perspective was still beyond my control, and images of Jean-Philippe alone filled my mental screen. As he yawned, stretched, and began to peel off his clothes, I decided that wasn't such a bad thing after all. It was difficult to entertain thoughts of another man when a piece of prime beef like Jean-Philippe was stripping off in front of you.

Obviously, I'd seen him undress before but never this slowly. I guessed lacking the incentive of another man in the room with him accounted for the reduced speed. Certainly if I'd been there in the flesh I'd have been all over him by now. Being forced to watch without being able to touch was a kind of pleasurable torture I hadn't tried before. Well, not with me as the restrained one.

Of course, another reason for Jean-Philippe's languor was his obvious tiredness, and I couldn't help remarking to myself that for a (hopefully) pornographic dream, my unconscious mind was working very realistically. Jean-Philippe looked as run down, if not more so, as he had when I'd seen him earlier that day. His face seemed even paler, more drawn, the skin rough and the dark circles under his eyes stronger. As stimulating as this peeping Tom scenario was, just for a second I found myself thinking maybe I should bring it to an end, try to wake myself up somehow, reclaim the use of my eyes and hands and maybe wank off to memories of my lover looking more French and gay than he did right then. But by that point, Jean-Philippe was down to his boxers. I couldn't say goodbye without just a little peek to tide me over.

With a sigh, Jean-Philippe perched on the edge of the bed and, no teasing preliminaries required, pulled the shorts down over his hairy shanks to drop to the floor. For once his cock didn't leap out playing "The Marseillaise", but even flaccid as it was it was a sight to make you catch your breath, a fireman's hose of a dick hanging heavy down the length of his thigh. Idly, he rubbed his hand over it and I perked up at the thought he might jerk himself off before he went to sleep. I wondered if he'd think of me when he did it. Would he moan and call out? Would it be my name? And if not, whose?

My hopes of a little hand-shandy action were dashed, though, as Jean-Philippe let his hand fall to one side, and then the bulk of his body fall back onto the bed. He closed his eyes and now, somehow, I was over him, looking down at this gorgeous hirsute mound of muscle lying below me, the chest and belly rising and falling slowly as he slipped into sleep. Vulnerable. Not a word I'd ever associated with Jean-Philippe before. Bizarrely, detached from my body as I was, I knew I was as hard as a rock looking down at him. There was something powerfully arousing about this defencelessness in so strong a man, an innocence that wank mags tried to capture sometimes in their pictures, though they only ever managed to turn it into "coy." I should have been frustrated as hell, hot to grab hold of those massive hairy tits, bite those nips, press my arse down onto his beautiful goateed face, feel his tongue working me, probing, teasing, moistening, relaxing, while his cock shot up straight and hard as a ramrod behind me. But I wasn't. I could have floated there all night just looking down at him, drinking him in. Somewhere, a wee small voice in the back of my mind whispered, *is this what it feels like to be in love with someone? To be happy just to look?* I shook my head (metaphorically) to clear the thought away. This was a dream, right? That was all. You could have all kinds of crazy thoughts in a dream.

Then the door opened a second time, and my dream began its slow metamorphosis into a nightmare.

It was Lee again. That I hadn't expected, and yet the rational part of my mind even then tried to explain it away. *Only logical,* it said. *He's been on your mind for fairly obvious reasons. He was in your dreams last night. Only to be expected that he should turn up again.* But I didn't want it, damn it! I tried, I struggled to take control of my dream, to change its direction, to turn Lee into Chris, into anyone, frankly, other than Lee, to just make him vanish so that I could be alone with Jean-Philippe. But he wouldn't go. He stayed, and with dreadful inevitability moved forward silently to the bed on which Jean-Philippe lay sleeping.

He was dressed in the same shirt and jeans he'd been wearing when last I saw him. Reaching the bed, he stretched out a hand and touched a bare foot that was projecting over the edge of the mattress. His skin looked so pale in contrast to Jean-Philippe's. Jean-Philippe moaned slightly in his sleep, shifted just a little, but then lay still and quiet again. Lee padded the length of the bed, trailing his hand up Jean-Philippe's calf, his thigh, the side of his body, up over his chest to his face. Jean-Philippe stretched as if about to wake up, but then subsided and slept on. *Wake up! Wake up!* I wanted to shout. I was screaming in my head, but could not make my voice heard in the dream world.

Lee stood now at the head of the bed, looking down at Jean-Philippe's recumbent body as I had done. But even my expression could never have been that possessive. Never that...hungry. He knelt and in a gesture of perverse tenderness reached out with both hands, placing them lightly on the wiry mounds of Jean-Philippe's pecs, smoothing them back and forth, drawing the rough hair this way and that, crossing and recrossing the tender softness of the broad nipples. I saw the familiar dark nubs harden under the forest of black hair, and Jean-Philippe moaned again but this time there was an undertone to the sound. It wasn't the pleasurable sound of a man being gently aroused, more the moan of a man dreaming of pain. I remembered the icy torture of my own dream. I saw Lee smile.

For long minutes Lee worked at Jean-Philippe's tits, his face a picture of cruel concentration. Jean-Philippe's groans grew louder, his breathing faster, inarticulate words gasped out amongst the guttural exclamations. Hands that could ordinarily sweep burly fullbacks to one side rose to protect the nips that I knew from personal highly pleasant experience were deliciously sensitive but were batted to one side with contemptuous ease by Lee. How could Jean-Philippe stay sleeping through this? Part of me knew.

Finally Lee sat back, withdrew his hands. Had he finished his torment? One look at his face, strangely white, disturbingly intent, made it clear to me that he had not. He had only just begun.

Silently he rose and walked in measured paces to the foot of the bed, dragging one hand the length of Jean-Philippe's body again, raking his nails over the now fast-pumping belly, through the thick black hair covering it, skirting for the moment the more luxuriant bush at the crotch to drag down one leg. He climbed onto the bed and knelt between Jean-Philippe's feet. Placing one hand on each of Jean-Philippe's ankles he pushed them slowly apart, splaying the legs, moving into his body more closely, still kneeling. Jean-Philippe's bulging thighs spread wide, Lee moved his hands up to his broad hips, shoved them down, round the broad curves of his buttocks until he was holding the meaty arse cheeks and then leaned back and pulled up, moving in still closer. Jean-Philippe lay, still unconscious, cock, balls, and hole completely open and vulnerable. Lee turned slightly, looking back over his shoulder, and he smiled at me, before turning to Jean-Philippe again, and lowering his head to his defenceless crotch.

He'd seen me! He knew that I was watching! He'd *smiled* at me! Oh God! Frantically, I tried to move forward, to reach out, to pull him off Jean-Philippe, shake my lover awake, do *something!* But now I could not move, my vantage point was fixed as if I had been tied to the spot, and all I could do was watch. All I could see now was Lee's back as he hunkered down like some feeding animal over Jean-Philippe's cock and balls, rocking slowly in and out, my lover's powerful legs splayed to either side of him. I remembered from my previous "dream" the twisted pleasure/pain Lee's frigid mouth had visited on my erection, the numbing thrill of his cold lips, the burning points of white fire I now understood had been his teeth, piercing the tight flesh of my taut dick skin. Sucking! He'd been sucking the warmth, the very life from me. And now he was doing it to Jean-Philippe.

Lee's head bobbed up and down, slowly at first but with increasing speed as he worked Jean-Philippe's thick shaft with his mouth, and over his head I could see the length of Jean-Philippe's body shifting on the sheets, arching, could see the sensations being inflicted on him reflected in his sleeping face, the twisted mouth, the frown; hear the small grunts and gasps coming faster and faster. His breathing quickened, his moans and cries grew louder, more helpless. His bulky body began to buck, his hips thrusting up from the bed, animalistically driving his huge dick harder into the mouth that was torturing him. His pumped arms rose blindly to push Lee away, and contemptuously Lee fended them off as if they had had no more strength than a baby's.

For long, agonising minutes I watched as the monster sucked on my lover, watched Jean-Philippe's thrashings become more frantic, his cries more urgent, even as his eyes remained closed, his mind as much a prisoner in his dream as I had been in mine. When he wasn't fending off Jean-Philippe's hands with ease, Lee was dragging his fingers over his victim's stomach like claws, and in the moonlight, I saw the glistening of something matting Jean-Philippe's belly hair that looked black in the moonlight but that I knew would look all too red in any other.

And then, all too quickly a point was reached, a terrible stillness. Jean-Philippe's handsome face grimaced like a man in the most awful pain or on the very brink of the most shattering orgasm. But I knew he wasn't coming, remembered from my own dream the impossibility of it in that bitter mouth. How long could a man be held at such a peak without going mad? But Lee wasn't going to hold him there, was he? That was the point to which he had brought me, and I had known then what he had intended for me. I had been saved by the intervention of that other person, but for Jean-Philippe there was no one, only me, and I could do nothing.

Lee's head rose from his ghastly work, and he looked over his shoulder at me. His mouth was wet, glistening with something. Saliva? Jean-Philippe's cum? "I warned you," he hissed. "Now try and stop me."

With a choked scream I awoke, shot up in bed soaked with sweat even in the usual chill of my rooms. Dazed, I looked around idiotically, reaching for sense, reassurance in the sight of familiar objects around me. Try as I did to dismiss what I had just seen as a dream, a larger, more primitive, altogether more urgent part of my brain told me that what I had witnessed had been real, that it had happened. That it *was* happening. Even now Lee was turning his attentions back to Jean-Philippe and there would be no one to stop him doing to my lover what he had nearly done to me.

I threw myself out of my bed and dragged on trousers, coat, and shoes and tried to marshal my crazily spinning thoughts. I knew that, like most of the exchange students, Jean-Philippe didn't have a room in college, that he preferred it as a way of keeping his extracurricular activities out of the notice of the college authorities. I knew he was in a hotel, and I knew he'd told me which one, but typically I'd not really listened. We'd both been more than happy for him to come to me for our trysts, so in my panic now, I couldn't call its name to mind. There was no way it could be The Regency, that was way out of his current budget. It had to be The Royal, grander sounding but altogether cheaper, and also within easy reach of all college buildings.

I ran, careless of the open doors I left behind me, careless of the night chill that struck through the hastily pulled on coat to the bare skin beneath, unable to care or even think of anything other than that image of Jean-Philippe at the mercy of whatever the hell Lee was now.

I'd given no thought to what time of night it was. The deserted, silent streets I raced through all seemed part of some half real, half nightmare world. As I reached the doors of The Royal I heard the distant tones of Old Mark, the bell of the College's most ancient clock tower, tolling three. The Hour of the Wolf in medieval literature. I shoved at the door, fully expecting it to be locked at that time, caught off guard as it swung open easily, depositing me stumbling into the foyer. A doorman sat to one side, his chair tipped back. His face was slack, his eyes closed. My stomach twisted. Was he...? I stepped up closely. No, he was alive, his breath whistling softly through his lips. At his feet lay the sports paper he had been reading which had slipped through his nerveless fingers. Briefly I wondered if I should wake him, ask for his help? Then what? Explain that I'd run through the streets of the town half-dressed because of a dream? Then I wondered why he hadn't woken up when I'd crashed through the door. I took another step towards him, reaching my hand out nervously. Somewhere from the distance came the sound of a door crashing to. That had to be Lee. Abandoning the doorman, I ran in the direction of the sound.

I might be an athlete in bed, but to claim to be such in any other sense of the word would be a lie. I was out of breath as I threw myself into the corridor the sound had come from. Up ahead was an open door, the light from within spilling out into the dimness of the corridor. Just short of the doorway I stopped, clenched my fists. What was waiting inside?

I knew what was inside.

But that was a dream.

I knew what was inside!

Fists raised, I forced myself through the door as if its threshold was the most impenetrable barrier I had ever crossed. Ahead of me lay the bed. On it lay Jean-Philippe.

He was so pale. The curtains had been flung back and he lay in a pool of moonlight that streamed through the window. I tore my eyes from him, looked sharply to my left, to my right, terrified of ambush. There was no one else there. I stepped into the room, closer to the bed. I looked down. "Jean..." The word died in my mouth, choked in my throat. I had never seen a corpse before. I'd always assumed it would look like a living person, like someone asleep. I knew now it did not.

"You're too late," said a voice behind me.

I whirled round to face the figure that had crept up noiselessly behind me and was standing now in the doorway, blocking my exit.

"Come with me," said Chris Bailey.

Chapter Nine

I should have stayed.

I should have grabbed Chris by the throat, smashed him up against a wall, and forced him to tell me what had happened.

I shouldn't have left Jean-Philippe.

But I did.

Somehow, I found myself back at The Regency with Chris. Somehow I found myself back in his bed. *I'm dreaming again,* I told myself. The silk whisper of the sheets; the spice of his expensive cologne; the warmth of his naked body next to mine—they all had that unreal, dreamlike quality of my dreams of Lee, my vision of Jean-Philippe. Except for that last image—Jean-Philippe cold and still on his bed. That image was a crystal clear picture of indisputable reality. However nightmarish or unreal the rest of my life had become, that much was undeniable fact. Jean-Philippe was dead.

"What...?" I began, struggling, to rise from the dreams, from the bed, from Chris's arms.

"Hush," he whispered to me. "You're safe now. Let me help. Let go."

"No. No, I..."

"Shhh." His voice was low, soothing, like a father. Like a lover. He was holding me tenderly, far more tenderly than he had the last time we'd been naked together, kissing my cheek, my neck, stroking my face, my hair.

"No."

"Shhh."

Jean-Philippe was dead. Lee Barker wasn't, but he was some kind of monster. I should've been with the police, should've been doing...something. But I was there in bed with a man I'd met only days before, and he was soothing me and, Lord help me, I was growing hard. Chris shifted next to me, and his hand was on my cock, gentle, cradling, and his lips were on mine, and I felt myself drowning in him, the sight, sound, taste, touch, and smell of him, and I wanted to drown, to sink utterly and forget everything but him.

I came in his hand like a teenager, again and again, great outpourings of cum, and when it was over, when I was completely drained, physically, sexually, emotionally, then I truly sank into a sleep so deep it was mercifully safe from dreams.

When I woke Chris was still with me, gently wiping my face as if I had just been crying. Perhaps I had.

"We need to talk," he said.

I sat up. "Jean-Philippe." Chris waited, regarding me steadily. A little to my own surprise I found I was able to speak calmly. "We have to tell someone."

"It has been taken care of."

"The police..."

"It has been taken care of," he repeated.

I looked at him. "Who are you?"

Chris nodded as if regretfully acknowledging something he knew would have to happen. "I'm exactly who I've said I am. There's just...more to me than that."

"You don't work for Aegis."

He gave that half smile of his. "Oh yes. I definitely work for them." He took a deep breath as if gathering strength for something difficult. "And so did Lee Barker."

"What!"

"I said *did*. Not any more. Lee went rogue. In the worst possible way."

"He isn't dead." It wasn't a question.

"Not...exactly."

"What the fuck is that supposed to mean?"

He reached out to stroke my hair again and I smacked his hand away, knowing all too well how easy it would have been to let myself sink back into that comfort. "Oh, Sean," he said sorrowfully. "You still haven't got a clue what really goes on here, have you?"

I shivered, even in the warmth of his hotel room, at the echo of those words from that night, still only over a week ago but seemingly centuries distant. "Lee said that."

Chris nodded. "We knew. He'd been digging for us."

"Digging?"

"For the truth. And he found it."

"What truth? You make him sound like a fucking CIA agent. Lee was a graduate in literature for God's sake. Specialising in Jacobean poets."

"One Jacobean poet."

"Yes, okay, *one* Jacobean poet, but that..."

"Which one?"

I blinked.

"Do you know?"

Again I was cast back to that last night with Lee. Our argument. My admission that I didn't know the subject of his final dissertation. "No," I confessed, with more guilt this time than I'd shown Lee then.

"The portraits," Chris said. "Have you had time to ask Rufus about them?"

My eyes widened with incredulity. "The portraits! No, of course I haven't fucking asked about the portraits! How can you still be going on about the portraits after what has happened here tonight?"

Chris was nodding again. "Okay, later maybe."

"A lot later!" I said heatedly. "Now tell me what the hell is going on here or so help me I'm going straight to the police. And then, if it still doesn't make any sense, I'm going to the police anyway."

"Your college is a lie," Chris said coolly.

I stared at him. "What?"

"Or, to be more precise, it's a lie founded on a truth only a few people know. A truth that's centuries old and a lot more powerful than you know." He looked at me levelly. "It's run by vampires."

Many men have rendered me literally speechless in bed by one means or another. None of them had done it through words before.

"Well, maybe that's not completely accurate," Chris went on.

"Right!"

"Run is perhaps overstating the case. Guided would be a positive way of looking at it. I suppose. Manipulated would be a lot closer to the truth. Preyed upon might come closest of all."

"Preyed?"

"I did say vampire, remember?"

Blood. That's what they'd said when Lee had gone missing, wasn't it? *Quantities of blood.* But... "There was no blood with...with Jean-Philippe."

"You're a student of literature. You more than anyone should understand the power of metaphor."

I shook my head slowly. "I...do...not understand what you are trying to say to me."

Chris tried again to reach his arm around me, and part of me really wanted him to. In the midst of this surreal, stomach-turning shit I was startled to feel just how strong my desire for him had become. Through the clinging satin sheets my cock was an easily visible ridge, and my balls were aching again at the thought of what he could do with those well-manicured fingers of his, coaxing, stroking, squeezing, pressing. What was wrong with me? I'd heard that danger was meant to be an aphrodisiac but the life of a college lecturer hadn't exactly brought me into much contact with it. Was that what was happening here? Or was it just Chris? Was this...chemistry? Was I falling for him? I flushed with guilt at such thoughts just hours after a guy I knew I'd...really liked had died. I pushed Chris's arm away again, aware of the lack of conviction in the gesture.

Chris sighed, and I found I couldn't look him in the face, afraid of what I might see there. Rejection? Pain? I felt rather than saw him lean back, close his eyes for a moment as if collecting his thoughts, and then he opened them again and in a calm low voice told me things that were simply fantastic.

"You more than most are aware of how our arts, our writing, poetry, prose, and drama, are filled with fantastic creatures, monsters of the supernatural. Why? Are they all simply make-believe? Why should people do that? How did they come up with the ideas in the first place?"

I went to open my mouth, went to deliver the sort of withering putdown I would have shot off at any first year undergrad who had dared to spout such speculative piffle in one of my tutorials. Then I thought of my dreams, of Lee, of Jean-Philippe, and I closed my mouth and forced myself to listen.

"We believe..."

"'We' meaning Aegis?"

Chris hesitated. "Yes. Aegis. We believe that all these incredible tales have their basis in fact. That they are warnings. We believe that alongside the human race is another race, maybe several, like us, maybe very unlike us. A very few might actually be benevolent. Most we believe are entirely indifferent to us. But a few might live by codes that are utterly alien to us. We would have to call them evil, and they mean us harm."

"Vampires?"

"That's just a word, and it doesn't cover everything, not by a very long chalk. But if you want, let's use it now."

"You're saying St. Thad's is run by vampires?" Even to me my laugh sounded unnervingly cracked.

He didn't blink once. "Yes."

"And when exactly did this takeover happen? You don't think that someone might have noticed?"

Chris was shaking his head. "That's because they didn't take over. They've always been in charge. Right from the very beginning. The Founding. What is the college motto?"

"Ex Tenebris Lux," I said without thinking.

"Which translates as?"

"I think you know very well."

"Indulge me."

"Bringing light to the darkness."

"A metaphor for education?"

"Obviously."

"If you translate it that way. But if you translate it, oh say, 'From the shadows, light'?"

I frowned. "Then you have a less convincing, clumsier translation."

"But if we stick with it just for a minute. How is the meaning different?"

"It... I don't know. What's the point? It's shoddy translation!"

"Light coming from shadows," Chris went on as if I hadn't spoken. "The idea being perhaps that the shadows have created the light, or are maybe using the light. What casts shadows after all?"

"Now you're moving from cod poetry to cod physics."

"Or perhaps I'm just taking you back to basics, helping you see the reality you've been too close to to see all these years. St. Thaddeus's isn't just one college. It's two and always has been. The one you're a part of, that functions in the light. And the other, the Shadow College, always in the background. Always...guiding."

"Or manipulating," I said slowly, thinking about what he'd said earlier. "Preying?" Chris said nothing, just watched me as the image he had planted in my mind slowly sank in. I shook my head. "It's absurd."

"Lee didn't think so."

"And Lee's..." I came to a halt, momentarily set back by the argument I had been about to put forward. I temporised. "And Lee was working for you?"

"Think of it more like sponsorship, the kind of thing most students try to get one way or another. We have quite an active sponsorship programme, actually, and you know how hard it is to find money for the arts these days."

"So what was he? Some kind of spy for you?"

"Does it sound better if we call it research?"

"Semantics."

"I thought that was what you were all about." His mood sobered again. "Lee was a bright boy. Apparently brighter than you." I couldn't help it. I bridled at that, but Chris laid a finger across my lips before I could speak. "He saw the truth of the Shadow College which seems to have eluded you, Sean. It intrigued him. Fascinated him. He wanted to know more. We agreed to help him, and he helped us. And then...something happened."

I shook my head again. Something wasn't adding up somewhere. "I can't believe that he knew all about this and never said anything."

"Were you close?"

"We were fucking for Christ's sake!"

"But were you close?"

I thought back again to that night. "*Just remember, later on, that I came to you first. That I tried to do things...properly.*" He had come to me, and I had turned him away. "So now he's what...?" I hesitated, unable to say the incredible words. "Undead?"

Chris looked away. "An old word. An attempt by people long ago to understand these shadow creatures. Like vampire. It will do for the moment."

"What do they want?"

It was an admission without words that I was actually starting to believe what Chris was telling me. He moved in closer again, put his arm across my shoulder, pulled me gently into him, and this time I did not resist. "What they have always wanted. Power."

I snorted. "What power is there in St Thad's?"

Chris punched me gently in a way I couldn't help feeling was very American, and actually not a little painful. "Typical academics. Too close to the wood to see the trees. You underestimate your position in this world, Sean. St Thad's is a top university. It produces men and women who go on to achieve positions of real power and influence around the globe in a variety of fields. St. Thad's isn't so much a base as a starting point. 'Give me the boy at seven and I will give you the man.'"

"Aquinas," I said without really thinking. "Roughly," I couldn't help adding.

"Right. Well, these vampires don't start at seven, nearer to seventeen, but the principle is the same. Their hooks, or fangs, are well and truly stuck into people by the time they leave this place, and so their influence spreads and grows. They've been doing it for centuries."

"But I was a student at St. Thad's. I never saw hair nor hide of these...creatures. And I'm..."

"...still there?" I shivered again. "Yes, Sean, you're still there, and I think you're starting to see a lot more than hair or hide of the Shadows now."

"So what? They've been waiting to reach out for me? They've been fattening me up or something?" Chris didn't immediately answer but reached across me to the bedside table and I saw he'd left his laptop there. He pulled it over and placed it down in front of us. At the touch of his finger on the keypad the screen lit up. "The refectory portraits?"

"Yes. With just a touch of Photoshop magic." I watched as he scrolled through the pictures, first a portrait, then a zoom in and crop of one part of it, again and again. "This is the man I was telling you about, the one who's in every portrait on the walls, one way or another." He was right. He was there, over and over, the same man repeated across the years, down the centuries in every single portrait from the dining hall, as a sculpture here, a carving there, a reflection, a miniature, a figure in the distance: so many different representations, but always the same man. "We think this is that mythical Founder you don't believe in, Sean," he said. "The real power behind the throne." I was only half listening to what he was saying. My mind was filled with the multiple images unfolding in front of me: the pale skin, the dark eyes with their steely gaze, the silver hair. "Recognise him?"

"No." The denial was out before I had time to rationally think about it. "Should I?"

"Perhaps. We asked you... I asked you to talk to Rufus..."

"I told you, I haven't been able to yet."

Chris waved a hand placatingly. "I know, I know. We'd already asked Lee to try and find out the same thing."

"So, what am I now? Lee's backup?"

Chris wisely ignored my peevish question.

"And anyway, how was Lee supposed to find out anything like that from Rufus? He was just another grad student and Rufus..." Lee had let it drop in my room that Rufus was helping him with his thesis. I'd thought he'd been grandstanding. Rufus himself had as good as denied it. But now... Chris nodded as if reading my thoughts. "So, did he find out?"

"We think so. We think Rufus was particularly helpful. You know he chose the subject for what turned out to be Lee's final piece of work?"

"Lee said something about that. A poet, but I can't remember who it was."

Chris pulled the laptop over to him, closed the file of refectory portraits, and called up another. "Richard Farjeon," he said.

I looked back at him blankly. "Never heard of him. Like I said to Lee, there were hundreds of minor Jacobean poets. Half of them weren't even known by the majority of the reading public at the time, which would not have been huge. Most aren't read even by academics today let alone laypeople."

"Hidden in shadows you might say." Chris turned the laptop so that I could see the picture he had called up. "This is one of only two known portraits of Richard Farjeon. Look familiar?" I gazed at a portrait of pale skin, burning dark eyes, and white hair. The man in all the portraits of the Masters. And more familiar than Chris knew. I used to talk about meeting the man of my dreams. This figure from my nightmares was never what I'd had in mind. It was the man in that first dream, the man who had stood by Lee when he had attacked me.

"I have to go."

I made to rise from the bed but Chris's arms were around me, pulling me back into the warmth of his bed, back to the comfort and reassurance of his body. "Where?"

"I...I don't know. Away. Somewhere to think. This isn't... This doesn't make sense. Jean-Philippe is dead and I... This isn't right!"

"Did you love him?"

I blinked. A simple question. An impossible question. Wasn't it? "I...I don't know." How could I answer that now? How could I answer it at all?

Chris let go and lay back. "Whatever we're dealing with here, Sean," he said softly, "isn't human. This"—and he ran one hand slowly over his smooth, tanned skin—"is. Comfort in times of sadness. Love in the face of death. It's how we fight back. It's what makes us human."

Slowly I felt my body relax, felt the impossible tension that had built within me lessen, my muscles unknit, and something deep within me let go. I don't know if I cried, all I recall is coming to sometime later, how much later, I don't know, wrapped in Chris's surprisingly strong arms, feeling protected and safe till, lulled by the sound of his regular deep breathing, I fell asleep.

But then I dreamed again...

Chapter Ten

At first there was just the darkness: no sight, no sound. I could have still been unconscious except I was aware. Then sparks, like fireflies, dim but gathering in intensity, swooping slowly in great circles around me until, as their light grew, I realised they weren't moving at all. I was.

As before there was a bed in the centre of a room, but the room itself remained much darker than the other, its details impossible to make out. It seemed alive with shifting, twisting shadows. The dancing lights slowly resolved themselves into burning torches fixed at intervals around the walls, and I understood the flickering of their flames created the shadow play that so disturbed me. Then I saw that what was in the centre of this chamber was not a bed.

It was longer, wooden, little more than a pallet, except for the devices at foot and head, and a man lay upon it. No, he was bound upon it. With horrified fascination and a movement I could not control I moved, or was moved, closer to him, so that I could see the rough ropes at ankles and wrists holding the legs slightly splayed, the arms drawn up over the head.

As I've said, my tastes are catholic. I've tried most things, many of them more than once, several times if I've liked them, so I can't pretend to be a stranger to the BDSM scene. Many a happy hour has been spent tied to a bed or—more often, it has to be admitted—tying someone else to a bed. But this wasn't a bed. This wasn't a scenario with playful protests and get-out-of jail safe words. This, I knew, was the real thing.

My head and stomach swam, and the torches lurched around my head in a dizzying freefall I couldn't control. I wanted to move closer again but could not, wanted to see the face of the man bound to the rack but it remained hidden in shadows. I could hear his breathing though, shallow, constricted by the tension of the ropes holding him stretched out, fast because of the terror he was struggling to contain.

The shadows moved again. A figure, two—maybe more, it was hard to make out in the drunken swirling of my dream vision—in black masks moved towards the pallet. The panting of the helpless man quickened. My own heart was pounding. Voices. Snatches of fragments of sentences, repeated, overlapping: *"repent...consorted with demons...consorted with men...foul arts...mercy... repent...your kind...stamped out...mean no harm... destroyed...mercy...hidden in the darkness...mercy... mercy...no!"* And then the dry groaning of a wheel being slowly turned, of dusty ropes creaking under gradually increasing tension, and a scream.

And that face! The face in all the portraits.

Richard Farjeon.

"Sean! Sean, what is it?"

That scream! I swear I could hear its echoes in my head, in the room. The room in the hotel. Chris's hotel. I was bolt upright in Chris's bed, my throat raw, and I knew then that the echoes were real. The scream had been mine. I had shrieked out loud even as the man being tortured had. "Turn the light on. For fuck's sake turn the light on." Chris hurriedly did so and I unashamedly clung to him, struggling to still my trembling and gasping, eyes stretched wide as if I could drink in the blessed electric light.

I heard Chris's voice as if from a great distance. "What is it, Sean?"

I tried to answer, but even as I went to speak a sudden hammering at the suite's front door made me start with terror. "It's okay, " Chris soothed. "It's okay. I'll be right back." He slipped from the bed, grabbed a dressing gown, and padded towards the door. It took me all my strength not to grab hold of him, force him to stay with me. I lay there, heard him in muttered conversation with someone, and used the time to try to recover my balance. I like being in control. Most of my life has been about making sure I am in control, one way or another. Leaning on someone, drawing on his strength in a time of need had its thrill, but I was damned if I was going to make a habit of it.

When Chris came back I was soaked in sweat, probably pale as hell, but I was more myself again. Chris slipped off the dressing gown, climbed back in and under the sheets with me again, and held me. "Your scream somewhat alarmed the management. I had to tell them you'd had a bad dream. I guess that's what it was, yes?" I nodded. "Jean-Philippe? Lee?"

I shook my head. "No. Farjeon."

I don't know what I'd expected. Probably that he'd tell me that was strange, or that it was only likely after we'd talked about him, and I'd seen his face again and again on

Chris's laptop. But Chris didn't say any of those things. Under the sheets, his hand touched my thigh, moved along its length. "Tell me about it."

I swallowed. "I'm not sure I want…"

Chris's hand was at the top of my thigh, sliding down between my legs, gently cupping my sac. His lips were at my ear, gently nuzzling my neck. "It's okay, Sean," he was whispering. "You're safe here with me. You can tell me about it. It's better you tell me about it. What was he doing?"

"He was…there was…a rack."

"He was torturing someone?"

I frowned. The dream had been so very vivid, and yet already, like all dreams, the details were falling away like grains of sand through my fingers. Chris's fingers were stroking my balls, squeezing gently, teasing. If on the one hand he was genuinely trying to find out about my dream why, literally with the other, was he so deftly turning my thoughts elsewhere? "Yes."

"So he had someone tied down?"

"Yes."

"Stretched out? Stripped to the waist? Sweating and groaning?"

"Yes. Stop it!" Convulsively I shoved his hand away from my crotch.

"What's the matter?" he breathed into my ear.

"You're turning me on, you shit."

He chuckled softly into my ear. "And you don't like that?"

"Not...not like this. I can still hear that man, still see him, you know? And you're making me hard. It's like... It's like you're getting me hard over the torture."

"It was just a dream, Sean."

I didn't say anything to that. Did I have to remind him how the difference between dreams and reality had been a little more strained than normal for me of late?

His hand moved back, though his tone became more serious, strangely at odds with his persistent teasing of my cock. "Didn't they ever tell you to laugh at bullies at school, Sean?"

I thought of the dark chamber, the cowled figures, the rack, the screams. "This was a fuck sight more than bullying."

He raised his head on one arm to look down at me on his pillow. The other arm stayed where it was, his hand cradling my lengthening, twitching dick. "Yes. Of course it was. So you meet it with a fuck sight more than a smile. Farjeon's evil, Sean, darkness walking. Death. This"—and his hand squeezed, and I couldn't hold back the small gasp of pleasure the action wrung from me—"is life. Light. Embrace it. Kiss me, Sean."

He lowered his head and I instinctively opened my mouth to take his. His tongue pushed deep into my mouth as his palm slid down my cock, pulling back my skin as his fingers searched out that spot that had made me a shivering wreck the first time we had shagged. "Tell me about the dream, Sean," he muttered as his strong fingers worked me. "Tell me what Farjeon was doing to the man on the rack."

"No. I don't want... I don't...Oh God, yeah!"

Sean mounted me, sliding easily over my skin, still slick with my nightmare sweat, rubbing, twisting, biting, his fingers stroking, kneading, pressing muscles and nerves, all the time asking me about the dream, the man on the rack, the inquisitors, and Farjeon. And I told him. Between grunts and gasps and groans I strove to recall the fast vanishing details, each one I could dredge up rewarded by Chris with a kiss, a bite, the soft caress of his tongue, the sudden unexpected insertion of a finger. I had thought I knew all the sensitive spots of my body. Chris found at least a dozen more and used them all. It was like an exorcism, each hellish moment of the nightmare wiped from my mind by cresting waves of sexual pleasure throughout my body until all that was left in me was a burning, quivering, undeniable need to come. I'd seen a vision of death, but now I felt so very, very alive!

I bucked, straining to drive my cock into his trim body, and Sean twisted, took both my wrists in his hands and shoved them up above my head, holding them there with surprising strength for someone so wiry, as he looked down at me, the bedroom light behind him shining into my eyes so that my vision blurred and I couldn't make out his features. He had me, stretched out on the bed, helpless, moaning and groaning—like the man on the rack: helpless, defenceless. "He was a handsome fuck, wasn't he?" Chris said, and I couldn't see his face, couldn't see his tan, blue eyes, gold hair. My mind was suddenly filled with those images of Farjeon, his pale skin, his dark eyes, his white hair. Looking down at me. Helpless.

"Yes. Oh fuck! *Yes!*"

I came and came in great shuddering spasms, sobbing and crying out as I did, and Chris laughed and shot his load wide and warm over my belly and chest.

When we'd finished I rolled to one side, curled up in a ball, and lay there, not wanting to close my eyes. Chris kissed me gently, on the nape of my neck and then at intervals all the way down my curved spine to the hollow above my arse, before putting his arms around me and pulling himself into my body so that we both lay there, curled together, his belly to my back, and I felt him drift away into sleep while I lay awake and waited for the daylight to return.

Chapter Eleven

"So what do I do now?" I asked the next morning.

Breakfast had been sent up, we'd eaten, showered, and dressed, and now, sitting in the luxurious lounge area with the pale early winter sun streaming through the window, I realised I hadn't a clue as to what I was meant to do next.

"You go on as if nothing has changed."

I laughed bitterly. "You have to be joking. My...one of my best friends was killed last night and you have told me that the college I have devoted my life to is infested by a nest of vampires, and you want me to walk back in there as if nothing has changed!"

Chris sat next to me and put one strong hand on top of mine. It was smaller than mine, which surprised me for some reason, the small patch of hairs beneath his little finger as gold as those on his head. "Yes. Exactly that. Sean"—and he fixed me with those blue eyes of his—"if your life was in any immediate danger do you think I'd say that? You've been at the college for how long now? If anything was going to happen to you it would have happened by now."

"But Lee..."

Chris looked thoughtful. "Yes, Lee. That's the sticking point, isn't it? Lee doesn't fit into the pattern anymore. But frankly I don't think you'd be safe anywhere from Lee."

"Thank you very much."

"Apart from with me."

"What do you mean?"

I ran my fingers through my hair. A sudden icy thought struck me. "Jean-Philippe!" Chris waited for what I was going to say. I could hardly bring myself to put it into words. "If he was killed by Lee, and Lee is now one of these...these..." The words we had spoken last night seemed wrong now, ridiculous even, in the bright light of morning. "Well, won't he become...one, too, the way Lee did?"

Chris shook his head, the pressure of his hand on mine increasing in a reassuring way. "Don't worry. We don't think it works like that. Besides, we...we took care of Jean-Philippe. He's at peace now."

I looked at him, so calmly, confidently bringing order to the madness, and I realised that I hardly knew him. "Jean-Philippe. The police. All taken care of. Who are you? Just who or what is Aegis?"

He regarded me with regret in his eyes. "I can't tell you at the moment, Sean. But trust me. We have your interests at heart. I think you know that now, don't you?"

I nodded. DI Marrin's words came back to me. *Friends in high places.* Now I knew. "So, I just have to ignore what's happened? What I've learned? Go on as if nothing has changed?"

Chris shook his head. "I didn't say that." He hesitated. "Sean. I...I don't like to say this, but this can't be allowed to go on. We've been working for a long time now, believe me, a very long time, to bring this Shadow College into the light and to an end. We need..." He stopped, took my hand properly in his, brought it up to his face, brushed it against his cheek. "We need someone on the inside to help us."

"Now that Lee's what...turned to the dark side?"

He gave a grim laugh. "If you want to put it that way, yes." I saw the regret in his eyes. "I can't ask you to do this. It might be dangerous but..."

"I am in blood steeped so far that returning were as tedious as go o'er?"

Chris blinked. "*Hamlet*?" he ventured.

I sighed. Some things, it seemed, never changed. "*Macbeth*. Can no one attribute quotations correctly any more?"

He laughed and kissed my hand before letting go of it and sobering. "So you will?"

I sat there gazing at his handsome face. Some good-looking guys can look as rough as a badger's arse first thing in the morning before they can get their hands on their facial scrubs and male moisturisers. Chris looked fantastic, fresh, renewed, like sleep had done what it's supposed to do and not what it usually does to me, leaving me looking like a bleary car crash victim as I crawl from my bed. I swear that might have been one reason why I hadn't had a long-term partner: they just couldn't take the morning me. So I looked at this vision across the breakfast table, and thought of how he had brought me through probably the most horrific night of my life. "What the hell," I said. "What do you want me to do?"

He sat back, unable to disguise his look of relief. "Like I said, just carry on as normal, doing exactly what you would have done before." He half smiled at me. Like a kid it made my heart flutter. "And one of those things, remember, was to ask Hamilton about his portrait. About the guy in the mirror."

Richard Farjeon.

*

Carry on as normal.

Yeah. Right. Easy to say. Bloody impossible to do.

I'd gone back to my rooms, changed clothes, and gone about my academic duties. I'd lectured, led a seminar, and now I was in Rufus's study, a pattern as familiar as that of one of his tweed jackets. And everything was different.

All the sights and sounds and smells, even the taste of the sherry he'd given me, were working their usual magic, making me feel more at home than I ever felt anywhere in the world, including at home, but inside my emotions were churning. Chris had told me Rufus was mixed up in some way with this Shadow College, with a monster called Richard Farjeon whose image was in his portrait, but this was *Rufus*. Rufus who had guided my career since the day I had entered St. Thad's. Or groomed? I shivered and swallowed a gulp of sherry as if it was medicine. I felt a complete and utter shit. A sudden thought struck me and I looked up hopefully. I'd hoped it wouldn't be there, but it was: the mirror, just as it was in the portrait. How had I never noticed it before? Then again, everyone seemed to be taking great pleasure lately in pointing out to me just how unperceptive I was. Maybe I needed to look less at the men in my life and more on what was going on around them. I regarded the mirror. Funny, vampires weren't supposed to cast reflections, were they?

"Vanitas vanitatum omnia vanitas," Rufus intoned.

I blinked. "Sorry?"

Rufus inclined his head towards the mirror. "Would you like a moment alone with yourself?"

"No. Thank you." I forced a laugh out. "Definitely not at the moment, thank you all the same."

Rufus looked at me keenly. "Are you all right, Sean? You seem a trifle...off colour?"

"I have had...rather a few things on my mind lately."

Rufus nodded slowly. "Of course. Of course. Lee." He stopped. *And Jean-Philippe,* I thought. Except he didn't know about Jean-Philippe. Or did he? "And maybe," he hesitated, "a certain American?"

"You mean Chris?"

"Mr Bailey, yes."

"Did you know?" I blurted out.

"Know what?"

Was that a stiffening of suspicion I saw there? "That Chris and I would...hit it off?" And was that a slight relaxation, as if I'd not given the answer he was expecting?

"I...had a suspicion that maybe you had some common ground to explore." As ever, the man had an ability to make comments that could work on so many levels.

"Well, you were right. It went well. I think we shouldn't have any trouble with that chair." The chair. I doubt we'd wasted above five words talking about it.

"I'm glad to hear it." Pause. "You've seen him since the meal in hall, I gather?"

"Had the St Thad's Irregulars on my tail, Rufus?"

Rufus shook his head and smiled though he wasn't looking me in the eye. "I believe I saw you together in the dining hall the other day."

Lunch, right. Not Chris's bed last night.

We both sat for a few minutes nursing our sherries. Such silences were not unusual between us: companionable moments when we could just sit, enjoy each other's company, and take a brief respite from the endless verbiage of the academic life. Except this silence wasn't companionable at all. I felt wretched, awkward, uncertain, and I was beginning to suspect Rufus was feeling if not the same then similar. Something had changed. "I think," he said eventually, still not meeting my eye, "I think you should be wary about Chris Bailey, Sean."

"Why do you say that, Rufus?" I asked, putting my sherry glass down carefully on the small table by the side of my armchair.

"I think...I think I might have misjudged him. It's so difficult to tell with Americans, isn't it? They talk a different language. So to speak."

Foreplay has never been one of my strong suits, and I just couldn't take this fencing any longer. "Who was Richard Farjeon?"

I'm not sure what I had expected. Bewilderment, real or feigned? Anger? Suspicion? What I hadn't banked on was Rufus's small nod and slight smile, and somehow that chilled me more than any false denial would have. He could have told me everything Chris had revealed last night had actually been a pack of fantasies, a lie, and I knew now that was what I had really wanted from him. His reaction, though, made it clear he was not going to do anything of the sort, and behind my horror and apprehension there was an absurd sadness as if I'd lost something very precious, not recognising just how precious it was until too late. "A remarkable man," he said softly.

"Jacobean?"

A hesitation? "Yes."

"So what? A poet, I presume? They all were then. Dramatist too? Philosopher? Politician?" *Vampire?*

Rufus weighed his words. "Many things at many different times. Like I said, a truly remarkable man."

"With connections to this college?"

Rufus looked up. It took me a second to realise he was looking in the direction of the mirror. "I think you know that."

"Yes. Now I do."

He nodded again, resignedly. "And why this sudden interest in Farjeon?"

It was quite obvious why. We had just been talking about Chris, but now I found I didn't want to talk about Chris with Rufus. "Lee was doing research on him." I regarded him closely to see how he took that but his expression now was unreadable to me, or was it that I knew I simply didn't understand him the way I thought I had?

"Yes."

"You suggested he research Farjeon." A statement not a question.

"It was the inevitable direction his studies were taking him."

"An odd way of putting it."

Rufus said nothing but sat, waiting.

"So, a Jacobean poet with connections to the college whom you thought worthy of a PhD dissertation by someone as gifted and talented as Lee." Rufus inclined his head. "But whom you had never mentioned once to me in all the time we've known each other."

"There are hundreds of…"

"Don't give me that line, Rufus!" I snapped. "Don't dare give that line to me! I've used it myself so I know how bloody patronising it is."

"I'm sorry, Sean," he said softly, and he sounded it. But did that mean he meant it? I didn't know any more. "There is—" he hesitated, cleared his throat as if he was having trouble speaking clearly. "—there is a time for everything. We would have talked about Richard Farjeon, you and I."

"How long after you'd talked to Lee about him?"

"Is that a touch of jealousy there?"

Yes! Yes of course it fucking well is! "Don't, Rufus."

"I'm sorry."

Two apologies in the space of less than a minute. Had to be my lucky day. "So tell me about Farjeon now." Rufus's eyes were fixed on his large hands. With one finger he was stroking the hair there. As ever I was struck by how strongly black it was. God, I wish we could have fucked at least once! "I know about the portraits."

"How did you...?" He stopped and then nodded to himself. "Ah yes. Of course."

"So tell me about Farjeon."

Rufus sighed heavily, the movement lifting his whole body. "Very well." He rose from his chair and walked across the office to a large oak chest of drawers. Pulling a key from his waistcoat pocket he opened one of the drawers. He glanced across at me, hesitated, and then sighed again. Reaching in, I saw him manipulate some lever out of my line of sight, and with a small click another drawer within spring open. A secret compartment. Well, not secret any more. Rufus hadn't bothered to conceal it from me. The time for hiding things, it seemed, was over. "Melodramatic I know, but you know I do have some small taste for that kind of thing." I remembered our first meeting, our talk of Stoker. I felt a sharp pang of nostalgia for something lost, even as I shivered at the realisation that the choice of subject might not have been as arbitrary as it had seemed. Rufus took something from within the compartment and held it in his hands as if weighing it before finally turning and walking back over to me. He stood before my chair so that I was obliged to stand, too, and face him. He handed it over to me. A book. "I hope you will understand," he said simply. "I hope you will forgive me." He turned his back on me, walked over to his study window, and looked out.

I stood holding the book in my hands, feeling there was so much I wanted to say to him, not knowing what on earth it was. Without another word I turned and left his office, not daring to look back behind me in case he turned round. I was out in the weak morning sunlight before I looked again at what he had given me. A diary, bound in dark, worn leather. I knew I should wait until I got back to my rooms before opening it. I could not. I opened it then and there to the first page, and there was Rufus's strong, angular, unmistakeable handwriting.

October 5th

Freedom! At last. Liberation from the prison of a provincial boarding school. Deliverance into the dreaming towers of St. Thaddeus's College...

I stopped. His own diary! From his first term here at St. Thad's as a student himself. But... I closed the book, looking again at its cover, at the date embossed on it in gold. But that would have made Rufus... I shook my head disbelievingly. There'd always been uncertainty about just how old Rufus might be, but that would have made him...

I abandoned the calculation, not simply because mental arithmetic had never been my strong suit, but because the numbers were adding up to a total that was disturbingly wrong. Clutching the book tightly to my chest, I hurried back to my rooms, closed and locked the door behind me, checked the window, poured myself a stiff measure of whisky, and sat in front of my fire. The book lay on my lap. I stroked its soft leather cover, caught a whiff of tobacco from it, Rufus's smell. How often had I dreamed of him opening up to me, really opening up? I'd never thought it would be like this.

Slowly I opened the book and began to read.

Chapter Twelve

From the diary of Rufus Hamilton

> *October 5th*
>
> *Freedom! At last. Liberation from the prison of a provincial boarding school. Deliverance into the dreaming towers of St. Thaddeus's College...*
>
> *I feel like a man released from a prison sentence that he had begun to fear was for life. Freedom! Escape from the petty tyrannies of school masters and prefects, from compulsory cold showers, obligatory rugby matches, shared dormitories. Release from the shackles of one's peers.*
>
> *Freedom to be myself.*
>
> *Or as much of myself as I am allowed to be. The liberty is intoxicating, but I must not let it fuddle my good sense. For such a one as I can never be free. Such a one as I must always stay apart. Alone. In the shadows.*

Enough with morbid introspection!

I understood years ago my nature and the kind of life it would lead me to. I will always live a life separate from others, but I need never be as truly alone as I was at school. Here at St. Thaddeus's I can finally devote my life to art, to literature. I can live for the beauty of other people's lives, even if my own life may hold no beauty of its own.

It is enough.

I am at peace at last.

I put the book down. This was what I wanted, wasn't it? The key to what was going on, as well as a better understanding of a man I'd felt so close to for so long. But finding out like this made me feel…uncomfortable. Dirty? And I don't know what I had expected to feel about Rufus, but sorry hadn't been it. *My nature.* I think I was pretty sure what that referred to.

I flicked through the following pages. Entry after entry about day to day, mundane matters, the routine of the fresher that didn't seem to have changed over the many years since Rufus had recorded his experiences. It made me smile, went some small way to making me feel that perhaps the link between us hadn't been completely cut yet. But as I flicked on the entries became shorter, more cursory. Days would be missed out altogether, and then an entire week, entries no longer dated, until I stopped at this one.

Late November

I wish I were dead.

How wrong? How wrong can one man be?

I thought it was my nature to be alone, but as I grow at last into manhood, as I begin to make my own way in the world, I see at last the truth of Donne's words: "No man is an island." I thought I could be, thought my defences were strong. But there is too much beauty in the world, too much life. It overwhelms me.

Jamie Kelley. In my weekly seminar group. He has hair like a raven's wing and eyes of an astonishing grey. He laughs at Chaucer and yawns carelessly through lectures on Shakespeare. I adore him.

Michael Logan. I saw him playing for our college's rugby team last week. He was like some careless young god. My heart was still singing hours later.

Frederick Wilson. He sat next to me at dinner in hall last night and chattered unselfconsciously for nearly two hours about binomial theorems. I didn't understand above one word in eight, and would happily have listened for another two hours if it had meant I could have carried on gazing at the curve of his lips, the fine line of his moustache.

I thought I had built a shell around my heart but I was wrong. I had gripped my heart hard and thought its stillness was death, but nothing can quell the fount of life within us, and now my heart swells and the harder I bear down on it the more painful it becomes. I live among fine beautiful young men. I adore them. And they would spurn me and hate me if they knew.

I wish I were dead.

Rufus! I tried to picture him as he would have been then: hair completely black, a burly young man even then I was sure, trying to be small, unnoticed. Brilliant and probably working hard to hide it so he could blend into the background, be safe. It would have killed me. It had been killing him. My heart ached for him. And then it turned to ice as I turned the page and saw the single word written at the top.

December

Richard.

I looked up from the diary, blinking like a man walking out of a cinema into the daylight, momentarily as confused as someone waking from a dream. Had that been a knocking at the door? I waited, unwilling to answer if it had been, waiting to see if the sound would be repeated. It was not. Good.

I returned to the diary.

Richard.

How long has it been now? Two, three weeks? I have to look at the last date in this diary to know when I am. Time seems so confused. Like in a dream. Maybe that's one of the reasons they talk about the "timeless towers of St Thad's."

It has been just over two weeks. Ten days since I first met Richard.

I have been reborn.

It was in the library. Where else? For so long I have lived my life in books. That was why I had come to St Thad's in the first place, to explore as far as I could the realm of literature and leave the pain of the real world behind. But I had not been able to do that, try as I might. Then Richard had come, just as I had been about to abandon all hope. He saved me.

"So much pain," he said.

I was sitting at one of the long tables in the library. It was late, I was alone. It was always late by the time I left and I was always alone. But this man had appeared without my seeing or hearing him approach. I looked up, startled. "What?"

He pointed to the book that was open in front of me. Dante's Divine Comedy. The Inferno.

"So much pain," he said, "in the poem. All those damned souls."

"Oh. Yes." Truth be told I had been sitting there for over two hours with the book, and hadn't read a single canto, sunk as I had been in my own misery. I'd thought he'd been referring to me. Now I knew he was not. Of course he was not. I looked into his face, long enough to take in the smooth pale skin, the angle of his chin and cheek, the slight upward turn of his mouth, the white hair so unusual in one apparently so young. I looked long enough to feel the beginnings of the familiar stirrings and yearnings, and looked down again at the unread book and waited for him to pass on and leave me in my world of misery, my own Inferno.

He sat down next to me. "Do you believe in hell?" he said.

"What? I...?"

"Do you believe in hell?" he repeated simply.

I kept my eyes fixed on the lines of unread poetry as if they were lifelines. "I'm...I'm not exactly religious. Not anymore."

"No more am I," the stranger said smoothly. "Though I do believe in hell. Hell is other people."

"Sartre is right," I said with very little hesitation.

"Then what does that make heaven? A place with no people?"

"Possibly. I think that, sometimes."

My unwanted companion reached across and took the book from me. I should have been annoyed, outraged even at this flagrant breach of British protocol. Somehow I wasn't. He did it as if he had a right to do so, and somehow that was what I felt too. "No," he said with simple conviction. "A place without people is definitely not heaven. Heaven is love. And for love, there must be...other people."

"But what if there are no other people one can love?" It was an anguished plea to a complete stranger, and I couldn't stop myself.

Richard rose with my book and walked round the corner of a stack to replace it on the shelves. "There is always someone" came his voice.

In spite of myself I rose to follow him. "How can you...?"

He was gone.

I dreamed of him that night. I dreamed of him every night that followed. Oh yes, I'd dreamed of men before then, many times, but those had been vague things, long dull inchoate aches, born of longing and ignorance and long-crushed hopes, unclear visions of half-remembered faces, unknown bodies, and uncertain fumblings. But these dreams were different. Like crystal. I saw Richard, I heard him as he whispered to me, the words unheard but the meaning clear. I felt the touch of his fingers on my face, on the unknown parts of my body, knew that I wasn't alone any more.

So as the snow was falling last night, the sound of Old Mark, muffled in the distance, tolling three, and I sat huddled by my small fire, when the knock came at my study door, I knew who would be there, and I had no hesitation inviting him in.

"You know what I am?"

"Yes. I've been waiting for you for so long."

His smile was heartbreaking. "You haven't waited as long as I have, Rufus."

"Why me?"

He smiled again. "Let me show you." As he had done in my dreams he reached to touch my face.

I hissed, startled, and drew back. "So cold!"

That fleeting smile vanished, replaced by that look of sadness I'd seen when he was talking of the Inferno. He stepped back. "Yes."

And now I reached out, my fingers trembling, and I touched his face. As cold and smooth as marble. "Let me...let me warm you."

The need in his eyes! The pain! For a second I thought he would pull back from me. But then we were embracing, fiercely, passionately, and I thought my heart would burst.

He was cold! The walk in the snow, I told myself, even as I knew that wasn't the truth. I didn't care. For the first time in my entire life I felt alive, and the heat of my life burned through my veins with warmth enough for us both. If he was ice then I was fire. For the first time in my life, I kissed a man with desire, and the blood beat in my lips, my head, my breast. It was all I knew and all I wanted to know.

Our clothes fell from us, I don't remember how, and we stood naked before each other. He was magnificent, like some Renaissance statue of a young god brought to life. His skin was smooth, unblemished, and beautifully pale. His stomach was flat, his chest broad, his nipples small tight buds of pale pink. I didn't dare to look at the manhood between his legs. Even as a child I had been ashamed of my body, ridiculously prurient about showing myself in front of others. As I had grown to manhood my maleness had confused, even disgusted me. I had denied my body, hidden it away beneath layers of unflattering tweed and deliberately shapeless garments. Now in front of the perfection that was Richard I knew even as I had found what I had always wanted I was about to lose it all. How could such as he want such as me?

He touched me on my chest, over my heart, and the skin burned. I flinched at the unfamiliar touch of a man in this way, ashamed of my fleshy hairiness. He murmured something that I didn't catch, sunk as I was in sudden misery. "What?"

He said it again. "So handsome."

I looked up into his eyes, expecting to see laughter, ridicule even. He was staring at my body, rapt. For the first time I had a sense of what it might look like as seen through the eyes of another, the eyes of a lover, and my shame, my self-loathing was burned away totally in that instant. I laughed out loud, threw back my head, closed my eyes, and let my lover do what he would with my body, proud in every sense of the word that he wanted it.

His hand moved to my face, stroking its side. Even at this young age I had grown my beard, more disguise, and the rasp of it against his fingers was loud in my ears. Then down the sides of my neck. I shivered. My neck! Dear God, I'd never known the touch of a hand on skin could be so exquisite. The sensations! The sensitivity! I felt the pressure of his fingers on the quickening pulse in my neck, felt him probe gently as if relishing its pace. Then down, over my shoulders, back to my chest, onto the thick mat of dark hair, tracing paths in its coarse length, crossing and recrossing my nipples, making me gasp each time he gently raked their puckered hardness. Before I would have run miles to keep a man from this, now I wanted him to grab hold of my fur with both hands, pull me to him, twist his fingers in it, no matter what the pain. My nipples ached for the abuse.

He moved down. My childhood "friends" had always teased me about the curve of my belly, scorned it as a symbol of how unsportsmanlike I was. Richard's touch, his obvious revelling in me, the sound of his quickened breathing destroyed utterly those memories. I felt strong, attractive, male. And then, dear God, his hand slid over my manhood.

I honestly thought I might die! I couldn't see. I could barely breathe. Lost in the sensation of his hand on my skin I hadn't realised how I had hardened, more forcefully than ever before, until his palm slid over my penis and I nearly exploded there and then in his hand. My testicles pulled up tight into my body and I cried out in alarm at this terrifying wonderful loss of control. Richard smiled and withdrew his hand slightly though I swear I could still feel it, inches from my twitching skin. He leaned into my ear. "Magnificent!" he whispered. With something like a sob I forced myself to relax. How many times had I struggled with myself, fought against this reaction that had sometimes threatened to overwhelm me as I sat next to some handsome stranger in a lecture hall, on an omnibus, in the refectory. It was wrong, I had told myself. Animal like. Worse than that. Twisted! Now I was naked, my penis longer, thicker, hard as oak, and I knew how wrong I had been. This was heaven!

Very carefully, Richard placed his hand again on me and pressed gently. I moaned helplessly, convulsively reaching round to hold his slim body like a drowning man reaching for salvation. He was still so cold. Trembling, I pulled him into me, even now some small inner voice crying out that he would pull back, that he wouldn't want me, that he couldn't possibly want me. He did not pull back. He wanted me as much as I wanted him. As I enveloped him in the hairy heat of my body I felt his flesh warm, felt him take the heat from me, and I was glad to give it.

I honestly don't remember the transition from standing to supine. If I was writing this in a novel rather than in my journal now, no doubt I would record that we consummated our passion on a bed of silken sheets. But we did not. Truth to tell, I have no clear recollection of anything other than his body and mine, and it was only the evidence of the next day that enabled me to piece out that we must have made love there on the floor, on the threadbare carpet in front of my small fire.

That night so much finally made sense: all the lyrics, the poems, the novels that had spoken of love I had arrogantly thought I understood because I knew about history and verse forms and derivations, they finally became real and not just collections of words on dusty paper. I finally understood passion. It was sublime and it was primitive. My soul was singing even as my physicality was thrusting and grinding, shamelessly greedy for more sensation, urgent to release at long last the pent-up sexual energy of years.

I could not touch him enough. My hands were on his stomach, his back, his arms and legs. My mouth was on his chest, his thighs. I knew no shame. There was no shame! My normal eloquence was reduced to inarticulate cries, pleading, begging, exclaiming, and it was more meaningful than anything I had ever said or written in my life. And then for the first time his mouth was on mine, his tongue pressed in deep, and I couldn't help myself. I spent myself then, the passion dammed within me for so long shooting up between our bodies, matting the thick fur of my belly, my thighs, sliding in thick rivulets over his alabaster skin.

I broke from his embrace, pulled my head back, gasping, feeling that very possibly my heart would burst. "I'm sorry!" I gasped. "I'm...I'm so sorry."

Richard whispered to me then, words of comfort, gently pulled me back to him, pressed his mouth to my neck and ran it the length of the muscle and, I swear to God, I screamed. It was as if he had ignited a cord of fire from the nerves in my neck down to the still drumming pulse between my legs. The sweetness of that first climax had been beyond description. Now, before I had had time even to begin to grow flaccid, he had roused me to a second crisis with just the touch of his lips. I felt that surely this time I would die. "Please, please," I gasped. "I...I can't. I need to...to..."

"You are strong, Rufus," Richard whispered in my ear. "So much stronger than you know. And you need to be strong. Strong to live. Seize it, Rufus. Seize your life." And his head sank again into my neck, his lips caressing, his tongue drawing itself the length of the taut tendons, and, sweet Jesus, his small teeth pinching at first gently and then with increasing pleasure at the tight flesh. My hands flew to his head, tried to push him away. I might as well have been an infant. He was immovable, like stone. All too quickly I no longer wanted him to move. All too quickly I was pulling him harder into me.

There was a roar, a guttural yell, from him, me, both of us, I didn't know. Once again I climaxed, the pain of it like steel needles in my vitals, the pleasure of it almost unbearable, an explosion of animal heat met this time by an answering explosion from Richard as his seed exploded over us both, heavy and plentiful and cold as snow in midwinter.

I lay, spent in every way it is possible for a mind and body to be spent, suspended between consciousness and unconsciousness. My last memory was of Richard looking down at me, an unfathomable expression on his face, bending down, closer and closer, his

*mouth near mine again, feeling that if again
he was to fasten on my neck I would surely
die from pain or pleasure, I wouldn't know
which, and knowing I was completely,
utterly unable to do anything about it.*

*I awoke over eighteen hours later. I was in
my bed, the sheets tucked in tightly around
me. The fire had died. Richard had gone.*

I looked up from the book, the transition from the
world of Rufus's diary to reality a jarring one. This time I
was sure. There definitely had been a sound, a tapping,
scraping sound outside. I rose, approached the door, put
my ear to it, listened hard. Nothing, or was that...? Taking
a deep breath, I yanked the door open.

A body hurtled past me. I yelled in reaction and
jumped to one side. The figure fell to the floor a
deadweight and lay there moving feebly. He looked up.
"Help me, Sean! For the love of God, help me!"

It was Lee.

Chapter Thirteen

Five minutes later, Lee was sitting in my chair in front of the fire, looking dully into the flames. I'd closed the door after having first checked that there was no one with him, and now I sat on another chair, pulled back slightly, watching him warily. Lee didn't return my look. He sat huddled, leaning towards the fire as if eager for its heat, though his hands remained fixed at his sides. He looked deadly pale. "Would you like something to drink? Something hot?" I said cautiously. "A blanket?" It was ridiculous. I was offering him hospitality. But what was I supposed to do?

He blinked and turned to look at me as if every slight movement cost him. I watched his eyes slowly focus as if they'd been fixed on something much further away than my small hearth and he was now having to force them to see me. "No," he said quietly and then again with more deliberate strength. "No. Thank you."

So what now? Having offered him a cup of tea and a biscuit was it okay to bash his brains in for what I'd seen him do to Jean-Philippe? In a dream. "I saw you," I said finally, simply.

He blinked again. "Saw me?"

His uncertainty was more unsettling than anything else he could have said or done. I pressed on, forcing myself to ignore the utter absurdity of what I was actually saying. "I saw you kill Jean-Philippe." Saying it out loud it just didn't seem possible, yet behind the words was still the dull, very real pain of what had happened.

Lee leaned towards me as if his hearing was as sluggish as his sight, as if he was having to work hard to understand what I was saying, and I had to work not to move further back in reaction. Slowly he shook his head. "No. No," he said with increasing strength.

"I saw you!"

"Where? When?"

"In..." I hesitated. "In a dream." Even to my own ears it sounded fantastic. What would Lee do now? Continue his denials? Laugh at me?

He did neither. He nodded, looked away from me back to the fire. "That's how they work," he said, so quietly I almost didn't hear him. "Through your dreams."

"How who work?"

Lee closed his eyes and covered his face with his hands. "You know who, Sean. I can tell. You finally know who."

"The Shadow College."

A faint sigh escaped from behind Lee's fingers. "How did you find out...at last?"

I passed over that one for the moment. "What do you mean they work through dreams?"

"It's their power, their strength. They actually have very few powers in the waking world. Well, more than mere mortals, of course, but perhaps fewer than the more fantastic literature would have you expect. But in dreams..." He paused. His fingers were clasped now in front of him so that I could see his eyes again, and they had that haunted look once more, as if he was seeing things far, far away on the horizon. "They can enter your dreams, Sean. Walk in them. Shape them. Make them over into whatever they want. Show you things. Make you...do things." He shuddered and covered his face again as if trying to shut out the things he was speaking of.

I looked at him. I hadn't wanted to admit to myself just what a bogeyman he had become to me over the past few days. The terrifying proportions he had assumed in my mind. But now, here, in reality... He was pathetic. Ordinarily, and not so very long ago, really, I would probably have been repelled by that, revolted even. They say arts students are big in empathy. I'd even had one woman try to convince me gay men were too. So as a gay English lecturer I should have been positively overflowing with the milk of human kindness. Thing was, somehow, I never had been. But now... I thought back over the dreams I had had in recent days, gut-wrenching sweat-soaked rides through terror. If that was what Lee had been through as well, on his own, without someone like Chris to explain and help him... But then he'd had... "Rufus. Professor Hamilton."

Lee started up, looked directly at me, and his eyes were focused now all right. They were burning. "He's working for them, Sean. That is...he's working for one of them."

"Richard Farjeon?"

Even at this point I was gratified to see Lee look surprised. "You...know about him?"

I nodded. "A little. Not as much as you. But then he was the subject of your thesis, wasn't he?"

"At Hamilton's suggestion. Oh God, Sean. If I'd only known."

Awkwardly I sat and watched as Lee's body was racked with sobs. I thought that maybe if I waited they would stop, but they did not. The minutes ticked by. I looked around the room. What the hell was I supposed to do? Hesitantly I stood up, took a couple of paces over towards him, and stepped back. Lee continued slumped in misery, oblivious to my prevarication. Oh, sod it! I walked right over to him, sat on the arm of the chair he was in, and put my arm around him. "It's going to be all right, Lee," I said. "It's going to be all right," as if repeating the words with emphasis and a small pause between each one was going to make them true. How the fuck did I know if it was going to be all right? From where I was sitting it was beginning to look as if we were all pretty much screwed. "Jesus, you're cold!" I added, which was probably less comforting but was my surprised reaction to the feel of him.

"I've been cold, Sean. Very cold." Lee's eyes were fixed on the ground again, but his hand reached up and round and fastened on my arm. "But I think I'm finally starting to feel warm again now." He squeezed my arm and I couldn't help but wince at the desperate strength of the gesture. "Thank you."

I'd forgotten how beautiful he was. How many different expressions had I seen play across that face during our all too brief dalliance? Lust? Of course. Playfulness? Occasionally. Seriousness? Only ever as a sort of brief foreplay. Anger? Unhappily. But this one was new. Gratitude. Simple gratitude? Something more? Was it because I felt sorry for him? I didn't know. This wasn't how I dealt with men. I'd thought he was the one grasping for a lifeline but suddenly, unexpectedly, it was me who was floundering. I'd wanted Lee back very much indeed over the last few days but mostly at first so that I would be off the hook for his supposed death and then because I thought he'd killed someone I really cared for and I'd wanted some form of payback. But now? His eyes. His lips. God, I suddenly wanted to kiss him. My cock was already hard and up, and I hadn't even felt it swelling, and I knew that Lee wanted it too.

I didn't even remember leaning down, but I must have because the next thing I knew his tongue was in my mouth and my body was shaken by the intensity of the sensation. I'd forgotten. How could I have forgotten just why we'd got together in the first place? The boy was fucking incredible! He was, I happily remembered, incredible fucking.

Looking back, I'd say that part of it was simply the release, the sheer bloody relief at being able to chuck all that sharing caring crap and self-flagellation over not knowing what to do for the right thing, and just being able to go with the flow, doing what came naturally, which was coming. My cock was an aching length of rock in my pants, and I tore Lee's clothes off him. I mean, I literally tore them off his back, ripping cloth, popping buttons, the lot, hungry, no, ravenous for his skin. He must have done the same to me, I don't know, I can't remember, but the next thing I knew we were both bollock naked and wrestling on the floor. Pale as ever, his skin seemed smoother, lustrous almost, more incredibly erotic than I remembered. I gripped him hard, pulled him in tightly, opened my mouth and ran my tongue the length of him. I wanted to feel him with every inch of my body, fill myself with him. Somewhere I heard Lee laugh, felt him pull my head hard into his body, force his flesh into my mouth. He spoke but I couldn't make out the words. I went to pull my head back so that I could hear more clearly but his hand pushed my face down still more firmly into his chest and I felt him lean down to whisper directly into my ear. "Bite me!"

Without hesitation, without thought, I bit, hard. It was like the words had gone straight to my brain and tripped some primitive animalistic instinct. Only then did some last vestige of reason surface and I tried again to pull back, alarmed that I might have seriously hurt Lee, that at any second my mouth would be flooded with the coppery tang of his blood. But Lee laughed again, a throaty sound unlike any I'd heard him make before, and held my head in a vice-like grip against his skin, and I knew he wasn't hurt. Or, if he was, he was loving it. And there was no blood in my mouth. *That's good*, I thought with relief. And I ignored that other unusual, unexpected thought stirring somewhere deep, deep down. Disappointment? I bit and bit again, the toughness of his pec muscle, the puckered softness of his nipples, any traces of restraint vanishing with every deep groan that each bite brought out of Lee. I thought I'd been pretty much of an animal when fucking in the past, but that had been nothing compared to this, and I hadn't even worked my cock up his arse yet. I was hot. I was on fire. Though Lee himself remained terribly, terribly cold.

Somewhere, amid the thrashing, moaning, arching, and twisting, I was aware of that. Lee's body was still very cold, and some inner ancient warning voice was trying to tell me that was wrong, so very, very wrong. But then what man has ever listened to his brain when his cock is having the time of its life?

Ever had a guy rub ice cubes over your nipples? Crap, isn't it? I mean, who learns his sex techniques from mainstream Hollywood films? But this...! The coldness of Lee's fingers made their touch that much clearer, made my sense of his body that much more acute. I was almost painfully aware of every single millimetre of the path his fingers traced over my heated skin: over each rib, each stomach muscle, over the roundness of my arse, the curves of my shoulders, the length of my neck, the impression lasting long after the fingertips themselves had moved on, like trails of ice water that shocked and exhilarated. He was ice and I was fire, and I was desperate to fill him with my heat, to pump my hot spunk up again and again into his twisting body, to make him sweat, to make him mine. I groped blindly for his cock, found it, and grasped it: a cold, thick length, bone hard, bone dry.

With a cruel jab, two of Lee's fingers stabbed into my arse, straight through the instinctively constricting muscle ring to poke into my prostate. I yelped. It was like a jolt of frigid electricity to my hot spot and I gasped helplessly, mouth open like a fish out of water. Lee laughed and jabbed again and again. That was...new too. Lee had always been more than happy to play the bottom, but now... "Hang on," I gasped, struggling to free an arm, "let me get some lube."

"No need," Lee whispered, "just relax," and his fingers were fucking me again before I even had a chance to try to do as he'd said. Cool and hard as stone, his fingers worked me, sending wave after wave of sensation through my nerves that damn nearly made me come there and then. When he pulled out my inarticulate cry of relief was mingled with a disappointment I couldn't hold back, but I needn't have bothered. Without pause for relief Lee returned to the attack, three fingers this time, stretching me harshly, unforgivingly. Amazingly.

And now his other hand was round my throat, his mouth clamped down on mine, his tongue thrusting deep. I was struggling for air like a man plunged into freezing water. And when I could, I was screaming out for more.

I must have blacked out. I can't remember just when Lee stopped finger-fucking me into a state of nervous ecstasy. What I do remember is coming back to myself on the bed, chest heaving like someone recovering from a heart attack. Groggily I assumed I must have come but as my mind found its way back to my body, my shaking hand confirmed what I could feel: my cock was still a stanchion, beating a tattoo on my belly with its muscle jerks, and still not fired off. I had to crack one off, I just had to. Weakly, desperately, I began to try to wank myself off. Lee, lying to one side of me, knocked my hand away contemptuously with one of his, while with the other he used one finger to trace lazy cold circles round and round one of my nipples. The fingernail dragged into the tender brown skin of my aureole. It hurt and I wanted him to stop but somehow I just didn't have the strength even to speak. All I could do was lie there, panting, waiting for the energy to come back, gradually becoming aware that it simply wasn't. My God. Had I actually had some kind of heart attack? I had to tell Lee. He had to do something. But for all my panicked efforts all I could do was move my head slightly so that it lolled to one side like a drooling idiot's. Lee looked down at me, calm now. "Oh Sean," he said.

He was propped up on one elbow, the earlier lustful eagerness gone, the anxiety of the time before that quite vanished too. Replaced by what? Confidence? Amusement? I tried again with all my strength to rise. Lee laughed softly and used his fingernails to nip the soft tissue of my nipple. I gasped and sank back, exhausted by the effort the simple movement had cost me, unable to stop his cruel pleasure. He laughed again, held the tit between his fingertips, pulled and then let go. "Oh Sean," he repeated. There was a wistfulness, a sorrow even in his words, though its insincerity was palpable. He leaned down to speak more softly in my ear. "I did warn you."

"What...? What do you mean?"

He moved his fingers from their lazy circle around one nipple across my chest to the other. I waited, waited for him to pinch that one too. He did. Hard. I hissed, and he laughed again as I knew he would. A bead of blood oozed from the wound he had made, a tiny globe of dark red that grew very slowly as if too gelid to flow freely. Lee watched it intently, the tip of his tongue on his lips as his eyes burned. "That last time we met, I warned you. I wanted to tell you, tell you everything. But you were so, you were so—" he paused, and for a moment his expression replaced by something else: sadness. "You were so cruel." I went to speak, I tried to say something, but I couldn't. I don't know if it was because of the terrible enervation that had me in its grip or something simpler though more difficult to deal with. Guilt. "You're wonderful, Sean, you really are," Lee was saying. "You're intelligent, you're witty, you're handsome. You are *the* best fuck. But...you're cold. Did you know that?" He laughed and pinched my tit again, smearing the blood, looking mildly surprised when I cried out as if he hadn't been aware he was doing it or hadn't known his own strength. He brought his fingers to his lips and licked the blood from them absent-mindedly.

"And now I've got it all," he continued. "Well, maybe not *all* of it, not yet, but I've got what I need right now. I've got more than you. I'm younger than you, and I'll stay younger than you. The only thing I don't have yet…is you. The one thing I wanted more than all the rest." He looked down at me. "I so wanted you, Sean. Didn't you ever know that?" He sighed, a theatrical gesture. "Of course you did. We could have had this together, you know. We could have been young for ever. Can you imagine it? Young. Handsome. Fucking our way down the centuries and not giving a shit about anything or anyone." He laughed and by this time all humour had been completely leached out of the sound. It was cold and bitter. "And you could have had this years ago, don't you realise that? Think about that, Sean. Eighteen, nineteen, twenty-one for ever. That could have been you." An expression of mock concern crossed his features. "Oh, don't get me wrong. You're not an old man. Not quite. Not yet." He moved his finger from my chest to my face, stroked the side of it gently with the edge of his finger. "But the years are starting to show. The lines are beginning to make their mark."

He took his finger away and stroked the side of his own face as he looked down at me, his cold, white, alabaster face. How could I have not noticed? How could I have not seen the sheer *inhumanity* of it? "But not on me, Sean. I'm twenty one, and that's how I'll stay. Forever."

Gently he moved down the bed and laid his head on my chest. In my weakened state it might as well have been a pile of bricks. I couldn't move under its weight. My arms lay helplessly at my side; I was unable to lift them to push him off, to protect myself. And the crazy thing was, even as I lay there as weak as a newborn, fear at the thought of just what it was Lee was going to do to my helpless body welling up inside me, my hard-on was like a girder thrusting up from my groin. Lee was ignoring it for the moment. I doubted that would last for long.

He went on. "Beforehand, before the change, I'd dreamed about killing you. It's easy now. I have the power and all those petty restrictions of law and morality, they just don't seem important any more. Rules and regulations to keep people in line for the brief time they're on this planet. Like good old St Thad's rules and regs. And as you have said, Sean, they're good for the freshers, but who gives a toss when you're here for the long haul? And then I changed." I struggled to speak again but Lee hushed me. "No, don't bother. It's done now. I changed, and I thought, well maybe I won't kill you. Maybe I'll just sit back and let you die yourself. Grow old and die. And I'd come back every now and again, every decade say, and just sit on your bed like this and look at you, when you're thirty, forty, fifty, sixty, seventy, watch you as you withered and shrank and dried out." And now he did run a finger the length of my twitching erection and the damn thing jumped, eager at his slightest touch. "And I'd just sit here and laugh. But then I had another thought."

Abruptly Lee sat up again, his voice quickening. "I could make you like me. I can do it now. They wouldn't like me to. *He* wouldn't like me to, and he hasn't shown me how to properly but I know I can. It could be just like I said it would, you and me. *Immortal beloveds.*" He sank back against the bedstead. "But what would be the point eh? You don't love me. You'd made that quite clear." And for one last time he shifted his body down the bed to lie in close at my side, breathing his words into my ear like a lover settling in for a cosy embrace. "So, I came back full circle to my original idea, and decided that, after all, I would have to kill you."

I lay there on the floor of my room, the fading light of the setting sun only just reaching through my dusty windowpanes, the dim glow from my fireplace dying fast, while this monster lay by my side and calmly talked about killing me. It was insane. It was the stuff of dreams, of nightmares. But I knew it was for real. This was what it had all been leading to. This was how my life ended. I tried to speak, to say something, I had no idea what, but Lee hushed me again gently, laying an icy finger on my lips and they were sealed. "No words now," he murmured and leaned in close to my neck. Like a lover. But as a killer.

Time slowed. I remember thinking that if he had been a lover leaning in to kiss my neck so slowly I would have felt his breath on my skin, but there was no breath from Lee. I wanted to scream as his icy lips brushed my throat but I could not. I clenched my eyes tight, the only protection left to me, waiting for the piercing pain of teeth tearing into my pulsing flesh. That was how they did it, wasn't it? Vampires.

He kissed me, and my pent-up terror bubbled out of me in a kind of strangled sob that made him laugh. He was playing with me. *Bastard!*

"No, no, no, Sean," he said in a singsong voice. "I told you, so much of what you've heard about them, about *us*, is wildly inaccurate. Oh, I dare say I could kill you that way, but it would be very messy. Besides, I really think it should be something a little more personal than a hickey on the neck, yeah? Something we can both enjoy a little bit more." Slowly he began to move down my body, dragging his cold, dry tongue over my chest, down my stomach, nipping occasionally with his teeth. "Jean-Philippe liked it." With a sick lurch I suddenly knew what he was planning. "Now that's more like it."

I couldn't look down the length of my own body, but I knew where he was. His cold fingers were gently caressing my tight ball sac, one finger probing the fleshy, fast-pulsing perineum, his face only inches from my straining dick. I felt him grasp my rigid shaft, braced myself for a savage pull, a twist, groaned helplessly as instead he softly stroked it up and down, up and down. God, I wanted so badly to come but I couldn't. As a teenager I'd read lurid porno tales of sexual torture, of men driven mad by being held at the very point of climax for hours, days. It had been wank-fodder tripe. I'd laughed at it even as I'd jerked myself off to it. Now I wondered if that was just another story with its roots in fact. Was that how Lee meant to kill me?

"Don't worry," Lee whispered as if reading my thoughts, which maybe he was. "You'll get to come. And trust me, it will be the climax of your life. *The blood is the life!* That's what they always say in those stupid horror stories, isn't it? Wrong again. That copious cream in your balls is the life. Your plentiful come, your bounteous spunk, your endless jism. Have you ever thought about what to call it as you pump it so liberally around the college into so many eager empty vessels? I doubt it. Thought was never your strong point, was it? Not in that area anyway. Well, I'm going to take it, Sean, your love juice, your man milk. Every last single drop. I'm going to drain you dry just like those story book vampires drained all those helpless shrieking damsels dry of their blood. And when the last drop is pumped from your shrieking, withered, dried-up balls...you'll die. *Dying on a kiss.* That's Shakespeare, isn't it? I'm sure you could tell me act, scene, and line if you were able. So I guess that makes this poetic justice." He kissed me lightly on my thigh. "Goodbye, Sean." He leaned in to my crotch and opened his mouth. I felt his lips pass over the hair of my balls, felt him take their weight on his tongue. I cried out and the sound emerged as a humiliating strangled wail. So this was how my life was going to end: with a bang *and* a whimper.

I only know what happened next because it was explained to me later. Two things struck me—literally: a sound like a great crash and then what felt like a physical blow to my whole body. Lee was abruptly gone from my crotch. Noises, crashes, cries from somewhere way above me. A struggle? A fight? Something rushed past me, a person running? And then there was silence.

I lay still, helpless on the floor. A yellow mist was gathering around the edges of my vision. Released from its torture, my body was simply closing down, seeking the only escape open to it. But even as I felt myself falling into blessed blackness I knew that someone had saved me. Someone had broken in at the last minute and thrown Lee off me, and I thought I had a pretty good idea who. A shadowy figure came and stood over me, the features invisible to my rapidly dimming sight. It didn't matter. I knew I could let go, sink into unconsciousness, safe in the arms of my rescuer. "Chris," I sighed as I finally passed out.

"Yeah. Right," said Sergeant Taylor.

Chapter Fourteen

When I came to again and found myself once more lying on the silken vastness of Chris's penthouse bed, I was convinced that what I thought I'd seen must have been some mistake. It had to be, right? My mind freaked out by the nightmarish experience I had just been through. Someone moved to one side of the bed and I turned my head towards the sound. The effort almost cost me more strength than I had. I felt drained, though happily not as drained as Lee had been planning to leave me. "Chris?" I croaked.

A face moved into sight looking down at me. "How many more times?" Sergeant Taylor said. "No."

"Though I am here," said a second voice, and this time it was Chris. He leaned down over me and kissed me on the lips and then sat down on the bed to one side of me. Sergeant Taylor looked on impassively. "You are one lucky son of a bitch."

Feebly I reached for his hand and held it as best I could. "I feel it now," I said, and it was true. Something about just having Chris there, caring for me, was making me feel stronger again.

"I'd tell you to get a room, but I suppose you already have. Nice room too," Taylor finished, grudgingly.

"What…" I stopped myself. I had been about to utter the most appalling cliché. Even now I could hardly bring myself to do that.

Chris smiled. "What happened?" he volunteered. I nodded gratefully.

"I saved your arse," Taylor said laconically. "Oh"—he jerked a finger at Chris—"and he helped."

I looked sceptically at Chris. "Actually," he admitted, "that isn't too far from the truth."

"Damn straight," Taylor said. "So to speak."

"It seems our Sergeant Taylor has made you something of a pet project, Sean."

"And you haven't?" Taylor said, the hint of an edge to his retort.

"I'm not currently stalking Sean, no."

"It's called surveillance, mate."

"Meaning you were outside his door listening in to private conversations?"

"Just as well I was, wasn't it? And need I remind you that you were only a minute or so behind me."

I raised an arm to silence them. Or rather I tried to. My arm only made it a few inches above the duvet before falling back again, but they both seemed to get the message. "Would one of you please just tell me what happened back there?"

Taylor snorted and stalked off to the far side of the room. Chris watched him carefully, and then, when certain that he wasn't poking around in anything that wasn't his concern, turned back to me and filled me in. It seemed I had indeed been the subject of Sergeant Taylor's "surveillance," luckily enough as it transpired. Doubly lucky in fact, as tonight he had been on the point of turning in for the evening having followed me to my rooms and assumed I was going to be there alone until the morning. It was only diligence or sheer bloody nosiness, I wasn't yet in a state where I could fairly decide which, that led him to make one final check on me. The voices he'd heard had surprised him given that somehow, he had failed to see Lee enter. The strangled gasps that had followed had, apparently, been less of a surprise given my reputation, but when something about the tenor of my exclamations had made him suspect that events were not taking their usual course in my bedroom, then he had applied his broad shoulders to my door and, it had to be admitted, saved the day.

"In flagrant breach of several laws of the land I should add," Chris concluded tartly. Taylor just snorted again from across the room. Chris, who had been coming over to see me, had arrived just in time to see my battered room door succumbing to the burly sergeant's forced entry, and had followed him in. It was Taylor who had actually knocked Lee from off me. Chris, he ruefully admitted, had been bowled over by Lee as he fled the room. "These creatures are formidably strong," he said, with just a hint of self-justification. I squeezed his hand as consolingly as I could, even as I nodded warningly in Taylor's direction.

"If you're worried about whether I know what he means by 'these creatures,'" Taylor said brashly, walking up to the bedside again, "you needn't worry. Yes, I do. Mr. Bailey has been so kind as to fill me in on all background details while you've been sleeping."

"Unconscious," I said with more asperity than was perhaps fair to a rescuer. "I was unconscious, not asleep. Did you believe him?" I braced myself for a flood of British police scepticism and scorn.

"It explains a lot," Taylor said.

I gaped at him.

He shrugged. "Don't you?"

"Yes. of course I do. I was the one having his cock sucked by some demon from the pit, but you're...you're..."

"A plod?"

Just for a minute I wondered if he was able to read minds too.

"The trouble with you ivory tower types," he went on, with commendable if unwelcome candour, "is you have no idea what's going on in the real world. We've got unsolved cases in this town alone that go back years, with details that'd make your hair stand on end. Well," he considered, "maybe not so much now after what you've been through. Fact is, though, it's as plain as the nose on your face that things have been going down here for a long time, a very long time, that just couldn't be explained by normal means." He folded his arms and gave me a look I could only describe as smug. "Surprised you've never picked up on any of them yourself. Too focused on your students I suppose." I glanced at him sharply but his expression was impressively inscrutable. "Some of us take an interest in them though."

"Marrin?"

Taylor gave a wry smile. "Let's say she's trying to keep an open mind."

"I don't think she's got much of an open mind when it comes to me. It was she, I assume, who put you on spy duty over me?"

"Let's just move on, shall we?" Chris said smoothly. "We need to work to put misunderstandings to one side so we can work together against...well, against our common enemy."

"Group hug?" Taylor suggested.

"Maybe later."

I smiled a little to myself at Chris's rejoinder and glanced quickly at Taylor to see if it had discomfited him. Apparently not at all. Interesting.

"Sean." I dragged my attention back to Chris who was addressing me. "You were going to speak to Rufus."

The memory of that sobered me up. "Yes. I did." I glanced at Taylor wondering if he'd get the hint that maybe he should leave now. I'd learned a lot about Rufus in the last few hours, and I didn't like the idea of sharing any of it with him, but he stayed resolutely immobile. I sighed, lacking the strength to protest, and proceeded to tell them both about the contents of Rufus's diary.

When I'd finished Chris looked grimly thoughtful. Taylor whistled. The sound was extremely irritating. "Lucky bastard," he said.

I refused to give him the satisfaction of asking just what the hell he meant by that. "So what do we do next?"

"We fight," Chris said grimly.

"We run away," Taylor said at almost the same time, before adding, "fast."

I looked at him incredulously. "*We run away!* How the hell can you say that! You're supposed to be a policeman, aren't you?"

"Bloody good one actually."

"So how can you suggest we just leave this and *run away*?"

"Because I am a policeman not a comic book vampire hunter. Since when did you become Peter Cushing?"

"If you mean since when did I become Van Helsing?" I began.

"Or Hugh Jackman," he went on with a smile on his face I was just longing to knock off.

"Do I have to remind you that someone has died? Or aren't bloody good policemen interested in murder anymore?"

The smile vanished from his face. Oddly enough that didn't give me half as much pleasure as I thought it would. "The French student."

"Jean-Philippe Morice," I said. I'd intended to snap it out but somehow the words choked. The wound was still raw. I saw Taylor look at me, and I turned my head on the pillow to avoid his eyes. I couldn't have stomached his pity.

"Yes. I'm sorry," he said slowly. "That will have to be...dealt with. But right now we are in way over our heads. Rushing in and doing something stupid would as likely as not only get us all into one hell of a worse mess than we're in already."

"So what exactly do you suggest we do, *sergeant*?"

"I suggest," said Chris, as calmly as ever, "that whatever we decide to do we decide to do it tomorrow morning. It is late and we are all, understandably, extremely tired." His calm deliberation should have been soothing. It was exactly what was needed at that time and what he was saying made eminent sense. In actuality, it infuriated me. The only thing that made me concede was seeing it infuriated Taylor just as much. I suddenly found I was indeed extremely tired. Delayed shock I supposed after what I'd been through.

"We'll discuss it again when you come back tomorrow," I said grudgingly to Taylor.

"No, no," Chris insisted smoothly. "We seem to be building ourselves a little team here, and from what I know of the genre we find ourselves in, it's never a good move to split a team. You can stay here, sergeant. There is a guest bedroom. You'll be quite comfortable. Unless there is someone you need to get back home to?"

Taylor shook his head. "No. There's no one. Thank you."

The idea of spending another night with Chris Bailey was a very appealing one, but the idea of spending it with Taylor under the same roof was somehow one I was not happy with. I wanted to protest, but was finding, just as Chris had said, that I was very, very tired. Indeed, I could hardly keep my eyes open. I watched as best I could as Chris showed Taylor out of the bedroom to his room. I even vaguely remember Taylor wishing me a good night, though I doubt if he understood my mumbled reply. The next thing I remember Chris had returned having presumably seen to it that the good sergeant had everything he required, and he was gently removing the clothes I was still wearing.

"No need to rush," I mumbled. "Le's enjoy it."

He smiled down at me. "You," he said briskly, "are far too tired to do anything more than sleep right now," and he resumed his businesslike and very unerotic removal of my trousers.

"At leas' gi' me a c'ddle," I managed to say.

"When you've got your strength back, I intend to give you a great deal more than that."

"Prom'ses, prom'ses."

"Yes. That is a promise." He pulled the duvet over my naked body and then sat for a moment at my side. "I'm worried, Sean," he said softly.

"*You're* worried!"

He smiled and smoothed a lock of hair back from over my forehead. "I mean about him. Sergeant Taylor."

I frowned. I knew that what he was saying was important but it was so very, very hard to concentrate. I felt as if I was slipping into a deep dark well. Chris leaned over me and his face filled my vision, while all around it was blackness. "I think we have to be very careful with him. He's made no effort to contact Marrin since we rescued you. I get the feeling she doesn't even know he was following you."

"Bu' why...?"

"I don't know. Yet."

"Bu' you asked him...t'stay."

He leaned in to kiss me. "Keep your friends close and your enemies closer. Works in business, and in...other ventures. Good night, Sean."

I wanted to return his kiss, to say goodnight too. I could do neither. With a completely dopey smile and a half-hearted hard-on, I slipped into a very deep slumber.

I should have known better.

The dreams were waiting for me. In the oblivion of my deep sleep I gradually came to an awareness of myself again and an awareness of something or someone waiting for me at the very edges of my consciousness, whispering, calling to me. I struggled hard, tried to will myself to deeper levels of unconsciousness, to hide myself utterly in the depths of sleep. It was useless. Memories of that last dream flickered in the darkness like shadows on a flame-lit wall. The torture chamber again. The creaking of the implacable ropes. The groans. The screams. And a voice calling out. "Tom! Tom!" and then changing, in timbre as well as words. "Sean. Sean. Wake up!"

With a strangled gasp I lurched up in the bed, feeling the harsh cruelty of ropes and boards slide from my body, morph into the soft rustle of silk sheets and a heavy duvet. I was drenched in sweat and completely, utterly awake, as if my previous exhaustion had never been. In the pitch black of the bedroom the light of the bedside clock made it easy to read. I'd been asleep less than twenty minutes.

I blinked, reached out for the clock, and dragged it closer as if proximity would change what I was seeing. It didn't. Less than half an hour and the bone-deep weariness I'd felt had gone. Surprising, but I found myself less concerned with thoughts of how that could be than with thoughts of what it meant I could now do. I reached for Chris. He wasn't there, and from the arrangement of the sheets I was guessing he never had been. Probably working, I thought, or on the phone to his bosses. Well, I could just lie back and wait for him to come to bed, surprise him with the strength of my ardour. I reached under the sheets and took hold of the satisfying length of my erection. Yup, plenty of ardour there. More than enough in fact to make me feel that waiting passively for Chris to come to me was not the happiest course of action. I got up and went in search of my handsome American. Mindful, and not a little resentful, that there was someone else in the apartment with us, I wound a hand towel around my waist. With no small amount of pride, I noticed it did little to hide the length of my eager member. I wondered briefly about finding a larger towel and then decided against it. Tough shit if it shocked any unwelcome guest. I headed out of the bedroom.

The main body of the apartment was empty and in shadow, the only light coming from across the length of it, spilling out from the partly ajar doorway of the second bedroom, the one Chris had given Sergeant Taylor. Voices came from it. Irritated at the thought that they might have decided to discuss already what to do the next day without waiting for me, I made my way across to the door. My intention had been simply to knock and walk in but as I raised my hand to the door I was struck not by the words I could hear so much as the way in which they were spoken. This room was separated from the one I'd been in by a considerable distance. My door had been closed and besides, I was supposed to have been in a deep sleep. There was no need for either Chris or Taylor to lower their voices. But what I was hearing was murmuring, the pace slow, this conversation nothing like the heated exchange of ideas we'd had earlier. Instead of knocking I lowered my hand and crept up to the crack in the open door and looked through. "Well, well, well," I breathed.

The bed was a smaller version of the one in the master bedroom, the silk sheets a deep red as opposed to the black ones I'd just risen from. Taylor, his clothes piled willy-nilly on the bedside chair, was in the bed, sitting up, a pile of pillows behind his back. Chris was sitting on the side of the bed, just as he'd sat on the side of the bed I'd been in not half an hour before. He'd taken his tie off, I noticed, unbuttoned his collar. He had that half smile on his face, the one he'd had when he'd first kissed me, and was making no attempt to disguise the focus of his attention on Sergeant Taylor's naked chest. Not that I could blame him. It was a very impressive chest, broad with a dusting of strong black hair and surprisingly large nipples. Framed by the chest hair they looked so soft and vulnerable. Tits like that just cry out to be licked. Sucked. Bitten. I shook my head. The idea of sinking teeth into a man's flesh had unhappy associations right at that moment. On the other hand, it had had plenty of much happier associations for a longer time before tonight. And what I wouldn't give to make the high and mighty Sergeant Taylor gasp and moan and yelp as I chewed on his dark-pink nubs. Even as I leaned forward to get a better view of the very pleasing sight the better to feed my happy imaginings, I was obliged to push my hips backward lest I gave myself away by having my eager cock poke through the gap in the doorway ahead of the rest of me.

Tearing my eyes away from Taylor's pecs, I finally got a glimpse of his face. I nearly laughed out loud. Taylor looked distinctly uncomfortable. His back was determinedly upright, his arms down close by his sides as if to pin the sheets close to him and prevent access by anyone else. The effect of this was actually contrary to his aims, as it merely stretched the thin material across his frame making the contours of his body stand out clearly, so that he was even more appealing than he would have been lying there stark naked. Not, I decided, that I would have objected to seeing him stark naked. There was a lot more to Sergeant Taylor's body than his ghastly off the peg police issue suit had led me to expect. Especially at the groin. Our pet policeman packed a sizeable truncheon indeed, judging by the size of the mound there, and that was while flaccid too. At least, I assumed it was. It was then I heard Chris speak my name and I forced myself to listen as well as simply look.

"Sean's no fool, not by a long chalk," Chris was saying, "but I don't think he really understands just what it is we're up against here."

"And you do?" Taylor said.

"Enough to get us safely through what has to be done. I've got the knowledge you need, the brains if you will." I watched as one of his hands moved, as if unconsciously, up and across to rest on one of the Sergeant's thighs. *He's not going to say what I think he's going to say, is he?* I thought. "What I need is the brawn." I could have groaned. Not at the casual betrayal you understand, but at the banality of the cliché. And the futility of it! Surely Chris must have known he was barking up the wrong tree with Taylor. What happened next surprised me.

I expected square-jawed, blunt, rough, gruff Sergeant Taylor to tell Chris exactly where he could put his pedestrian compliments, and his hand. But he didn't. Taylor looked down at the hand. I saw him swallow, look even more uncomfortable, but he said nothing. And he made no move to dislodge the hand. Chris laughed softly and squeezed Taylor's thigh. "You are *so* tense," he said. "Your muscles"—and he kneaded the thigh making Taylor swallow again—"are hard as rocks." He moved his other hand to the sergeant's other thigh.

"You...you moonlight as a masseur?" Taylor said, the words apparently costing him an effort.

"Sometimes. For...friends," and he leaned forward to kiss Taylor.

I held my breath, waiting for the outburst, the explosion from the sergeant. I swear I could hear the rasp of the strong dark stubble on Taylor's cheek against Chris's smooth tanned skin. But that was all I heard. No protest. I couldn't believe it. Had I really so badly misjudged Taylor? Chris pulled back slightly, and I could see Taylor's face, head thrown back slightly, eyes closed, mouth slightly open as if he was stunned. And then he gasped hard, arched in the bed, and Chris smiled. I looked down and saw why. One of Chris's hands had moved down to that ample bulge at Taylor's groin and was extending the massage to an altogether more sensitive area. As I watched the bulky lump beneath the material grew rapidly more than a handful at Chris's skilful ministrations. Taylor's breath was coming in short gasps now, his tongue flicking between his teeth, his eyes tight shut. His hips lifted slightly from the bed and then fell down again as if he was fighting the urge to drive his crotch up into Chris's hand. Chris laughed softly and Taylor's hips rose again, then again and again, pushing stronger each time, quickly abandoning any pretence of resistance, the hardening cock under the silk rammed repeatedly into the palm of Chris's hand.

Unable to tear my eyes away I reached for my own cock, now well beyond any hope of concealment beneath the small towel around my waist. Like a schoolboy fearful of discovery in the dorms but desperate for relief, I eagerly wanked myself off to this unexpected visual feast.

"That's right, sergeant, that's right," Chris said, like a father soothing a child. "You like that, don't you? And I like doing it to you. I've wanted to since the first time I saw you. You scratch my back and I..." He grasped the sergeant's cock and gave it a strong squeeze and twist that wrung a helplessly loud gasp from Taylor. "Well, I think you get the picture." He was letting his other hand roam over the Sergeant's wide chest, teasingly avoiding the tender aureoles that were just crying out for attention. *If he so much as touches those I'll shoot right into the room,* I thought. I so hoped he would! "We can all help each other, don't you think?" Taylor gurgled something inarticulate. Chris laughed again. "You'll have to speak up, sergeant," and he squeezed again, the shape of his hand suggesting he had Taylor's cock *and* balls in his grip this time, Taylor's cry and grimace suggesting the proportion of pleasure and pain was more questionable. "I said we can all help each other. Yes?"

"Yes."

"What was that?" *Squeeze. Twist.* "I couldn't hear you." *Squeeze.* "You'll have to speak up, sergeant." *Twist!*

"Yes. Yes! *Yes!*"

Close to climax myself, suddenly, and against all of what I would previously have called my better instincts, I stopped. Unexpectedly, and maddeningly, I found myself...unsure. While one part of me, by far the largest, loudest, most urgent part of me, wanted to carry on watching this arrogant sod being jerked off and coming joyously to the sight and sound of it, another part of me found itself...disturbed. Taylor looked and sounded too helpless, and I'd been there myself that night. This wasn't some semi-kinky consensual scene. I might have got this

PC's AC and DC all mixed up, but I knew I wasn't too far wrong about what he felt about Chris. And there was Chris himself, the things he was saying. The way he was saying them. The look on his face. Taylor's eyes were still shut, almost as if he *couldn't* open them, so Chris's expression wasn't for him. It was all Chris. It wasn't love, but it wasn't lust either. I think I could have dealt with that. It was something far colder, far more impersonal. It was *ownership*. This was business!

"Let's just make sure of that, shall we?" Chris murmured. He released Taylor's cock and Taylor gasped with relief, sinking back onto the bed. But Chris hadn't finished with him. He reached for the edge of the sheets and yanked them down the length of the policeman's body. When his cock was unveiled I literally had to take my hand off my own swollen knob and stuff it in my mouth. Talk about the long arm of the law! The son of a bitch was huge! Thick and long, gleaming with precum and tapping out a tattoo on his stomach with its nervous spasms. Even Chris's eyes flickered with something like astonishment at the magnificent sight. "I might even enjoy this," he breathed, as he leaned in to finish the job he'd started so well.

Enough was enough.

Pausing only to rearrange the towel, to very little purpose, I shoved open the door and marched in. "Is this a private citizen's arrest or can anyone join in?"

Startled, Chris whirled round at the sound of my voice and lost his balance. The hand that had been reaching out for Taylor's giant cock landed square on it, Chris's unbalanced weight pushing down hard on its girth and the hairy balls hanging below it. With a roar Taylor's body arched and bucked, his eyes sprang open, his mouth a huge and silent "o" as a fountain of cum erupted from him. For a full ten seconds the man orgasmed helplessly, rope after rope of thick white seed driven high into the air from balls worked to bursting point by Chris's "massage" to rain down on him and Chris. His cobs finally drained, he flopped back onto the bed panting like a man who'd run a marathon. He rubbed his hand shakily across his face. "Wha...wha...?" he spluttered.

I looked to Chris, expecting either an expression of frank amazement at the volcano of jism we'd just witnessed, some sort of guilt for having left me behind while he went to see to the handsome young policeman, or maybe a mixture of both. In the event I saw neither. Chris had drawn a spotlessly white handkerchief from his pocket and was using it to wipe some of Chris's enthusiasm from off his trousers. It was a large handkerchief, and still wasn't up to the task of dealing with all of Taylor's output. "Just trying to make our guest more comfortable," he said smoothly, rising from the bed. He made as if to put the sodden handkerchief back in his pocket, grimaced slightly, and casually and very precisely lobbed it into a wastepaper bin across the room. "If you want to come back to bed now, I can do the same for you if you like." He walked past me, pausing only to lean into me while passing to say in a low voice, "And if you want a larger towel there are several in the bathroom."

Chris gone, I turned to Taylor. He was blinking like someone woken from a dream or a nightmare, looking around himself dazedly, gazing incredulously at the cum soaking into the sheets as if it must have gushed out of someone else's balls. "I don't... I don't..." He looked up at me and if I hadn't been stirred up by a whole lot of other feelings, none of which I wanted to look at too closely at that precise minute thank you very much, I might have laughed. "I just don't," he said lamely.

I stood there, nodding, putting together the best reply, the most withering put-down I could think of. "Yeah. Right," I said, and turned and left the room.

I spent the night on the couch.

It was more comfortable than the bed in my rooms.

Chapter Fifteen

Perhaps after all, I decided, there is something to be said for an American corporate mindset. I presumed it accounted for Chris being able to begin the next day as if nothing had happened the night before. And after all, I told myself, repeatedly, nothing had really, had it? I was hardly one to lay down laws of sexual fidelity or morality. Chris wasn't my boyfriend. Taylor *definitely* wasn't my boyfriend. So why should it bother me if they wanted to shag themselves stupid all night? Okay, maybe it was tacky to leave the guy you've just gone to all that trouble to save asleep in a bedroom while you sneak off to fuck someone else, but I was supposed to have been unconscious, wasn't I? I mean, if I'd been conscious enough to have been up for it Chris would have chosen me, wouldn't he? *But would Taylor?* I couldn't help wondering about that. He'd shown me what could only be described as contempt since the day we'd first met. He'd shown Chris a hell of a lot more. What had Chris got that I hadn't? I tried to clear my mind of such adolescent crap. Next thing you know we'd be comparing dick sizes. Even as I thought that I found myself mentally picturing our members. Side by side. One on top of the other. Rubbing backward and forward, backward and forward against each other. Very slowly at first, and then...

"Looking thoughtful," Chris murmured as he put a plate of croissants on the table in front of me.

I shook my head to clear it. "I have things on my mind. And I am not a morning person." Chris made some noncommittal gesture and headed for the bathroom.

Taylor emerged from his room. From the look of his hair he'd showered, but his five-o'clock shadow was now as respectable a growth of beard as most of my students could manage in a week. He was, of course, wearing the same clothes as yesterday. Their crumples, I thought with what I considered justifiable viciousness, reflected the crumples on his face, particularly around his eyes. He looked as if he hadn't slept much last night. I think if I'd knocked one off with such vigour I'd have slept for a fortnight. "Morning," he said. I grunted something in reply. He hesitated and then sat down at the table with me and reached for the coffee.

Two minutes passed in strained silence while we both pretended to be completely absorbed in the breakfast. "Look," he said finally, "about last night..."

I laughed mirthlessly. "Please, I heard enough clichés in your pillow talk with Chris."

I watched him grit his teeth and plough on with what he had to say. "I didn't want..." he began slowly.

"Yes," I interrupted. "I could see just how much you didn't want. It was particularly outstanding."

Taylor slammed his cup down so hard it set the rather fine china on the table to clattering, pushed his chair back as if to get up and leave, and muttered something under his breath that sounded very much like, "Fuck it!"

Chris came back into the room, his crispness and briskness contrasting markedly with Taylor's creased look. Mine, too, I had to add as an afterthought. "Well, if you've both gorged yourselves, I guess we need to get down to work."

"Sure you wouldn't like me to leave you two alone? I wouldn't want to cramp anyone's style."

Taylor looked to Chris. "What work? What leads do you have, apart from a few dreams and some very old stories?"

"I have...resources that go a little beyond anything the police can come up with."

The pair of them were, it seemed, determined to ignore me. "Oh I'm not sure I'd ever be surprised again at just what the police can come up with, if pushed." Even I was appalled at the level of my childish insults and petulance. But fuck it, I just couldn't seem to stop. Seeing the two of them there, talking calmly as if nothing had happened. It was really getting under my skin. Taylor should have been with me not... I shook my head. No, that's not what I meant, was it? *Chris* should have been with me. "Oh, fuck the pair of you," I muttered with all the grace of a jilted sixth former.

At that moment my mobile went off and I made a great show of excusing myself and standing to one side of the table to answer and make the point that I had a life that went beyond the pair of them. One glance at the small screen before accepting the call cooled my petulance.

"Rufus." Rufus never used his mobile. It was a source of mild humour in the Senior Common Room (where humour was very mild) that he even had one of the things in the first place, and I'd known when he gave me its number that firstly I was being honoured, and secondly I would never have cause to use it. And now he was calling me. "Rufus?" I said quietly. I was aware that Chris and Taylor immediately stopped talking, and I was the centre of their attention again.

"Sean." Rufus's voice was calm, but even over the mobile's small speaker I could sense the falseness behind it.

"What's wrong?"

"There's someone here who'd...like to speak to you."

There was the rustle of the phone changing hands but even before I heard the second voice, I knew who it would belong to.

"Hello, Sean," said Lee. "Have a good night's rest? I hope so. Our little tête-à-tête took a lot out of you. Not as much as I'd hoped it would, of course, but there's still plenty of time for that."

"What do you want, you bastard?"

Lee laughed. "Jesus. Do people have to spell everything out for you? I want you. I'd have thought that was perfectly clear by now. I want you dead and I want to be the one to do it."

I heard a noise in the background, a scuffling, a soft grunting, and then one of Lee's low laughs. "Rufus!" I called out.

"Don't worry about our erstwhile mentor, Sean. Nothing's happened to him, and probably nothing will. If you do exactly what I tell you to."

I nodded, listening hard to what he went on to say, twisting my head so the other two wouldn't be able to overhear. Give them credit, they waited a full ten seconds after I'd finished the call before they asked me what was going on.

The deal was simple and hardly unexpected. "He wants me in my rooms at midnight. Alone. If I go there then he'll let Rufus go."

"Why the hell should we worry about Rufus?" Taylor demanded. "Isn't he in on all this?"

Chris was shaking his head, regarding me closely. Great. When I wanted his attention he was off shagging policemen. Now, I just wanted him to leave me alone. "I don't think things are that clear anymore. There's more going on here than we might have expected."

"What, you mean like some kind of falling-out?"

Chris nodded slowly. "Perhaps. The relationship between the Shadow College and the Masters of St. Thad's seems always to have been a fluid one, though in the end there's been little doubt where the real power lies."

"I don't see Rufus as someone out for power." Even now, I couldn't help speaking up for him.

Chris gave me a small smile as if pleased at my loyalty for my friend. Taylor just rolled his eyes. "Perhaps not, but I have to warn you: nothing and nobody is what it appears. We can trust no one." He didn't need to tilt his head in Taylor's direction. I knew what he was saying. But then last night... Suddenly I thought I understood better. When Chris had said you had to keep your enemies close I hadn't realised just how close he'd had in mind. Cold? Maybe. I shivered. But then so was the enemy. "So, what do we do now?" he said.

"What? So now I'm in charge?"

"This affects you most closely."

"Thanks." I took a deep breath. "It was a rhetorical question anyway."

Chris nodded. "We must try and rescue Rufus."

"Yes, of course we are going to rescue Rufus." I went to gather my coat. "At what point did I start to sound like a kid from a Saturday morning cartoon show?"

"At the precise moment you started to act like one! Have you lost your fucking marbles?" Taylor exploded. "Where do you think you are going?"

"To my rooms." I stared back defiantly at the two faces in front of me. "It's going to be all right to go now, isn't it? It's morning. Lee's just made it perfectly clear he won't be there for hours. In the meantime I really would like to get out of these underpants and into some new ones. My own, of course. Then I'll be back and we can lay our plans, make our strategies, or whatever the hell it is we're supposed to do."

And with what I thought wasn't at all a bad exit line under the circumstances, I left the apartment.

One thing about my long and colourful love life: it's made me a bloody accomplished liar.

Chapter Sixteen

"You came?"

"Did you think I wouldn't?"

"You're a complete bastard, Sean. Yes, I thought there was a strong possibility that you wouldn't."

"Thanks. Rufus, are you all right?"

Rufus sat slumped in one corner. I wasn't even sure he was conscious but at my direct question he raised his head and looked at me, nodding once sadly before looking down again as if unable to hold my eyes. I was relieved. There was no obvious sign of injury. "No, I haven't hurt him. Not physically anyway," Lee said in that unnerving way he had of answering my unspoken thoughts. "There's been no need. Rufus has been a foolish old man for a long time now but even he isn't so stupid as to try and fight me. He knows all too well what I'm capable of now, don't you, Rufus?"

Rufus didn't look up again. His voice was low and heavy. "What you are doing is wrong, Lee. There is still time to..."

"Shut up!" Lee's voice cut like a whip crack through Rufus's words, and Rufus fell silent again.

Lee rounded on me. "And you, Sean? Have you been stupid again? Have you come alone like I told you to or is your band of *friends* going to come hurtling in at the last minute in a bid to save you?"

I shook my head. The late afternoon sun was bright through the windows of my room, but it would fade quickly at this time of year. "Midnight" indeed! I wasn't surprised Taylor had fallen for that piece of Hammer Horror folklore, though I had worried that Chris might have been suspicious enough of its melodrama to question me more closely. But he hadn't, and here I was. Alone. Defenceless. With a creature that had made it perfectly clear what it wanted most in the world was to kill me. What the fuck had I hoped to gain out of this? I glanced at Rufus. *He* was what I had hoped to gain. I just hadn't given very much thought to *how* I was going to gain him. No, strike that. I hadn't given *any* thought to it. Typical bloody Sean Sinclair. How can a so-called intellectual get through life without thinking very much? "No," I said heavily. "No one will come."

Lee sniggered and then made an obvious effort to sober up. "It wouldn't have made a difference either way. You!" He spun on his heel and spat the word at Rufus. "Go, now." Rufus didn't stir, didn't even look up. Lee nodded slowly as if he had expected that. "Very well, your choice. You get to watch. I always thought you were someone who preferred to watch, Rufus." He turned back to me and I knew before he spoke this was finally it. "No more words, Sean," he said, almost tenderly. He took a step towards me. "No more words."

"No."

Lee stopped. I thought he was toying with me again but then I saw his face, the expression of surprise shading into consternation quickly subsumed by fury. There was a sound to one side of us. It was Rufus. He was sighing, and his head was lowered even more, in his hands, covering his eyes.

Very, very slowly, Lee moved again. It took a visible effort of will, but inch by inch he forced himself to take one step and then another towards me. His arms rose, reached out for me, but it was as though he was fighting some invisible force that was pulling them back, keeping him from me. His features twisted with the effort and his emotions, and there, finally, was the very last emotion I had expected to see on Lee's face. Fear. One more jerky, abbreviated step towards me, and that new voice spoke out a second time. "Stop."

"This isn't right!" Lee cried, the sound strangled as if whatever force was holding his limbs had him by the throat as well.

"No," said the voice. "It isn't."

"He is mine! It is my right!"

There was another sigh, very like the one Rufus had made a second before. "It is not. It is mine."

I could see Lee's mouth working, see the stretching of the muscles in his neck as he tried to force the words out but the power that had him in its grip was too strong and was preventing that too. All he could speak was the one word. "Why?"

"Because it is wrong," and at last I felt able to tear my eyes away from Lee, knowing for the moment at least I was safe from him, and look to the source of the new voice.

No door or window had opened, but he was there in the room with us, and the light from outside that I had thought good for at least another hour or so was suddenly dimmed as if some huge cloud had crossed the sun, or night had descended early on St. Thad's. When I spoke, my own voice came out as little more than a whisper. "Richard Farjeon."

Farjeon didn't look at me. His burning eyes were fixed entirely on Lee as he walked, step by step towards him. Frozen, Lee could do nothing but watch, the way terrified prey watches the approach of its predator. "You promised me," he croaked. "Promised."

"Dreams, Lee. I promised you dreams. Not this."

"But what... What is the point?"

Farjeon stopped. He was within reach now of Lee. "There is no point," he sighed.

"Help me! Stop him!"

I blinked. From somewhere, some depth of panic or despair, Lee was crying to me for help. No! No, that wasn't true. He wasn't calling out to me. He was calling out to Rufus.

Rufus lifted his head. "Richard?" he said haltingly. Farjeon shook his head.

Now Lee was calling to me, desperately. "Sean. You can't let them... I mean, I know... I was wrong. I'm sorry. I wouldn't have... I won't. I promise you. I swear!"

I shook my head. "I don't know. I don't understand. What...what the fuck is going on?"

"What must," Farjeon said. He reached out. His fingers brushed the side of Lee's face, and Lee moaned. With one finger he traced a line across his cheek, across his lips. Lee closed his eyes. I watched the fear in him fade, felt the tension lessen. Farjeon laid his palms, first of one hand and then the other, on the sides of Lee's face, and leaned in to kiss him, gently, on the lips. I just caught the one sound, more like a sigh than a word, that escaped from Lee. "Richard."

With one swift twist of the head held in his hands, Farjeon snapped Lee's neck, held him for a second, and let him fall to the floor.

And then he turned to me.

I wanted to run, but his expression stopped me in my tracks. What had I expected? Ferocity? Hatred? Anger? Some twisted animal-like mask from a movie special effects vision of evil? Farjeon's expression was nothing like that. There was only one word I could use to describe the depth of emotion I glimpsed in that face then. Desolation.

Farjeon walked slowly towards me, hands outstretched, stepping over Lee's fallen body, and this time I did try to run but now it was I who was frozen, as incapable of motion as Lee had been. And like Lee I turned for help to the only other human being now in the room. "Rufus!"

Just as he had done before, Rufus let his head sink into his hands and said nothing. Richard Farjeon's fingers brushed my face. I had an instant to do something, anything, but could think of nothing. And then a world of darkness embraced me.

Chapter Seventeen

I woke, and the air was blessedly warm, heavy with the scent of heather. I lay back on the stone, stretched my body, and let the sun's rays soak into my flesh, into my soul. It should have been hard, this rock, but it never was. I could have been resting on a bed of moss, or the best bed in my family's home, the one with the duck down mattress. Lazily I let my head fall right back.

"Your pardon, sir, I didn't see you there."

Reluctantly, I opened my eyes. A boy, upside down from my vantage point, peasant I'd say from the look of him. I should have been annoyed. This was the one place I thought I could come to be alone with my thoughts, my dreams. But the day was too good to spoil with ill temper. I sat up, intending to graciously grant the lad the pardon he asked for, and send him on his way, maybe even give him a penny to speed him. But my restoration to the perpendicular gave me a better sight of him, and what I saw was pleasing. Very pleasing.

He was no boy, although not yet a full-grown man. A lad then, probably no more than nineteen summers. The beginnings of a beard, black though sparse and still soft. His smock marked him out as some kind of farm worker, and I racked my brain to think if I had seen him before around my father's house. Father was always saying I did not pay enough attention to the running of our estate. I knew that sooner or later I would have to do so. The sight of this lad made me think that maybe now was the time to start. "That's all right, lad. There is no harm done."

The lad bobbed his head in a grateful gesture, stepped backward as if to move away, but stopped uncertainly. His eyes were directed down towards the ground as was meet and proper, but I could tell that he was looking up at me through the downward-hanging curtain of his black hair. Perhaps he was trying to place me, too, though that seemed unlikely. I might have been lax about my duties but this was my family estate, and though I had been away at university, I was the eldest son and had otherwise lived my entire life here. "It's Master Richard, lad," I said, half teasingly.

"Oh I know, sir, I know." He gave a quick smile which he then tried to hide, probably for fear I should find it impudent. If truth be told, I found it quite the reverse.

"And you are...?"

"Tom, sir." He bobbed his head.

"And what are you doing here, Tom?" I racked my brain but still couldn't place him. I looked more closely at his dress. "Looking for a lost sheep?" I ventured.

"Save us, no, sir," he said, with a laugh that made me suspect I had said something wrong, perhaps even silly. "I'm not one of your shepherds, sir. I just...I just likes to come here."

I span round on the rock till I was sitting on its edge closest to him. "Do you, Tom? Why?"

Unbelievably, delightfully, Tom blushed. "I...I dunno. I just likes it that's all. It's quiet, peaceful, away from people." He shifted a little as if uncomfortably aware that he might have just been rude. I laughed and he smiled, encouraged. "I likes to sit here sometimes and...and think."

I nodded, as if I understood what this uneducated working boy could mean. Quite possibly I actually did. "What do you think about Tom?" I wanted to know, but I also wanted to watch him as he spoke. He had a strong jaw, full lips. I'd never really looked at field labourers before. They were just there, in the background, toiling as was their lot, and their work in the open coarsened them, aged them so quickly. Sadly, that was what would have to happen to young Tom here, and sooner rather than later. But just now he was young and beautiful, a full-blown flower before it is blown, an ear of corn before it is plucked. He was like something from a pastoral idyll, and I had long adored pastoral idylls.

Tom raised his head, swept back his hair with one hand, and looked directly at me for the first time. His eyes were an exquisitely deep blue, almost exactly the shade of the small flowers that grew at the base of the rock. "All kinds of things, sir," he said in a low voice. "I don't mean to but sometimes it's like I falls asleep here, without closing my eyes, and I has the most wonderful dreams."

I leaned in closer, more interested than he knew in what he was saying. "What kind of dreams, Tom?"

"Dreams of places I've never seen. Places far, far away. And people I don't know. Sometimes I dreams of the stars." He stopped abruptly, and once again looked down at his feet as if frightened he might have said too much. "There's some as says that's where this stone comes from—the stars. My dad he just laughs at that, says that stone has always been here, but my gran, she's nearly fifty—" He paused so I could register surprise at such a great age. "—she says she can remember the stone being here when she was a girl but that her gran couldn't." He stopped again. "I'm sorry, sir." He gathered himself together, presumably realising he had said far more than he had meant to, far more than was really appropriate between two people of such different stations in life. "You'll be thinking I'm a bit touched. I'd best be on my way."

"No, Tom, wait!" The words were out of my mouth before I knew it and without thinking I sprang from the rock to my feet and stretched out a hand to stop him. "I don't think you're touched at all. Or if you are...so am I." Tom regarded me quizzically, perhaps even a little suspiciously. "I have those dreams too."

And then...

...then it is another day. I don't question how I know that, or even how it has happened. I just know it. I'm seated on the stone again and Tom is with me but this time he is sitting by me, as if it's the most natural thing in the world for a landowner's son and one of his father's menials to be sitting side by side, talking about any and every kind of nonsense. For us, it *is* the most natural thing in the world. Perfectly ordinary, and perfectly marvellous. The sky is blue and the sun is golden in the way they always are in perfect memories or perfect dreams of this kind.

I couldn't tell you what we spoke of, not the words. But I could write you a sonnet about Tom, a whole sequence of sonnets that would put *Astrophel and Stella* to shame. A dozen on his eyes, a hundred on his skin, a thousand on his laugh. My writing was praised in my university circles. People said I was the heir to Sidney and Spenser, that college had polished my natural gifts, made me a true poet in spite of my father. I'd believed them, drank in their praise and let it intoxicate my ego. Until now. Sitting next to Tom, feeling my heart in my throat at the heat of him, the smell of him, feeling the thrill along my limbs as I gazed on his, the ardour in my loins as I dreamed open-eyed of his, I knew I hadn't been a poet at all. It had all been words, words, words, totally without meaning. Now I finally understood what yearnings lay behind those words I had bandied about so carelessly. I loved Tom, and I knew he loved me. And we consummated our love on that stone where we had first met. Mayhap it had and mayhap it hadn't fallen from the stars. The love we found by it transported us beyond the narrow boundaries of our mundane world.

He lay on the stone that looked like rock and felt like velvet to our skin and let me lift up the smock that covered his body, push it up and back over his head, laying bare the naked torso beneath. His skin was soft and pale. I traced the lines of each rib with my finger, kissed each one and Tom sighed and moaned softly at my lips' touch. "Someone will see," he whispered.

"Do you care?"

"No. I love you."

"And I love you, Tom." With his arms thrown back I nosed at the black hair in his armpits, the good honest smell of his sweat like fine liquor to my senses, quickening my pulses and the stiffening of my manhood. I leaned back, dazed by the beauty of him, unable to believe that Earth held anything so wonderful. I gazed in stupefied wonder at his nipples, puckered pink skin with the first bloom of black hair round each. A fierce desire possessed me to suck as I must have sucked when a child at my wet nurse. What had I done that God had chosen to lay such beauty before me? Almost guiltily I raised my eyes to his. Tom lay back looking at me, smiling. "You are beautiful, sir," he said.

I felt as if my very heart would explode with bliss. "Don't call me sir, sweet Tom. Call me by my name. Call me Richard."

"You are very beautiful...Richard."

I fell on him then, my mouth hard on his as if I could by that kiss snatch the very soul from out of him and make it one with mine so that they both might fly to heaven. Laughing and struggling for breath I sat back just long enough to rip off my doublet, heedless of the costly fabric's tearing. I threw it to one side of the rock and then descended on my Tom again, to feed on his mouth with mine, press my body's flesh against his, so that bodies and souls we could be one.

I lowered my hand to his breeches. His cock was hard and long, thrusting up strongly against the roughness of the coarse material. I grasped it as one would a poniard, and he gasped and twisted uncontrollably at the unaccustomed surge of hot sensation. "Sir!" he cried. "Sir, I..." Laughing out loud, I pulled again at his stout manroot, thrilled by the solidity of it in my palm, aroused by the heat of it I could feel even through his breeches. He cried out loudly and pulled back from me.

"What is it, Tom?"

He was breathing so quickly, trembling like a leaf. My passion instantly fled, or rather transmuted into something else: a fierce tenderness, an overwhelming urge to protect. For one horrid moment I feared that I had hurt him,

"It's... I do not know. It's..." He twisted his head so that I could not catch his eyes.

Tenderly I reached across, rested my fingertips on the side of his face, and gently turned him round to face me again. The heart of me caught in my throat. He looked as if he might cry. "What is it, Tom?" I breathed. He shook his head, regarding me with such dumb misery and confusion I thought my heart would melt with the pity of it. And then I understood. "You don't know, do you? You don't know, of the love between a man and another man? You don't know what it can be?" He shook his head. I leaned in and kissed him softly on the cheek. "It is nothing to be afraid of, Tom. Let me be your teacher and this your sweetest lesson."

Carefully I pushed him back, ready at the first sign of refusal to stop. In his eyes I saw still the uncertainty, the fear of this thing he had probably only ever heard whispers about, but I saw also his trust, the willingness to let me do anything I liked with him, and the flame of love that burnt in me was the sweetest pain I have ever experienced. When he was lying underneath me, his back to the stone, I carefully undid the cord at his waist, never taking my eyes from his, and pushed down the worn breeches he called a hose. Only when he was completely free of them did I look down, and the sight near took my breath away. His young cock stretched long and proud. I was accustomed to think of myself as prodigious in my excitement but even I couldn't match this boy for length, and though my girth was greater, in time, when Tom came to full manhood, I would most likely be bested there too. The thought sped the blood still faster to my own member. Slowly, like one bending to pray, I bowed my head to his loins, rested my lips on the round wet crown, and kissed it.

Tom cried out and I tasted the spurt of salt on my tongue. "I will shoot. I will shoot!"

"No, Tom," I whispered. "You must not spend yourself, not yet." I sat back looking down at him, smiling, speaking softly, sweet nothings, until the small crisis was passed and he was ready for my attentions again.

I removed my own hose, their silk such a contrast to his dowdy rags, and sat astride him, my bare buttocks on his belly, his cock pressed into the cleft of my arse, the two of us naked as young bucks atop that rock in the open air with England's sun warming our flesh.

I waited as Tom gazed down his own body at my hard member jutting out far over him. Nervously as a child he reached out and lightly touched it. Sir Proudstaff jerked at his touch like a skittish colt, and we both laughed. Tentatively he reached out a second time, touched me. I watched, my breath held, willing him on. He wrapped his hand around my cock. I felt the calluses of his palm, the gentle nervousness of his hold on me. I closed my eyes, swallowed hard, and hissed. "Take care, Tom. I am as close to spending as you were, and do not want to cast my seed yet."

Tom quickly let go, the suddenness of his reaction to my words nearly pushing me over the edge there and then. Swiftly I held out my hand, gesturing him to be still, do no more, as I struggled to master myself. When I was sure I was safe, for the moment, I opened my eyes once more, and with them alone dared him to do what he would. Like a boy bracing himself for a cold plunge in unknown waters, Tom raised himself on his elbows, leaned in, and kissed me then as I had kissed him, and I swear I nearly covered his face on the instant. "Carefully, my boy, carefully."

For time beyond counting we remained there, he on his back looking up, me astride him looking down, touching, stroking, fondling, our chests, bellies, arms, shoulders, and cocks, stoking the pleasure until near all reason was consumed and I knew I must have him then and there or die of the need. "Turn over, Tom."

Without speaking he did as I bid him, lowering his weight carefully onto his engorged cod, pressing it between his own young body and the hard rock on which we sported. I looked down at the upturned hard buttocks, paler even than the rest of his fair skin. These nether parts had never seen the light of open day before, never known a man's hand on their firmness, never known the unforgiving iron of a man's hardened cock thrusting unstoppably between them, penetrating deep into the warm musk of the cleft. I stroked their curves with one hand, pleasuring him, tormenting myself sweetly with restraint, murmuring meaninglessly, and he sighed under me and stretched out on the rock. I repositioned myself, held my weight on my forearms, and then slowly lowered my hips onto his arse.

What happened next happened all too swiftly. The feel of his tense buttocks against my madly sensitive cock crown was like a charge of gunpowder in my stomach. My entire being shook as if wildly palsied, my hands slipped on the mossy stone, and I fell down and forward on to Tom's body, my full weight driving my stiff flesh ramrod deep into him, like a sword into his guts, the free flow of my anticipation making the passage swift and easy, for me. I gasped out loud at the thrill of sudden penetration even as he shrieked at the unexpected violation of his tight, secret ring. I cried out, wanting to beg his forgiveness, wanting to hold back, be gentle with him, but my words emerged as animalistic grunts, and my restraint vanished as swiftly as morning mist touched by sun as near unbearable ecstasy flooded my body, through my loins, to my stomach, my heart, and head. I fucked him hard, my hips bucking back and forth, back and forth, ramming my engorged cock into the sweet tightness of his virgin hole, and my better self was lost quite under the flood of terrible, wonderful sensation. Tom groaned and writhed, the squirming of his body under mine only enflaming me still further, driving me beyond all hope of reason to greater and still greater efforts of physical violation. "I'm sorry, Tom! I'm sorry!" I sobbed, even as I reaved him on that rock.

And then with one glorious cry of mingled defiance and triumph, Tom's hips and arse reared up, pressed back and into my body, his hidden muscle closed about my cock with a hot, fierce grip, and, Lord help me, it was my turn to shriek. I howled. With delight. With amazement. Pleasure. Pain. I could no longer tell. "Tom! My sweet, sweet Tom!" I ploughed my dear farm boy with yet renewed vigour.

Man and woman, that's what the priests say, isn't it? The union of opposites. What do they know? What joy can a man take in the pale love of a milky maiden when he can burn in the fire of another man's passion? What pleasure can a true man take in that? We were two men, yet there was the union of opposites nonetheless. I avow it, we rutted like animals. We ground and thrust, grunted and howled, slapped and clawed and bit in our transport. And yet we were like gods too. I had never been more alive, never felt such a complete oneness with everything around me as when I finally reached the moment of ecstatic release. As I spent myself again and again and again in Tom I felt as God must have felt on the morning of creation. I was complete at last. I had found the reason for living that I had, all unknowing, been looking for all my life in my books, in my poetry. I had found it all there on that rock with Tom. I loved him, and I knew I always would.

When at last I had gently withdrawn from within him, I carefully turned him over again, pulled him to me chest to chest, and covered his face with kisses. "Thank you, my boy, my sweet Ganymede. Thank you. Thank you." I looked fondly to his lap, his cock lying exhausted the length of his thigh. I frowned, looked past him to the spot on the stone where it must have been pressed hard under the heaving weight of both our bodies. "Did you...? Tom? Are you...?"

He looked wonderingly first at me, and then down at the stone, touching it as if surprised before looking back to me. "Yes. Yes, Richard. I had thought I would die, that I could not stop until all that was in me was spent on this stone." He laughed. "I had thought we could swim from it, but now." He brought his fingers back up from the stone. They were quite dry. "The rock has drunk it quite," he said.

I wrapped my arms about his slight body and pulled him tightly into me. "As I shall drink from you, my boy. And you from me. We shall practice all the ways of love. I shall read to you of them and we shall follow them. And then we shall find new ways of our own."

And we did.

Through that long summer we essayed physical love that would have amazed and astounded the most goatish of the Roman poets, and knew true affection that would have made the court poets of our own age sick with jealousy. With our bodies we sought and found pleasure in ways neither of us had known before was possible, while in our hearts we grew closer and still closer. The time we spent rutting was of almost inexpressible dearness to me, but equally as dear were the times afterwards, when we lay side by side in each other's arms, the sweat of our exhaustion cooling on our naked skin, on the rock. Sometimes we would speak of this and that, more often we would say nothing at all. And frequently, as we slipped into the blissful sleep men seek after doing what it is that men do best, we would dream, as we had both done before on this rock. We were young. We thought we had forever.

We were wrong.

Chapter Eighteen

The scene changes.

The light of those golden summer days is gone, replaced by the flickering darkness of some tower cell. The sweet scents of summer are vanished quite. In their place the sourness of stale sweat and old blood. The softness of the moss on our rock against my back becomes the roughness of a wooden pallet. "Held at Her Majesty's pleasure." The mealy-mouthed phrase used to hide the hideous truth of Her Majesty's torture chamber in the tower. But it is not the old Queen who takes most pleasure in the plight of those brought there.

"Repent!" hisses my Lord Waldron as he stands over my near naked body, bound with thick hempen rope at wrists and ankles, stretched out on the implacable cruelty of a rack. His hands held in front of him in a parody of prayer though they are clasped into fists, the knuckles pale, Lord Waldron watches as his minions slowly turn the wheels at my head and feet.

"Mercy!"

"Repent!"

"Of what?" I gasp for the hundredth time. I know it is futile.

Yet again my Lord nods to his men and first the one at my head and then the one at my feet turn their wheels and to the creak of wood and rope my body is stretched out another fraction and then still another, each turn increasing my agony tenfold, a hundredfold. Impossible to measure the pain. Impossible to believe it can grow any greater. But with each application of the wheels it does. I groan helplessly, and my Lord's fists grip the air even more tightly, the knuckles bone white now. His eyes glitter. Constrained by the inhuman tension on my ribs, I struggle to draw air into my lungs. My breathing is short and shallow, and so is my Lord's.

At either end of the rack my cowled torturers are sweating from their exertions. One is stripped to the waist, the thick hair on his bulky body matted against his skin. When his hands are not at his work, I see the one at my feet covertly rubbing his chest as if to wipe off the sweat. His thick nipples are thrusting proudly through his mat of grubby fur and I see him rasp them over and over with his coarse palms, pleasuring himself at my plight when he thinks Lord Waldron isn't looking. But Lord Waldron is never looking at him. His attention is fixed entirely on me.

Lord Waldron is sweating, too, his upper lip beaded. I see his tongue flick out to lick the sweat away, again and again. In my pained delirium it makes me think of a snake. The Devil came to man first as a snake, did he not? And yet my Lord Waldron has said it is I who am in league with the Devil. *"You have consorted with demons!"* There is a joke there somewhere. I try to laugh but all that escapes my lips is a cracked moan that rises to a helpless cry as once again the wheels are turned. My world falls away into blackness.

When consciousness returns my first awareness of it is the sensation of something wet on my face. Blood? I have perhaps a second to register that it is water, that my Lord or his men must have thrown it on me to revive me so that I am conscious for their sport before the pain along my arms and back returns in a searing tide and burns away all other awareness. Dimly, I note that the men at the wheels are no longer there; it is just my Lord standing immoveable over me. "Please..." I try to speak but my throat is parched. I try to lick at the water dripping down my face. It is foul, rancid, but I struggle for it all the same. My Lord watches but does not move to help. "Repent," he says.

I close my eyes. Does Waldron intend to continue the racking himself? I think not. It is widely held that it is my Lord's pleasure only to watch. "I have done no wrong," I whisper.

"Her Majesty believes otherwise."

"I am faithful to the Queen and the new religion and to my country," I cry out with as much force as I can muster.

"There are those who say otherwise."

"There will always be those...who speak ill of others. Especially...if those others...are of wealthy families. Eh... my lord?"

Waldron's eyes flash dangerously as, for the first time since my ordeal began, he leans down to bring his face close to mine. "Your father is dead, boy. Your family's famed wealth is now yours. But if you die here—" he pauses, mocking me. "—your chattels and estate pass to the Crown. I am the Crown's faithful servant. And the

Crown rewards her faithful servants." He straightened. "All you have to do to save yourself is repent."

"You mean...*confess*. And what is the punishment for that?"

Waldron shrugs. "Terrible it is true. But swifter than this." He gestures to the rack.

"I...have...done...no...wrong!" The words are wrung from my soul with all the strength I can find. They are swallowed by the dank blackness of the torture chamber leaving not even an echo.

Lord Waldron laughs softly. "You are deep in sin, young Farjeon."

"Is it not sin to take joy...in the pain of others...my lord?"

"And," he continues as if I have not spoken, "we have here the proof." He gestures and at the corners of my vision I see movement. I grit my teeth hard and close my eyes against the return of his minions and the resumption of the racking. When the turning of the wheels does not begin anew I open my eyes again slowly. Waldron's torturers are standing to one side, and fast in their brawny arms is the very last thing I want to see in that pit of hell. "Tom!"

"Richard!" My lover is stripped near naked. The bruises and weals on his body are clear testament to his treatment at the hands of our captors. As I watch helplessly, one of the hooded henchmen clamps his hand on Tom's breast, squeezes and twists. Tom cries out and struggles but his slight strength is as nothing to the muscular devils who hold him, and the one tormenting him merely laughs. When he lets go the marks of his fingers are white on my lover's breast, turning quickly to a deep angry red. Too shortly they will match the other blue, black, and yellow marks that are everywhere else to be seen. Lord Waldron affects not to notice. My bowels turn to ice at the thought of what they might have done to Tom already, of what they might do to him yet. My suffering on the rack has been great. It is nothing compared to the suffering I now feel at the sight of Tom in their hands.

"The boy calls his better by his Christian name. Is that meet?" Waldron barks.

"He is of my estate. Leave him be. Let him go!"

"Your concern is touching and surprisingly strong for a mere farm labourer." He circles the rack, making his way to where Tom is being held. He reaches out and rests his hand on my boy's chest, on the vicious mark just left by his man. I hear Tom hiss with pain, see him flinch as much as he can in the brutal grip of the men who hold his arms pinioned. "So smooth," Waldron muses, tracing the outline of his henchman's imprint with one gauntleted fingertip. "Surprising." His finger moves upwards, up Tom's neck, to his chin, pushing his head back, moving over the chin, to the lips. "Like a girl, and yet..." For a moment Waldron simply stands, one finger on Tom's lip, silent as if lost in thought. Then abruptly he draws his hand back and then brings it swinging round to crack across Tom's face. He stands then, watching, watching, until a trickle of blood begins to ooze from the corner of Tom's mouth, upon which he nods, turns, and makes his way back to me, wiping the back of his gauntlet on his breeches as if my lover's skin is contaminating. "You have consorted with demons, Farjeon. And you have consorted with men. This man. Do you deny it?"

I close my eyes again. "Yes," I say weakly.

"You have been seen in congress with this catamite!"

I say nothing. I know now it is hopeless.

Waldron stands at my side. He reaches out, his hand over my body. Drawn out hard as I am there is nothing I can do, not one fraction of an inch I can move to evade whatever he wants to do to me. He brings his hand down, and I think at first he means to grasp my manhood. Before they bound me to this rack, they made great show of the various other instruments they have at their disposal: the pliers, knives, and screws. The thought of what he might do to me almost makes me faint away again, but at the last minute his hand moves slightly higher, comes down to rest on my stomach. He lets it lie there, surprisingly gently. The feel of his leather glove is cold against my bare skin but it quickly warms. He is moving it very slightly, almost imperceptibly, perhaps so that his men cannot see. He is stroking me.

A madness momentarily possesses me, a moment of insane hope. My Lord Waldron's enjoyment is clear. If I join with him rather than resist him, if I try to please him in the strange ways he wants to be pleased, might he not let me go? Incredibly, I feel my cock stir between my legs, shift against my thigh. My Lord's eyes flit to my crotch, the rags around my loin hiding little from sight. He looks then at me. There is a moment of silent communication more meaningful than any of the words we have shared these past few days. I want him to touch me there, and I see it in his eyes that he wants that too.

He looks away and the contact is lost. He continues to stroke my stomach, lifting and flattening the line of fine hairs that cross it, and his refusal to press down lower becomes a new torment of its own. "Do you love this boy?" he asks softly.

"I love him...as I love all the members of my household."

Waldron laughs again. "Of course. I believe you." He pauses as if thinking something through and then raises one finger as if suddenly struck by an idea. "And I shall give you the chance to prove it." He signals to his men. "Make our young friend here comfortable. And bind his mouth. I have had my fill of screams this day."

The two burly monsters drag my boy to the second rack that has stood waiting by mine through my ordeal, and bind him to its wheels with strong ropes and leather cuffs. His exhausted struggles are no match for their pitiless manhandling. One forces a filthy rag between his teeth and ties it off tightly behind his head. As yet there is no tension on the ropes binding him and he pulls futilely at them. I know how useless this is. I know he will not be able to do it for long. Once the wheels start turning his freedom of movement will become less and less until all he can do is lie on the pallet and groan at the ever-increasing pain.

Waldron comes and sits carefully on the edge of my rack, arranging his short cloak fussily as though he were seating himself on some fine divan. Something slips from within his doublet, a small device on a chin hanging round his neck. He pushes it carefully back so that it is hidden again close to his breast. My Lord's crucifix no doubt. "A proposal for you, my lord," he says with exaggerated jollity, as if suggesting some pleasant wager in a tavern. "One of you shall walk from this chamber this night. One"—and he gestures first at me and then at Tom—"will die horribly. Your boy there seems unable to speak for himself, so the choice must really be yours." Again he leans in closely. His breath is rank and this close I can see the specks of foam on the grey flesh of his lips. "Speak, and I will release him. He can go free. Say nothing and my men will rack him as they have racked you, and beyond. And then you may go free. I think you know well now how much young Tom will enjoy my men's attentions."

He gestures to his torturers and they reach for their wheels, ready and eager to do his bidding. With sadistic slowness they begin the cranking of the winches. Tom's gasp of horror is smothered by the gag in his mouth, "Make your choice quickly, Farjeon," Waldron urges. "The time for play is now passed and my patience is exhausted." He gestures again, a sharp twist of his fingers. "My men will turn the boy's wheels more quickly than they have turned yours. You have perhaps five minutes before they break him. One word from you and they will spare him, cut him free from his ropes and let him...crawl from the room. And then they will return to you. Oh, and one other thing." He lowers his voice to a harsh whisper so that Tom cannot hear it. "After they have torn your body in two they will turn to your mother and your sisters. We still have them here in the Tower. At the moment they are safe. But without you to protect them..." He spreads his hands wide and shrugs. "So speak, my lord. You say you love this boy as you love all the workers on your estate. But do you love him more than your own life, more than the lives of the distaff side of your family? Tell me you do. Confess it. If not, well, what boots the death of one farm boy when it secures your freedom and your family's?"

I watch with helpless horror as the torturers wind the winches, notch by unforgiving notch, watch as the ropes binding Tom lose their slackness, pull with ever-increasing strength at his limbs. His smooth chest pumps harder and harder. He looks at me, his eyes wide over the gag in his mouth, imploring me, begging me.

"Please! Have pity!"

Waldron is breathing heavily, pacing excitedly from one rack to the other, gazing down at first one victim and then the other as if he cannot decide whose suffering he most wants to savour. "Just one word, Farjeon!" he cries. "Just one. Say it. Say it!"

"I...do not believe you! If I speak for Tom, you will take that...for proof of a love...you would decry. You would kill him...and me...for that alone."

"It is abomination!"

"No love is abomination! You cannot know...because you cannot love! This is an abomination, this torture! You...are a foul creature! Twisted! Evil!"

"But I am not on the rack! I am not condemning my lover to hellish torment, in this world and the next." Waldron calls out to his men in a voice that cracks. "Faster! Turn the wheels faster!"

"But my lord...!"

"Faster, you dogs, or I'll have you roasted alive over a grid once this work is done!"

My head is reeling. Dazed by days of painful torture I can barely think. My body has been taken to limits of pain I had not dreamed it could endure, but this final device is Waldron's masterpiece. If I call out Tom's name he will be free, and I will then die, a sacrifice I am more than happy to make, except for the prospect of what will happen to my sisters and mother. If I say nothing my family and I will live, but Tom will not, and my heart will surely break. And above and beyond all that lies the bleak fear that Waldron is lying, that no matter what I say or do my poor Tom and I are doomed for death anyway. Waldron wants more than to break just our bodies. He wants to break our spirits as well, and by forcing me to condemn either my lover or my family, that is what he most certainly will do. How can I escape? How?

Tom's head falls back, his mouth wide beneath its soiled gag in a silenced scream. "Enough! No more. Let him go! Let him go! Take me!"

Waldron barks a short incredulous laugh, revelling in his triumph. "Do you confess it? Do you love him?"

"Yes! Yes! I love him. Let him go. Let him go!"

Waldron stands, eyes closed, the look on his face that of a man who has climaxed in his lover. I shout out again. "Stop the rack! Let him go! You've won! You've won!" Shakily, as if he has not heard me, Waldron withdraws an embroidered handkerchief from somewhere in his cloak and wipes his face with a shaking hand. He says nothing, looks almost stunned, gazing down at the damp cloth in his hand as at something wonderful. Finally, he collects himself, turns, and nods to his men. "Release him," he says, in a hoarse whisper.

I let my head fall back on the hard wood of the rack's pallet and close my eyes. I hear the staccato rattling of the other rack's wheels spinning as their pinions are released, hear the men cutting the heavy knots on the cuffs, pulled too tightly beyond all hope of simple unravelling now. I hear them lift my lover from the table. "Let me see him," I croak, "before...before..."

"My lord." It is the guttural voice of one of the masked torturers. "He's dead."

I open my eyes, but do not raise my head to try to see. I stare up at the stone ceiling of the chamber.

"He was only a boy," growled the other. "Couldn't take it. We could have made him last longer but you was hurrying us."

Waldron nods. "Indeed. Indeed. It matters not. His master has confessed to debauching him. He would have had to die in any case. I had intended it to be...in some other manner. But so be it."

He walks back to me. I know he is there though I do not see him. I had not cried for my own plight but now my eyes are awash with tears. I see nothing. I feel nothing other than the agony of my broken heart. "Kill me," I say softly. "Do it now."

Waldron nods. "Yes." He takes one deep breath. "Now I can. Now there are none who can say it is wrong. But not like this. Not like this." He is rubbing his hands up and down his doublet, over and over his thighs. I know where he would have pressed them if he had dared, if there had not been witnesses. I know my Lord Waldron's cod is hard and aching, and the thought sickens me. When he speaks again there is a broken giggling tone to his voice, like some small, overexcited child. "You fancy yourself a poet, I believe?"

I do not speak. What do I care about a madman's ramblings now?

"There are many punishments reserved for the sin you have at last confessed to." Waldron's voice grows almost dreamy. "Not the rack. The rack is merely a tool, a way of getting at the truth as we have here this night. No, for sins such as yours there is always the fire. But why rush to the flames when you will be burning therein for all eternity, eh my lord? No, for you I have something else in mind. Tell me—" He swallows twice, at the corners of his mouth a thin line of silver, a trickle of spittle edging down and over his chin. "Have you ever seen a man pressed to death?"

I know what horror he is proposing but I will not speak. I am determined that this monster will hear but one more word from my lips, and when its time comes it will be the name of the one man I had loved and had failed so badly.

"Rocks are placed one after another onto the chest of the man who is to die. One after the other, building, building, until the man can take no more, he cannot breathe, his chest is crushed and...and...God's will is done. But for you, my lord, I will show mercy. Not many rocks. Just one. Just one. This one."

There is a rumbling, scraping sound to one side of me. I do not wish to look but Waldron presses his hand on my face, forcing it roughly to face the means of my death. At first, I cannot understand what I am seeing and even when comprehension at last dawns I cannot believe what I am seeing. "You...are...mad."

"Oh, I'll admit it took a great deal of effort to bring it. My men here complained loud and long. But I had to. As soon as I saw it I just knew I had to. It seems so...right. Do you not find this poetic justice, my lord?"

Suspended on a cradle of ropes and poles is a huge rock. It could have been any rock, more than heavy enough to crush the life utterly from my frail mortal body.

But it is not just any rock. I know its angular lines, recognise its particular colours even here in this chamber. It is the rock from my family estate. The rock on which I had dreamed. The rock on which I had made love to Tom. "You monster!"

Waldron laughs as his lackeys wheel the device over the rack on which I lie helplessly stretched out and lock it into place. The rock hangs a foot or so above my body, gently swaying in its cradle of rope. "It took many strong men to drag this rock up here to the Tower, but now it will only take one to finish its journey. Leave us." Impatiently he waves to his men who leave the chamber grudgingly, the thud of the heavy wooden door closing behind them like a solemn bell tolling my end. Waldron circles the rack and the cradle, savouring my last moments. I go to speak. My throat dry and raw with grief makes my voice almost inaudible. "If you have any pity, man, get it over with now."

"No, no, no." Waldron shakes his head. "It must be slow, very slow." He stops at the foot of the rack. He reaches out, draws his hand back again quickly as if he has touched fire, and then extends it again, carefully, deliberately. "Some say that at the point of death men achieve the most potent sense of manhood they have ever reached." His hand hovers over my crotch, lightly, and then presses down, reluctantly at first as if he is fighting some inner resistance in himself, then harder, firmer, his hand squeezing and mauling, his breaths coming in ever increasing grunts. In spite of myself I cannot prevent groaning which seems only to feed his frenzy. "Is it so, my lord? Does the prospect of your slow death send the blood driving to your root?"

"Not so much as it does to yours. You are the unnatural here, not I. I damn you, Waldron. When it comes your turn to cross to the other side of this life I will be there waiting for you, waiting to drag you down into hell."

Waldron withdraws his hand and gazes at it wonderingly as if it belongs to another. "Mayhap," he mutters distractedly. "Mayhap indeed." He turns to the lever that will lower the rock onto my helpless body. "But you will be there first. And your journey begins now."

The device is cunning, a devilish engine drawn from a fevered and distorted mind. With a sharp pull of the lever Waldron sets the device into motion. Wheels clack and turn slowly, tooth by tooth, and the crushing weight of the stone begins its descent to the rack's pallet and my all too frail body. "Tom," I whisper. "Tom." I will go to my death with his name on my lips.

Waldron is circling again, drinking in my plight from every angle, taunting me as the rock sinks lower and lower. "Was it on this stone you first had him, Farjeon? Did you fuck him hard, make him cry out and beg you to stop but you kept on, driving yourself again and again into his sweet young arse? Did he spill his hot young seed over it?" I see his ghastly face, twisted as if he is in pain himself, his chin wet with spittle as the words spew from his mouth, see the spasmodic jerking of his hands at his crotch and know that, his minions gone, Lord Waldron has abandoned any last shreds of pretence. His breeches are unlaced, his thick blunt cock out and in hand, and my Lord is driving himself to crisis. He will climax over my death. I turn my head, close my eyes, and welcome death. The rock touches my chest, lightly at first, and then bears down heavier and heavier still. My ribs begin to bend.

"Do you feel it? Do you feel it, my lord? The terrible irony of it all?"

Waldron has outlined his sick idea of what happens to a man at the point of death. Others say what happens at that point is that a man's entire life passes before his eyes before he dies. It is not like that for me. Only one part of my life do I see again: the best part; my all too brief time with Tom. The rock bears down on me with all its terrible weight, crushing the last breath from my lungs, and I welcome it as if it is my lover's body. "Tom!"

There is a scream. I know not if it is mine or Lord Waldron's.

There is no more pain.

I die.

I lie beneath the rock and know that I am dead. But I am aware. I hear the strangled sob as Lord Waldron spends himself over the rushes on the dungeon floor, hear the rapid rasp of his breath, the rustling of his clothing as he hurries to conceal himself again. And then the muttered prayers, the desperate cries for forgiveness for what he has just done. Not for his murder of me. For the pollution of his body. I know all this, and I wait. All pain is gone, except for one: the burning in my heart that cannot be assuaged. His prayers petering out, Waldron turns again to his device and uses the gears and pulleys to begin the task of lifting the rock from my corpse. I wait.

I hear him gasp at the sight of my unmarked body, and I smile.

He shrieks like a woman when I tear the ropes that bind me as effortlessly as if they had been threads. He tries to run, but with speed I had never known in my human life I catch him easily and raise him with one hand round his throat. I pin him to the dripping stone wall. "So, my Lord Waldron," I whisper, my face so close to his he would have felt my breath on his skin, had I still been breathing. "It seems 'tis you who will be greeting Satan first."

I kill him there. And I do not make it easy for him.

Chapter Nineteen

My scream tore at my throat.

My mind was in pieces. Two conflicting sets of memories were at war in my head and I could no longer tell which were real and which were not. But that was the terrifying thing about it. Both were real—I knew that with a bone-deep knowledge—but only one of them was mine.

"Sean Sinclair! I am Sean Sinclair!" Saying it out loud helped, gave an anchor of sorts, but it didn't make those other memories any weaker. Richard Farjeon's memories. I had been reliving Richard Farjeon's memories. *No!*

I screwed my eyes tight and grasped my head with both hands as if I could physically block out those images of horror from the Tower. What had been done to Farjeon. What I...what *he* had done! I had to concentrate, focus on my memories as Sean Sinclair. What was the last thing I remembered, *really* remembered?

Lee! Rufus. And Farjeon! Farjeon had killed Lee. Just like he had killed Waldron. No, not like that. I wiped my mouth with the back of my hand, the memory of what Farjeon had done to his tormentor making me sick to my stomach. No, nothing could be quite like that.

From one side of me there came a sound. Wary of moving my body, I let my eyes scan my surroundings but there was nothing. I mean, literally nothing, a blackness so complete that for one sickening second I thought I must have lost my sight. Then there came the sound again, a scratching, rasping sound, and suddenly light burst back into my world, the startling explosion striking into my eyes painfully, and I instinctively raised my arm to cover them. Blinking rapidly, I forced myself to lower them again, and as my sight adjusted I took in my surroundings, what little of them was revealed.

I was lying on the ground, rough grass. I was outside. It should have been cold—it was winter—but it was not. I pushed myself up, leaning on my forearms, and looked around. In front of me was a stand holding a burning torch, a rough length of wood wrapped in an oil-soaked rag that for a moment reminded me horribly of Waldron's long-ago torture chamber. A man stood next to it, observing me silently, unblinkingly. I thrust myself upright onto my feet and looked around but there was no sign of Rufus. The flambeau cast a small circle of light and beyond it nothing was clearly visible. Farjeon and I were an island of illumination in an infinity of blackness.

"Where are we?" I demanded.

"Don't you recognise it. We're in The Quad. The Quad at St. Thaddeus's."

I squinted, trying to see what lay outside, in the darkness. For an instant I thought I saw it, the outline of the buildings, the familiar rooms that should have surrounded us, the pinpricks of light signifying the students and tutors within, safe, normal. But then the flickering light made the shadows shift and it was gone, in its place a suggestion of empty spaces, dark, desolate fields. I rubbed my eyes, trying to make sense of it. Maybe I was concussed. Or maybe...

"Quit playing bloody mind games with me!"

Farjeon was silent for a moment, his eyes dark, unreadable. "No games, Sean," he said at last. "I am sorry."

"Right. Okay." I took a deep breath. "If you won't give me a straight answer to where I am, tell me why you've brought me here? What was...?" I stopped, unwilling even to talk about the vision of hell he had just put me through.

"I am trying to open your eyes, Sean. Trying to let you see the light."

"The light!"

"You were always meant to come here. You have been treading the path that led you here since the first day you entered St. Thaddeus's. Perhaps even before."

I remembered what Chris had told me, about how Farjeon and his people groomed St. Thaddeus's men. "You've been...watching me?"

"From the beginning."

I struggled to keep my tone level. "Why?"

There was a motion, little more than a shadow around his lips. Had Farjeon smiled? "Are you really telling me you don't know why, Sean?" I should have bristled at his casual use of my first name but somehow it seemed...right. "You do seem to spend a great deal of time making the answer clear to those around you."

I looked down, for a second unable to meet that dark gaze. "You mean because I'm..." and now it was my turn to hesitate.

"Brilliant? Exceptional? Unique?"

His words stung. He could have been quoting me. Damn it, he *was* quoting me. It was the sort of thing I said to impress the undergrads, the words I reeled off to woo men into my bed. It was the sort of thing I had said to Lee.

Lee.

"Tell me about Lee."

For the first time it was Farjeon who looked down, as if unable to meet my eyes. "What of him?"

"You killed him."

"I...ended his life."

"That's not much of a distinction."

"He would have killed you."

"You made him what he was."

"I opened his eyes."

"Like you want to open mine?"

"I gave him the knowledge he sought."

"You gave him power."

"If you will."

"And that power corrupted him. Destroyed him."

Unexpectedly, shockingly, a sigh. "Yes. Yes, it did. He was not ready. A mistake."

"A mistake?" My incredulous echo hung in the air between us.

Farjeon raised a pale hand. "Now you are looking for answers before having fully grasped the question."

"So? Tell me! What is the question?"

Farjeon moved. Gracefully, slowly he moved around the torch and walked up to me until he was standing by me. Carefully he extended his hand. "Come." I did not take his hand. He inclined his head, turned, picked up the flambeau from the bracket holding it. "Come." Without waiting he walked away, the centre of the circle of light moving away with him. I had to follow or be left behind in the darkness.

We did not walk far, I think, the journey dreamlike, motion without any sensation of movement. Unable to see anything other than Farjeon ahead of me, the only thing that told me I was moving was the steps I was taking, the faintest whisper of air across my face. Around us everything was blackness, shadows that only hinted at the reality behind them, buildings or emptiness? Without warning Farjeon stopped, turned, and stepped to one side so that I could see what we had reached.

"The Founding Stone?" I shook my head. Perhaps I had been wrong. Perhaps I never had woken up, was still caught in that horrific dream and what I was seeing was just some collection of random images my subconscious was using to try to tell me something. The idea was almost appealing. It held the promise that if I really tried I could wake up, escape this madness. So tempting, and also, I knew, not true. This was reality. I stepped up to the stone and looked closely at it.

It was as I had always known it to be. Large, flat, a slab of greyish rock, run through with veins of something that caught the candlelight and sparkled faintly. It was nothing special.

"The one constant," Farjeon said softly. "Waking or dreaming, past or present. Probably what is yet to come too. Sometimes they all seem one and I cannot tell them apart with ease any more. But the Stone is constant. Literally a rock in the river of time." He held out his hand again. "Touch it, Sean."

I looked down at the rock, at the place where his hand rested. It wasn't hurting him. But he wasn't human, was he?

"Touch it. It's where it all began, Sean. It's where the answers lie."

The veins glittered, pulsing in the reflected light of the torch, like the constant faint throbbing of a living being. Almost against my own will I stretched my hand out but stopped inches above the surface. That mark, that stain. Some kind of lichen? Rust? Blood? For a moment I was back in the Tower again, looking up as the Stone was lowered slowly onto my body. Farjeon's blood? This was the stone that Waldron had used to crush him to death. This was the stone on Farjeon's estate where we, where *he* had first met Tom.

"Touch it."

I felt his will beating against my own, seductive, irresistible.

"No!" I snatched back my hand. "You can't make me."

He regarded me, as unreadable as the Stone itself. "I can. But I won't."

And knowing that, but keeping my eyes on him, I reached out and put my hand firmly on the Stone.

"My lord. He's dead."

"He was only a boy. Couldn't take it. We could have made him last longer but you was hurrying us."

No! Not that! Not again! I tried to look away, but it didn't matter where I attempted to turn my physical eyes. All I could see was poor broken Tom on the rack. *It's just a dream,* I kept telling myself, or at most a memory. Another man's memory, not mine. But it was no use. The images might not be real, but the love I felt for this boy swelled my heart even as the pain I felt at seeing once again his cruel death was sharp enough to stop my breath. "I don't want to see this again!"

"You must look!"

"It...hurts too much."

"You think I don't feel the pain?"

"It's *your* pain, damn it, not mine!"

"But you must understand. Look again! Look more closely. Look at my Tom."

And I looked, and I saw the pale skin, the black hair, and I remembered him when he first came to me—*to Farjeon!*—on the rock. And I began to understand. "Lee!" I snatched my hand back from the rock as if it had been burned.

Farjeon stood across from me on the other side of the rock, regarding me steadily and nodding his head slowly. "Lee," he whispered softly.

"Why didn't I see it the first time? The resemblance, it's... How could I have missed it?"

"We see what we want to see. And sometimes we see what others want us to see. This is true in your world and in mine. It has always been that way."

"Bullshit! This is more of your head games, isn't it?"

"Listen to him, Sean. For too long now your attention has been fixed on what's in your trousers when what you should have been focusing on was what was under your nose."

I whirled round to face that new voice, fearing for a moment another vision, uncertain whether to believe that who I saw was actually... "Rufus!"

Rufus Hamilton stepped into the torchlight. For just one moment I thought he was circling me and was wary of some attack, but I quickly realised he wasn't and felt oddly guilty for considering the notion even briefly. He was merely moving closer to Farjeon, and stopped when next to him. They stood. They didn't touch, didn't hold hands or kiss or anything as banal as that. But I knew. It was perfectly clear. They were lovers. I remembered Rufus's diary, the passion in his words. I could sense it still between them, still strong after all these years.

"Maybe I'm not the only one being led by his cock." It was a cheap shot, and even as I said it I cringed at its coarseness, the vulgarity of the words and their obvious wrongness. The unspoken reproach in Rufus's eyes was an added sting. I turned on Farjeon again, lashing out at him in an attempt to dull my own sense of shame. "So why the hell did you kill Lee then if he was the spitting image of your country yokel boyfriend?"

Farjeon's face was marble, but something, the slightest tensing of his posture, the faintest glint in his eye made me immediately regret my rash goading, and fear for its consequences.

It was Rufus who answered. "Lee was a...mistake." He spoke the word with great difficulty.

"A mistake!" My laugh had an edge of hysteria to it. "Now you're just aping him! What the fuck do you mean, *a mistake*?"

"He should have been you."

Rufus's answer hit me like a hammer blow. "What... what do you mean?"

"Oh Sean. Your problem, my young friend, is that you go through life thinking everything is about you. And the one time it really was, you never saw it."

My head was reeling. I felt oddly detached from everything, the sensation heightened by the absence of any trustworthy visual information beyond this bubble of wavering light we stood in, and I reached out for something solid, something I could use to literally ground myself, recalling myself just in time to prevent my hand touching again the only other thing in the circle with Rufus, Farjeon, and me—the Founding Stone. Okay, so it was just me, no physical props at all. I gritted my teeth and spoke clearly, slowly and loudly, the emphasis more for my sake than theirs. "What the fuck have I got to do with any of this?"

It was Richard Farjeon who replied. "After that night," he said, and I knew which night he was speaking of, picking up again the threads of that terrible vision. "After I had...changed, I fled this land, afraid of what it was becoming. Afraid of what I had become. I travelled far and wide, saw many things, and learned much, but I could not stay away for long. I was bound to this place." As he spoke, he rested his hand lightly on the Founding Stone, stroking its surface. "So, I returned and knew that I had come home. England had changed. There was a new spirit of toleration in the world. But it was a fragile thing and I feared the forces that were arrayed against it, the forces that had already shown their hand against me."

"You mean Waldron?"

"Waldron was their first, barely human face. There have been others since. Call them the forces of ignorance or fear. Or just call them the Shadows."

"Call *them* the Shadows?" Farjeon paused at my question. "No matter. Never mind. Go on."

He gave me a quizzical look but continued. "They have had many names, they don't matter. I determined to set myself against them. I knew then that my...life was destined to be long, and I dedicated it to the fight. I set up my College to be a beacon of light in the night, a torch for those who needed help to see." As he said that he fixed the flambeau in a new bracket standing next to the Founding Stone. I hadn't noticed it there. Maybe Rufus had brought it with him. Maybe he had not.

"Wait a minute!" I struggled to take in what this creature was saying to me. "A beacon? A torch? Are you trying to tell me *you're* the good guys?"

"You're talking like a first year undergrad, Sean," Rufus said with the sort of mild reproof I did indeed remember from my first year tutorials with him when I would come up with some particularly crass statement. "Life, and what comes after it, is more complex than that."

"I founded this college," Farjeon went on. "A place to inspire, a place where men could think. A place where they could dream."

"Creatures of dreams," I murmured, remembering what Chris had told me in his room. This was a new interpretation.

"A place to draw the brightest and the best."

"To feed off them?"

Farjeon laughed. "Yes! As you fed off them when you were a student. As you feed off them now you are a teacher. For the growth and good of all."

"And to make more of your own kind."

Farjeon's eyes narrowed. "You are determined to give a perverse interpretation to all I have done, Sean. Yes, to make more of my kind. As a father hands down his ideals to his son and to his son after him. I cannot bear children. My legacy needs must lie elsewhere. It lies in St. Thaddeus's College."

"Wait! Wait!" I held out my hands as if to physically stem the ideas he was throwing at me. "Your *legacy* is the type of creature you made Lee. The type of creature you are." I forced myself to face him squarely as I spoke the fantastic word behind his truth. "A vampire."

"Vampire?" Farjeon spoke the word with incredulity. "Vampire! Why do you call me that?"

"I saw what you did to Waldron, remember? You made me watch!"

"And you saw what he did to me! To Tom!"

"I saw what you did to Lee!"

"Lee was..."

"A mistake, yes I know, you told me."

"Lee was twisted inside. Wrong. Corrupted by his own ambitions and by his thwarted love of you."

"What! So you're saying that was my fault?"

"Not entirely. Had you been less self-absorbed you might have seen the nature of his obsession before it was too late, but as it was..."

"He nearly killed me with whatever goddamn powers it was you gave him just because he reminded you of your dead boyfriend."

"Yes!" Farjeon's admission rang out, and involuntarily I stepped back. His lips were drawn back in a snarl. This was it! I looked to Rufus, the only other human there. He was gazing, stricken, at his lover. I looked back to Farjeon and realised I'd been wrong. That wasn't anger or crazed blood lust in his face. His lips were drawn back in a grimace of pain. His face was a rictus. He looked ready to howl with grief. I felt ashamed. "Yes, I have said it. I was blinded. I saw his face and I saw again sweet Tom and I could not help myself. I had to give him what he wanted." He stopped and I watched the visible effort it cost him to regain control before he looked up at me again. "Have you never loved someone so much?"

Lee? Jean-Philippe? Rufus? I couldn't meet his eyes. "No."

"Love. That more than anything has been what you call the power behind my college down the long centuries."

"Love!"

"Yes, Sean." It was Rufus who spoke now, moving forward just slightly to be that closer to Farjeon. "Don't be so quick to sneer."

I regarded them both, the way Rufus gazed at Farjeon, the way he looked at me, and somewhere in the battered lump I like to call my heart, I think I began to understand maybe just a little more of what was going on around me. "You seem to know whose side you're on." It was another cheap shot but this time I couldn't even fake any conviction.

Rufus gave that sad little smile of his and shook his head. "It's the Master's job to see both sides, to be the link if you will between the two colleges, waking and dreaming. That's what we do. But I've been doing it for too long now. The time has come to step over the line," and now at last he took Farjeon's hand, the two men looking at each other tenderly. Then Rufus looked back at me. "And for someone else to take my place."

"Me? As Master?" It took a full three seconds for his full meaning to register. Yeah, I know. Stupid!

"Please don't look surprised, Sean. It's what you have wanted practically since the day you first walked into my room. You deserve it too. You are vain, self-centred, far too preoccupied with the pleasures of the flesh, and yet—" he paused, enjoying my discomfiture. "—you are brilliant, I believe underneath it all you have a heart just waiting for the right man to find it and, at last, you have opened your eyes to see the truth. Or at least," he added, "most of it."

Before I could ask him just what *that* meant Farjeon released his hand and spoke. "We offer you this, Sean Sinclair. Mastery of St Thaddeus's College. We put into your hands the responsibility of guarding our secrets, guiding the best, the brightest young minds that pass through its gates. You will earn great respect, have the position you have long coveted. You will have a long, full life. But you will grow old until eventually. Perhaps, you will choose, as Rufus has, to step out of the waking world for ever. Or"—he stepped closer to me—"you can step out of the waking world now." And he held out his hand to me.

I tried to step back, away from him but once again I found I could not move. "You mean..." I stopped. My voice was little more than a whisper, my mouth dry. "Become like Lee?"

"Become like me. Here, before the Stone, I can make you immortal. You could not be Master and you would have to step to one side of the waking world, but you would stay as you are now forever. Young. Beautiful. You have loitered too long on the path to this moment—" Was that an exchange of looks between him and Rufus? "Now you are at the crossroads and must choose your path. There is no going back."

Once, not so very long ago, the casual flattery would have pleased me. Now my mind was too full of conflict to even register it. Young forever. That was what Lee had offered me, wasn't it, a teasing prospect he had snatched away from me even as he held it out. But Farjeon was serious. All I had to do was say yes and he would give it to me. I remembered those earlier words of Lee's that last night in my rooms, the vision he had painted of my growing older and older as the men coming through my doors got younger and younger. I'd thrown him out because of it. Hadn't I just been trying to throw out the image he'd planted in my head? Because it was true? Because it was all life had to offer?

"Lee became a killer."

"The evil was in him from the start."

"No. It can't have been." I tried to remember. What had Lee been like when I had first met him? There'd been no sign of a bloody killer then. Of course there hadn't. So what had there been? Why had I gone with him? I racked my brain but couldn't remember. It hadn't been love, I knew that, but had there been any affection there at all? The slightest shred of something more than pure animal physical attraction? Chris had told me Lee had come to the college with an agenda. Had that included bedding me as well? And if that was all men were, rutting machines, then what else mattered? Literature, the Arts, being Master of St Thaddeus's College, it was all meaningless. If you had to stick around and muddle through it as best you could why not do it as a young man forever? What else was there? "It's the Stone," I said faintly, almost without thinking, as if something inside me still fought against the offer Farjeon was making.

"The Stone?"

I pointed at it. My hand was shaking. "What is it? Where does it come from?"

Farjeon did the last thing I expected him to do. He shrugged. "I have lived long and travelled far. Most today would say as Tom did that it had fallen from the stars, but there are still some people in this world who do not draw the line between dreams and waking as our people do. They would say that perhaps the Stone came from dreams. The Stone is drawn still to dreamers and their dreams."

"And their blood!"

Farjeon frowned. "It did not seek blood. It has never sought blood."

"It's steeped in it. It killed you!"

"Bloody acts were forced upon it, unnatural, bloody acts."

"Maybe acts it brought about. It made you an unnatural monster."

Farjeon blazed. "I, a monster? Not Waldron?"

"The first thing you did after you…changed, was you killed. Horrifically."

For long seconds we glared at each other across the Stone. In the end, this time, it was Farjeon who looked away. Rufus stepped up to him as if to take his hand again but Farjeon moved from him, his gaze fixed on the rock between us. "The Stone gave me life again. Perhaps it was an accident, perhaps not. Perhaps it was God's will. Whatever, it was not a curse. What I did was evil, *that* was my curse, and ever since then I have striven to make amends." For the last time he looked up at me, his eyes a bloody golden colour in the light of the flaming torch. "Believe it or no, now is the time you must make your choice."

"How the hell can I make a choice? Everything I've been told, everything I've seen tells me you're monsters. But you tell me you're on the side of the angels."

"It isn't about us, Sean," Rufus said quietly "It's about you, about your understanding yourself."

"Sorry, Rufus, but again that is just so much bullshit."

"You have been given all the information you need but still you won't see."

"Again with the not seeing! Why can't somebody just *tell* me something. Instead of letting me find out for myself."

"Too many people have been *telling* you things."

"What does that mean?"

"Look again."

"What?"

Farjeon leaned forward urgently. "Look again into the past. Touch the Stone and let it show you."

Resolutely I shook my head. "Never. That thing's force-fed me more horror than I ever want to know again. I'm not letting it take me back there. And what's the point anyway? How do I know you're not just making me see what you want me to see? Like Lee did."

"What Lee showed you in dreams was true," Farjeon said. "And whatever you see while touching the Stone is the Stone's gift of truth."

"Sean." Rufus came and stood by me. For the first time in all the years I had known him, he took my hand. Never so much as a handshake before, not even at my graduation, not after all those years of sitting across from him in his study, thinking, wondering, fantasising, and now he took my hand. "If you won't trust Richard, will you trust me?"

I pulled my hand out of his grasp more roughly than I meant to, more roughly than I wanted to. I turned and faced the damn Founding Stone. "Shit!" I said, and thrust both hands palm down onto its surface.

"He was only a boy. Couldn't take it. We could have made him last longer but you was hurrying us."

Not again! Not that again! Tom on the rack. The torturers' surly apologies for a job done too well. Waldron's febrile sick excitement. Why did the Stone keep taking me back to that scene? What was it I was supposed to see that I hadn't seen before in all its blood-soaked vileness? I could feel it again: the violence of Farjeon's pain and grief, swamping my senses. I had to fight it, struggle to remain me, stay Sean Sinclair, a watcher only, detached from the scene not part of it. I forced myself to look away from the pitiful sight of Tom, all too aware now of how very much he resembled Lee. How could I not have seen it before? What else was there that had been hidden from me?

Waldron. His men. My stomach knotted with animal terror at the sight of them. Those cruel eyes. The stale sweat smell of them. The matted chest hair. The powerful arms.

The arms!

One wore a jerkin. One was naked from the waist up. One was smooth while the other's hair spread thick across his chest, shoulders, and down his back. But I hadn't noticed the similarity before, the mark both bore on their upper arms. A mark I'd seen before. A surge of excitement rushed through my body. I didn't know if it came from me, the Stone, or Farjeon. I strained to see more, to distinguish the mark in the gloom of the chamber. Tattoos of some kind. Bright light flashed in my eyes and I squinted. Waldron had moved, was sitting in front of me, fussing at his clothes as he taunted me. His crucifix had slipped out and he was pushing it back into the folds of his doublet. The light reflected from that had caught my eye. I looked at it, looked more closely. It was not a crucifix. A decal of some kind, a design in metal. The same design inked on his servant's brawny upper arms. The same design...

I snatched my hands away from the Stone and stepped back, unable to take another second of that fetid place.

"What did you see?"

"You don't know?"

Farjeon made no response, waited for my reply.

"I...I'm not sure. Signs. A symbol of some kind. On a pendant and marked on men's arms."

"The Enemy marks its men in many ways. What was it exactly?"

I shook my head. The image was fading so quickly, the way a dream evaporates in the morning. But that hadn't happened with the other visions the Stone had shown me, much as I might have wished it had. This was different, as if something else was trying to force the memory from my mind. "I...I can't remember. I've seen it before. I know I have. But where? Where!" I squeezed my eyes shut, clasped my head in my hands as if the physical contact could help to squeeze the answers out of my brain. Images were whirling in my head, spiralling fragments of the past few days of my increasingly mad life, and I knew there was some way they all linked up, but I couldn't see how. Farjeon, Rufus. Lee. Jean-Philippe. Taylor. And...

"That would be on me, I think. Oh, and by the way, nobody move."

"Chris!"

"Yeah. And me," Taylor was saying. "In case you hadn't noticed."

"Thank God!"

"If you like," Chris said. He and Taylor had stepped into the circle of light, standing at its edges, looking in at the three of us, and the Founding Stone at the centre. Taylor appeared confused, almost dazed, alternating between looking at us and glancing back over his shoulder into the shifting darkness as if uncertain how he had come to be there with us. Chris seemed confident, triumphant even, and I couldn't help a small thrill of pride and relief at his presence. His arm was outstretched and steady, the gun he held pointed unwaveringly at Farjeon. Okay, that was an unexpected touch, but not exactly unwelcome.

"How did you know?"

"Sean, your overconfidence in your abilities is one of your biggest problems. And hopeless lying is another."

"You should rescue me more often. It's worth it for the compliments alone."

"He's right," Taylor said. "More than just a pretty face, y'know. More than just a pretty... Worked out what was going on...and where you would be. Brought us here too. Wherever...here is."

Taylor's words were slower than usual, almost slurred. Was he drunk? It was hard to tell in the light of the one torch but it did seem as if he was struggling to stay conscious, or to fully wake up, unable to focus completely on the scene around him. As if he was caught in a waking dream. I began to experience the first twinges of a bad feeling insinuating themselves into my possibly premature relief. "Yeah, right. Look, let's just get out of here, right?" Taylor made as if to move but Chris remained steadfast, his eyes fixed on Farjeon. Taylor stumbled to a halt. No one else moved. "Guys?"

"You do not imagine that your weapon can really do me any harm, do you?" Farjeon said softly.

"Actually, yes I do," Chris replied calmly. "I imagine it can do a great deal of harm, especially if I was to use it, say, to blow your head from your shoulders. Our research suggests an awful lot of your supposed invulnerability has more to do with your ability to warp perceptions than any actual imperviousness to harm. But then"—and he shifted his gun slightly so that now it covered Rufus—"if I'm wrong I can very easily get off a second shot and dispatch your good friend the Professor here who certainly doesn't have your abilities."

"Chris?" Against a shifting background of shadows I struggled to make sense of suddenly shifting relationships. "What are you doing? There's no need to point that thing at Rufus. Let's just get the fuck away from here, right?"

"Alas poor fool, how they have gulled thee," Farjeon said.

"Yes," Chris added conversationally. "You are a fool you know, Sean."

"Hey, now look. Wait. Just...hang on a minute." Taylor stumbled forward, blinking with the effort of trying to focus, holding out his hand to Chris. "I don't..."

Chris moved the gun fractionally, just enough to make it clear he had carefully positioned himself so that he could shoot just about anyone he pleased at a moment's notice: Farjeon, Rufus, Taylor, and me. Taylor stopped in his tracks, but his eyes suddenly looked one hell of a lot more focused, like he'd just had a sobering bucket of ice water thrown over him. "No, you don't, do you?" Chris said pleasantly. "You know, this could have gone a whole lot more easily if I'd been able to finish that rather pleasant interlude back in my apartment. One good fuck..."

"And you'd have fucked with his mind."

"Bingo, as you say over here."

"Like you fucked with mine." Making me forget about the tattoo on his chest, the mark of the enemy that had literally stared me in the face, that I'd sucked on for fuck's sake, and had then forgotten about, because he'd made me. Like he'd made me distrust Taylor, distrust Rufus even. Like he'd made me lust after him. Or had that just been me? Was I simply ready to fall for anyone with a cute arse and a cock that just won't stop? I suddenly felt very sick, and very foolish. Chris simply inclined his head as if accepting some great compliment.

"I had honestly hoped we could try again. I've never—what might one say?—boffed a bobby? But needs must..."

"When the Devil drives?" I was impressed. I hadn't thought Taylor was in the market for witty line-capping. At least it suggested his brain was more in gear now. "That why you let me tag along? Hoping we'd find time for a quick shag in the bushes?"

Chris smiled, and the expression seemed a whole lot colder than it used to. "Not exactly. Merely keeping my options open. Though who knows what we could have pulled off if there'd been time." The smile, false as it was, faded completely. "But the time for games is now well past."

"So you can do what they do? Mess with minds? Walk into people's dreams? Are you...like them?"

"Yes. And no. Which brings us to the nub of the matter. We've learned a lot from Farjeon and his ilk down the centuries. It's helped us greatly in our goals. But we're still very much human. What we lack in natural abilities we make up for"—and he tipped the gun in his hand—"in other ways." The gun came back to rest squarely aimed at Farjeon. "But you've become strong over the years, too, my friend. Your influence is pervasive and very, very irritating. You've managed to undo much of what we have struggled to achieve. It took us a long time to track you down to this godforsaken little country school. That was good. Realising this was where it all began for you was even better. But finding this was best of all." He was looking at the Founding Stone, and I knew that expression on his face. It was the look of expectation of possession he'd had when he'd first stared down on me sprawled naked on his bed. Only much stronger.

I cleared my throat. "Brilliant. Okay. So your brain is at least as big as your dick. Metaphorically speaking of course. So what are you going to do now? Lift the bloody thing up onto your back and take it away with you?"

Chris sighed as if finally tired of my stupidity. "I can sense what you've been through tonight, Sean, even if you aren't aware of quite how much yourself. Did you have to lift the bloody thing?"

I went to answer, but stopped. The opportunities for witty retorts seemed to be drying up alarmingly.

"That's all I have to do, Sean, now that m'lord has so obligingly blurred the boundaries between past and present, dreams and reality, for his affecting little heart to heart with you. Touch it. That's all. Trust me. My mind is considerably more ready for the experience than yours. I have been trained all of my life for this moment. I'm more ready for the power this Stone offers now than even Farjeon's was when it took him." He spun to face Farjeon again. "You think you've unlocked its powers? We think you haven't even scratched the surface. And I intend to do very much more now than scratch the surface. Gentlemen, stand aside."

"No."

Chris smiled at Farjeon's exclamation, and there was more genuine humour in his smile than any I'd seen before. Genuine and cruel. "No?" he mocked. "Do you still not understand what is at stake here, Farjeon? Are you really so willing to see another lover sacrificed to a greater good?"

"Another...?"

"The Aegis's records are extensive, and Lord Waldron may have been a fool who didn't know what he literally had in his hands all those years ago, but he was a meticulous diarist. We've read everything he ever wrote about you, and he wrote an awful lot, you know. Indeed, he was quite obsessed. So we know all about young Tom Fellows. Waldron even made several sketches of him. And you. Quite a favourite subject of my lord. Tom was quite an outstanding young man, I'd say, based on his lordship's draughtsmanship. Of course there may have been an element of wishful thinking there. I dare say after he'd had your young lover in the Tower for a while he could have drawn us a much more accurate picture, correct in every last detail. But unfortunately, you killed him, didn't you, before he had the chance to record everything for posterity. Still, I hope he enjoyed 'Sweet Tom' as much as he planned to. He really had some very shocking things in mind for the lad's body. Ah-ah!"

The warning came as Farjeon lurched forward a step, hands held out like claws towards Chris. He stopped as Chris's gun swung swiftly to point at Rufus. "As I said," Chris continued, "are you really so willing to put another of your lovers to the sacrifice?"

"Do it, Richard," Rufus said, and there wasn't so much as a quaver in his voice. I gaped at him, standing straight and proud, calmly meeting Chris's cold gaze. God, if I thought I'd loved the old goat before I could have fucked him then and there. He looked magnificent. "A few more years or not, what does it matter? We're all mayflies next to you, so why not get it over now? He mustn't touch the Stone. I love you, my dear. Now do it." Rufus closed his eyes and raised his chin.

Farjeon wavered. Waking and dreaming I had watched this man kill savagely, without hesitation, twice. Now, he vacillated, looking from Chris to Rufus, and then...to me. And I saw it in his eyes, the pain of losing Tom, the agony I had shared with him through the Stone. He had lived on down the centuries and that pain had lived with him. He had survived, but he and I both knew he could not do so again. He would not sacrifice Rufus to Chris. Chris was going to win, with God knew what consequences for us all.

I cleared my throat. "All down to me then," I said.

Chris blinked. "What?"

I began to walk, very slowly but with as much of an appearance of outward calm as I could manage. Complete bollocks of course. Inside I was terrified, utterly, utterly convinced that I was about to die and hating the idea with every fibre of my being. But I had no choice, did I? "It is a far, far better thing..." God, I'd always hated Dickens. One step closer to Chris. "You could always leave, you know." Another step closer. "Just put the gun down and leave." Another step closer.

"Don't be a fool, Sean."

Another step. "But I am a fool, aren't I? That's what everyone has been telling me for the past hour."

Chris raised the gun, pointing it straight at my heart. "Sean, you were a good lay..."

I stopped. "A *good* lay!"

"But that's as far as it goes. Believe me, I really, really will not have any compunction about killing you. The stakes are too high."

I nodded, took another step closer. "I know that, Chris. I don't doubt it for a minute." Another step. "And if it was just you and me here now I'm guessing you'd have shot me long ago and done what you came to do. But you haven't. Because it's not just you and me, is it? You could kill me, but in the two, maybe three seconds it takes to do that I'm betting our friend Richard here could jump across the stone, pin you to the ground and"—I grinned, and tried to put every last bit of malice I could feel about that bastard into the expression—"well, I won't go into details, but I've seen what he can do when he's angry. It's very nasty. Very...messy."

Chris laughed. It was gratifyingly shaky. "Well done, Sean. You've shown more backbone than I'd have given you credit for." His gun was still unwaveringly targeted on my chest, but on his lip I saw a single bead of sweat. It was the sweetest sight I'd seen for hours. He wasn't finished yet though. The consummate businessman, he'd kept one last deal up his sleeve. "There is still another alternative, you know. Join me."

"Why should I? Going to make me young forever?"

He shook his head. "That's their game, Sean, not ours. One lifetime is enough if you live it well. Live it with power. We can give you power. We can teach you to do what we can do. Imagine it, being able to bend the will of any man you wanted to yours."

"Make them want me?"

"Yes."

"Make them want to fuck me?"

"Yes."

"Make them want me to fuck them?"

"Yes!"

"Is that all you think I am?"

Chris frowned. "Isn't it?"

"You bastard!" I jumped at him.

I died.

As I flew across the remaining space separating Chris and me, and as I saw him squeezing the trigger, I died. My life was at an end, and I knew two things. Firstly, I hadn't done half the things with it I thought I should have done. Secondly, what I was doing now more than made up for that. It was the right thing, and I'd never felt this way before about anything. I was ready to leave life. I died.

That's how I saw things afterwards, and Rufus in that kindly, scholarly way of his made it clear to me that I was talking a lot of bollocks and my mind had been rationalising furiously to cope with all the insanity of the moment. What I do know was I was convinced the solid thump that hit me in my shoulder was the bullet from Chris's gun. I cried out, of course, but even as I did I recall being surprised at how comparatively painless it was. That, at least, was a blessing, I thought, as I crashed to the ground. What I couldn't understand was why the yelling sounded so loud, and why I seemed to have some great weight on top of me crushing the air from my lungs.

"Keep your head down, you fucking idiot!"

"Taylor?"

"Now he remembers my name. Oh shit!"

Frantically I pushed his bulk off me. That other yelling had been him. But he'd been way away from me. He must have thrown himself across the Stone to hit me, to knock me out of the way of... The bullet! Shakily I raised my hand to my face. Wet. Red. Blood. Taylor's blood. "Oh shit!"

"I just said that, didn't I?" Taylor grinned weakly and then his eyes fluttered, rolled up white into his head, and closed.

"No. No! Taylor, stay with me. Fucking well stay with me! Taylor! Rufus!" I looked up desperately, and the sight that met my eyes stopped my exclamations.

Farjeon had seized the advantage of Chris's momentary distraction to launch himself at his enemy. The two men now were grappling hard. From what I knew of Farjeon his strength was enormous and I didn't think for a second that Chris would be able to hold anything like his own against him, but yet again I was to realise there was a lot more to the enigmatic Mr Bailey than had met the eye. The two men rolled and grappled on the ground, Farjeon grasping his foe's wrist and smashing his hand against the earth until the gun was dashed from his grip.

Rufus dodged and circled them, trying to come to our aid. "Here." He'd removed his jacket and was bundling it up, pushing it up under Taylor's shirt to his shoulder from where the blood was darkly welling.

There was a crash and the world seemed to wheel around us. The stand holding the torch had been flung to the ground. Standing directly over the torch, unperturbed by its flames, Farjeon had Chris by the throat. With a terrible grimace he hoisted him up high, the American's black patent leather shoes kicking ineffectually at the air.

"We have to go," Rufus gasped. "Help me lift him up."

"But..."

"Just do it, Sean. It's all over here."

I knew he was right. Chris's feet kicked at emptiness as his hands scrabbled at the cold white fingers squeezing, squeezing at his neck. I shoved my arms under Taylor's dead weight and Rufus and I hoisted him up. "Which way? I can't tell."

"Any way. Away from the Stone. It'll all become clear again. Just move."

We struggled, half carrying, half dragging Taylor. I was talking all the time, saying I have no idea what, trying not to accept that Taylor was saying nothing in reply, was making no sound at all.

"Sean!"

The scream twisted my head around like a physical thing. I didn't want to look but I had no choice. Farjeon had dragged Chris over towards the stone. Chris's face was black with blood, congested and free-flowing, one hand still flapping futilely at Farjeon's chokehold, the other hanging limply at his side, the arm possibly broken. His head lolled grotesquely to one side. Bulging eyes looked directly at me. He couldn't have spoken. There was no way he could have formed words with Farjeon's hand ruthlessly crushing his windpipe. But I swear I heard his voice. "Sean! Please!"

With a roar Farjeon lifted him high with one hand and killed him, above the Founding Stone, his flesh never touching its surface. As the blood flowed freely from his body, it spilled down onto the cold stone surface, pooled, spread, and then slowly disappeared as if absorbed deep into the rock.

Gagging, I turned my head and pressed on with Taylor and Rufus away from the Stone and into the warm lights of St. Thad's which were blooming into undeniable reality around us, like morning light chasing away bad dreams.

Chapter Twenty

"So how come you didn't know?"

"What Christopher Bailey's real agenda was?"

"Yes, that little thing."

Two days had passed since we had dragged Taylor from the Quad and back into the waking world. Four, maybe five days since I had last been in this study with Rufus? It felt like an eternity ago. It looked and smelled the same. But everything was different.

Rufus sighed and stared into his schooner of sherry as if assessing its vintage by sight alone. "What can I say? I made a mistake."

I set my own untouched glass down. "You, too, eh? Farjeon makes a mistake over Lee. You make a mistake over Bailey. Doesn't seem to be much hope for us mere mortals, does there?"

Rufus inclined his head and contrived to look apologetic. "I'm only human."

"Are you?"

"Yes, Sean," and for the moment all pretence was gone. "I am indeed only human."

"You're old."

"You're tactless."

"You know what I mean. You're older than you look, older than you *are.*"

"What can I say? A good diet and a clean conscience." Rufus raised his hand to forestall my objections to his prevarications. "Yes, yes. I know. My...relationship with Richard has had some small effect on my weathering the years. But"—and he spread his arms as if displaying himself for my inspection—"as you can see I am not the sprightly young thing I was when first I met him. I have aged. I am indeed old." He let his arms fall to his side again. "And I'm now ready to move on."

We sat in silence for a moment, the only sound in the room the crackling of his small fire, and I pondered what had happened, what he had just said and all that was to come. "You're mad," I said softly.

Rufus arched an eyebrow. "In what particular way?"

"Grooming me for Master."

"With your qualifications, intelligence, and now, experience? I can't think of a better candidate."

"My experience." I laughed at the euphemism. "Yes. That. So now you're sure?"

"Yes, I'm sure."

"But you wouldn't have been if I hadn't gone through that...experience?"

"No." The admission came reluctantly. Rufus eyed me, trying to work out where I was going.

"Just as well I went through it, then, isn't it?"

"I suppose," he admitted grudgingly, "that it was really."

"Just as well I had temptation put in my path and was able to work out for myself what was the right way to go."

"Yes."

"Couldn't have worked out better if you'd planned it really. Could it?"

Rufus pursed his lips. "No. I suppose it couldn't."

I leaned forward. "That was a bloody dangerous gamble, Rufus."

Rufus nodded. "I had faith," he said simply.

"Like I said, mad. And not just for that reason either." This time Rufus waited silently for my final proof of his insanity. "You love him, don't you?"

There was no need for either of us to say who I was referring to. Rufus nodded once. "Yes."

"And you could have been with him, couldn't you, I mean *really* been with him, like him, as young as you were when you first met him?"

"Yes. Yes, I could."

I shook my head. "So why didn't you?"

He sighed. "Don't think I didn't consider it, very seriously indeed. I thought that life, this mortal life, had little to offer me except growing old and dying."

"So?"

"Richard persuaded me not to."

"*Richard* did? But I thought he loved you too?"

"He does. Very much. Perhaps not as much as..." Rufus sighed again. "Well, we'll never know that, will we?

Richard loves me. Young or old that's not going to change. He saw one lover's life snatched away too soon. He didn't want to see that happen again. He persuaded me to wait. He was right. I've had a long life, and I've enjoyed every minute of it. I wasn't ready before, the way poor Lee wasn't ready. Now I am. Growing old isn't something to be scared of, Sean."

"Yeah, right."

Rufus looked at me, and his expression made me more profoundly uncomfortable than anything we had talked about that morning. It was the simplest pity. "You've faced some terrible fears in the last few days," he said carefully. "Don't you think you're ready now to face that one?"

Outside the wind blew a flurry of snow against the glass. I shivered, in spite of the cosy warmth of Rufus's study. "Oh come on!" I muttered, trying to brush the conversation away from a direction I myself had steered it in. "It's not that." Rufus continued to fix me with that mild gaze of his, the one that could cut through all crap. "I'm not frightened about... It isn't that..." My objections faltered and ground to a halt. My eyes fell to his hand holding mine. It's just that sometimes," I said slowly, "quite often, actually, I...can't see the point."

Rufus nodded, his eyes unfocused as if looking back across his own history, perhaps to when he had written those despairing diary entries. "You're going to him tonight, aren't you?"

I stood up, gently removing my hand from his, and reached for my outdoor coat. "Farjeon? Yes."

"He'll ask you again."

"I know."

"And what are you going to tell him?"

I thought of all we had talked of, of the arguments that had been going through my head in the days since the fight in the Quad. Of the promise of eternal life, everlasting youth. Of leaving behind the mundane world. Of the blood soaking into the stone without a trace. "I...don't know. Plenty of time, though, till tonight," I added with false cheeriness. "Besides, there's someone I really ought to see first."

I'd wondered if Rufus would get up as I was leaving, wondered if he'd actually do something terrible like hug me, and what the hell I'd do if he did. But he didn't. He remained seated and didn't even look after me as I went to the door, but as I was stepping out of his study he called after me. "Sean, if you've learned anything from what's happened here it's that you have the most awful tendency to miss what's under your nose." He closed his eyes as if very, very tired. "Don't make the same mistake again will you, my boy?"

Now, what the fuck was *that* supposed to mean?

*

I'm turning into a voyeur, I thought. *My life just recently seems to have been all about watching other people, conventionally and supernaturally. And here I am doing it again.* The sight, though, was worth it.

Don't get me wrong. A little pain can be a pleasurable thing, if you know what I mean, but I'm not into the real McCoy in any significant way, and definitely not into wounding. So it wasn't the sight of the huge bandage on

Taylor's shoulder that was turning me on. It was what it represented. He'd taken the bullet that had been meant for me. And it hadn't been some automatic trained reflex either, the sort of reaction that made bodyguards throw themselves in front of their charges. He'd been pretty much in a fugue, his mind overloaded by what had been going on that night in the Quad, but seeing Chris about to draw the curtains down on my life had been enough to jump start his reason and send him flying across the air to save the day. Well, my day anyway.

And of course, there was that whole thing about a sexy, good-looking, strong man in a vulnerable position. A bed. Stripped to the waist. That didn't hurt with the attraction either. Rearranging my coat so that the bulge in my trousers wasn't obvious, I pushed the hospital ward door open and strode in. "So, this is why the streets are full of crime? All the policemen are lying around in bed!"

Taylor put down the magazine he had been reading and hurriedly shoved it under a box of tissues on the bedside cabinet. *Interesting,* I thought, and sat myself on the small chair right by it.

"And this is why our nation's youth can't read or write? All its teachers out visiting hospitals!"

"Touché."

"I'm touched."

Neat. "How are you?"

Taylor struggled to sit up in the bed, the movement drawing the bedsheet still further down his torso. Very nice chest. I was guessing the local cop shop had a decent weights room. I remembered Chris toying with those fabulous nips. The memory in context was an unpleasant one, but manfully I forced myself to concentrate on the positive and expel the negative. Yeah, those nips! They really were amazingly broad and tender-looking. With an effort of will I dragged my eyes up to meet his. Great eyes too. A beautiful deep brown. I had, I realised, had my fill of blue eyes just lately.

"Feeling better day by day, thanks. They should be kicking me out day after tomorrow all being well. I am, I am told, very lucky."

"Yeah. You are."

A nurse walked by and we both turned to look, grateful for the distraction. She walked the length of the ward and turned out of sight. We both waited a couple of seconds, as if hopeful she might return, slowly returning to our awkward conversation when it became clear she wasn't. Embarrassingly, my eyes, as if they had minds of their own, turned back to Taylor's bare chest. Once again I forced them to rise to meet his. "No grapes then," he ventured.

"Hate 'em."

"I quite like them actually."

"Ah. Right."

Another silence.

"Look..." we both began.

"You first."

"No, you."

"Okay, I'll start." I drew a breath. "Why?"

"Why what?"

"What do you think? Why'd you throw yourself in front of that bullet?"

"I tripped."

"Bollocks."

"I..." Taylor stopped. He really looked as if he was at a loss for words. Not so very long ago that would have amused me very much indeed. Now...I almost felt sorry for putting him on the spot. Almost. I had to know. "It's my job," he said simply.

"No, it isn't," I replied with equal simplicity.

"God, you are such a prick."

"What?"

"You really can't..."

"Don't! Don't say it! If anyone else says I cannot see what is right in front of me, I'll..."

"Be very sarcastic at them?"

I drew myself up in mock dignity. "I am ironic, never merely sarcastic."

"Right." He was laughing at me, with his eyes not his lips. I'd have liked to see his lips smile. Like to have touched them with my fingers, with my own lips, felt them part, felt... "Okay then, you tell me why."

"What?" I dragged myself back from my wool-gathering.

"Come on, you're the smart one. Tell me why I'd want to risk death or worse..."

"Oh please!"

"...*or worse* for you?"

A challenge. It was there in his eyes, the way Lee used to challenge me with his eyes, but not like Lee at all. "Because..." They were like dark chocolate, those eyes. I'd never done that chocolate stuff, you know, covering juicy bits of anatomy in the stuff and sucking it off. It always seemed a bit vanilla, if you'll forgive the mixed metaphor. But now I couldn't help imagining a pan of the stuff, melted to body heat, being poured slowly over Taylor's pecs, backward and forward, left to right, the thick, rich liquid oozing over his nipples, sliding in a slow, sweet wave down his stomach, filling my mouth as I dragged my tongue up his body, licking, swallowing... I coughed, my throat suddenly dry. "Because you fancy the pants off me and want to fuck me into the middle of tomorrow." There! I sat back and waited for the denials, the protestations and the inevitable movement onto safer, more neutral topics. God, I could have murdered a Snickers!

Taylor grinned. "Yeah," he said.

Bastard!

"And no."

Fucking bastard!

"What's that supposed to mean?"

Taylor leaned forward as much as he could, wincing from the pain the motion caused him. I went to do something, help him or stop him I'm not sure which but he waved me off. "I don't just want to fuck you, even though you do have one of the sweetest little arses I've seen in a long time, and from the way the guys fall over themselves to shag you I bet you're a great lay. I want to talk to you, have a meal with you, go to the cinema with you. Anything. I'd like to get to know you, Sean. And *then* I'd like to fuck you. You're self-centred, conceited, and aimless. But you're also intelligent, witty, brave, and very good-looking. I think you need someone decent to look after you and keep you from making a complete prat of yourself every opportunity you get." He fell back onto his pillow with a small grimace. "I don't just fancy you, you idiot. I think I've fallen in love with you."

"Oh."

"Eloquent. Your turn."

I opened my mouth to speak. Then closed it again. "Can I have a minute?"

"Take all the time you need."

All the time you need. That was what Richard was offering me, wasn't it? All the time I could possibly need. And he hadn't called me a prat. Not in so many words. "So, when...when did this all start then?"

"This...?"

"This...falling in love."

Taylor rolled his eyes. "I was proceeding along the main road in a westerly direction when..."

"If you don't give me a straight answer I'm getting Attila the Nurse over there to give you a bed bath!"

"All right! All right!" Taylor smiled dreamily and I wondered if they'd got him on painkillers. That would explain all the romantic stuff, wouldn't it? "It was that first meeting at St. Thad's in that little room with the funny man."

"Harry."

"Right."

"And what...did it?"

I swear his bloody eyes twinkled! He was enjoying this, and I could tell he was toying with the idea of not telling me, of keeping me in suspense. If he'd tried, I'd have ripped that bandage off and poked my finger in his wound. "It was watching you stand up to Marrin. That woman scares hardened criminals. I've seen her reduce drugs barons to quaking wrecks. But she just couldn't get a rise out of you, and you left her steaming."

"Yeah?" That was nice to know.

"Funny really. She likes me because I'm the only man in the service who'll stand up to her."

"And who doesn't want to shag her?"

Taylor went on smoothly. "She hates you."

"It's mutual."

"But I can talk her round. And then I stood back and watched as you got yourself deeper and deeper into shit."

"Thanks."

"But you just kept going."

I shifted uncomfortably on the bed. My own memories of my recent conduct didn't seem quite so admirable. "I didn't have a lot of choice."

"You ran to your friend, to Jean-Philippe when you thought he was in danger, and then you risked yourself to save Rufus." I opened my mouth though I had no idea what I was going to say. Taylor reached across and laid a finger on my lips and the unexpected pressure and intimacy of the gesture silenced me more effectively than a poleaxe. "And you were going to do it again, weren't you? To stop Bailey you were about to throw yourself at him. You'd almost certainly have been killed." He let his finger fall away and I really, really wished he hadn't. I could feel its pressure still. "And that's when I knew for sure."

He lay there looking at me, and I sat looking back. He'd come on to me. A million guys had come on to me. (Okay *slight* exaggeration.) That was no problem. It was easy. You made a gag back, flattered them, and made an appointment if there wasn't a private horizontal surface immediately available. But this... Taylor hadn't been talking about my cock, or his cock, or my cock *and* his cock. He'd been talking about...me. I think. What was I supposed to say? "So, when do you get out?"

Taylor sighed. I think he'd been expecting more. "Tomorrow morning, all being well."

"Back on the beat?"

"I've been given leave for a week. Marrin will probably have me back at my desk a couple of days before that."

I nodded. "Right." I stood up abruptly. "I have to go."

"So soon?"

He looked gratifyingly disappointed. I almost hesitated. But what would have been the point? "Life goes on. So to speak. Things to do. People to see. And I hate hospitals."

"The smell?"

"The mortality."

"Heavy!"

"Yeah. Yeah, it is. Take care." I turned to leave.

"Wait!" Taylor impulsively reached out and I turned back, as much because of the small gasp the sudden movement cost him as for the gesture itself. "That sounded... Are you...?"

I regarded him from just far enough away that he couldn't actually touch me. "Yes. I'm all right. I really think I am. You know, I think I'm finally seeing things clearly. It's a bit like waking up." Taylor gave me a worried look and I smiled, just to reassure him really. And I couldn't leave him on a sad note, could I? "Talking of seeing things clearly..." Before he could stop me, I had stepped forward and snatched up the magazine he'd taken such care I shouldn't see properly. I inspected its cover incredulously. "*Model Rail* magazine?"

Taylor looked wonderfully sheepish. "I'm a fan of model railways. Since I was a kid."

"Toy trains!"

"Scale models. And what can I say? I'm just an overgrown boy."

I couldn't help a last glance at the appetising lump in the sheets at his crotch. That hadn't all been there when first I arrived. The bed bath nurse would need her biggest loofah if that didn't subside. "A thing of beauty and a boy forever, eh?" Wouldn't that be nice? "Taylor?"

He lay there looking so hopeful it hurt. "Yeah?"

"What the hell is your first name?"

"It's... It's what I'll tell you on our first proper date."

I could have found out. I could simply have walked to the foot of his bed and read it from the clipboard there. But what would have been the point? I just nodded. "Goodbye, Taylor." I left the ward without looking back.

*

So, here I am, midnight in the gothic gloom of St. Thaddeus's College Quad, not because the time has any mystical significance, more because I think if you're going to make a literally life-changing decision then you might as well choose a portentous sounding time. Without hesitation I had walked out across the grass to the Founding Stone and without looking I had known that twenty-first century St. Thad's had faded out around me, replaced by some earlier St. Thad's, or by a dream of the same. In the darkness at the centre he was waiting for me, and so was the Stone.

"You have decided?" Richard Farjeon asks.

I look into the bloody-golden eyes of the creature that is offering, or threatening, to make me immortal, and I think. Of Farjeon and Tom. Of Rufus. Of Lee. Of Jean-Philippe. Of growing old. Of never being afraid again. And of Taylor. I smile.

"Yes," I say. "Yes, I have decided."

About Jack Stevens

Jack Stevens did a degree in English at a university suspiciously like the one in *Dark Master*. Since then, he's travelled, worked in factories, offices, up trees, in schools, and on stage. These days he mostly sits in front of a blank computer screen hoping for inspiration. He still hears from his old university vampire friends.

Other NineStar books by this author

Wrestling for Top Part One
Wrestling for Top Part Two
Wrestling for Top Part Three
Wrestling for Top Part Four
Wrestling for Top Part Five
Wrestling for Top Part Six
Wrestling for Top Part Seven
Wrestling for Top the Complete Collection

Also from NineStar Press

The Vampire's Witch by Damian Serbu

The Vampire's Witch welcomes readers back to the world of vampires, witches, and magic.

Jaret Bachmann's life spins out of control after a handsome stranger saves him from an attack along the bike path on Lakeshore Drive. His estranged high school sweetheart stalks him, the enraged ghost of his ancestor destroys his family, and his bike path savior-cum-lover abandons him after learning Jaret is a powerful witch.

A horrific family tragedy sends Jaret into deep depression. Struggling to find his way afterward, Jaret searches for comfort in the unlikely friendship of a secret vampire community.

Over time, Jaret's friendship with the vampires strengthens and he forges a new family connection with Xavier, Thomas, and Catherine. But he and Anthony are estranged, and though their souls are entwined, their hearts are another matter.

Xavier, Thomas, Anthony, and Catherine return in this, the third book in The Realm of the Vampire Council series and a sequel to *The Bachmann Family Secret*.

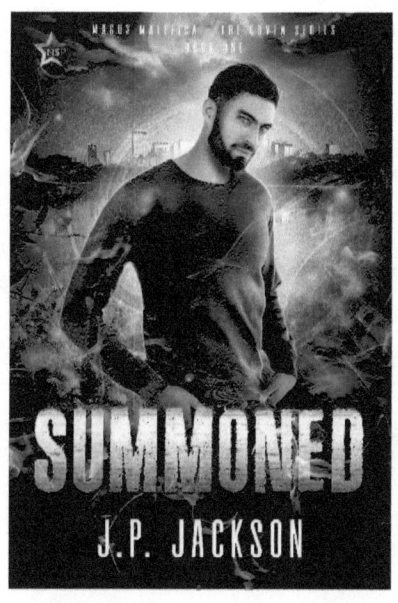

Summoned by J.P. Jackson

Devid Khandelwal desperately wants to experience the supernatural. After years of studying everything from crystals to tarot to spellcasting, nothing has happened that would tell him the Shadow Realm is real. And that kills Dev. As a last-ditch resort, he purchases a summoning board, an occult tool that will grant him his ultimate desires.

Cameron Habersham is Dev's best friend. Cam loves Dev like a brother and will do anything for him, as long as he looks good doing it. So when Dev asks him to perform the summoning board's ritual, he reluctantly agrees, but he knows nothing will come of it. Nothing ever does.

However, within a day, Dev and Cam's lives are turned upside down as wishes begin to come true. They discover the existence of a supernatural world beyond their imagination, but peace between the species is tenuous at best.

Dev finally gets to see the Shadow Realm, meets the man of his dreams, and is inducted into the local male coven. But for all the desires that were summoned into existence, Dev soon realizes the magical community dances the line between good and evil, and Cam ends up on the wrong side of everything.

The old adage is true: Be careful what you wish for.

Awakening by Connal Braginsky and Sean Ian O'Meidhir

Nathen was recently diagnosed with autism, and he's a newly created vampire. His maker, a multinational corporation with its finger on the pulse of the technology industry, has recruited him to stop a terrorist plot. In the process, he meets Cameron, a telepath and psychologist, who has a troubled past he keeps locked up in the shadows of his psyche.

Nathen is confused by social cues and Cameron can barely block out the thoughts of others.

Together, they find common ground, and with the help of their friend Syn, they work out the secrets of the terrorist group and learn that the plot is far greater than they could have imagined.

Connect with NineStar Press

www.ninestarpress.com

www.facebook.com/ninestarpress

www.facebook.com/groups/NineStarNiche

www.twitter.com/ninestarpress

www.instagram.com/ninestarpress